# Immortal

# GILLIAN SHIELDS

# Immortal

SCHOLASTIC INC.
New York Toronto London Auckland
Sydney Mexico City New Delhi Hong Kong

ISBN 978-0-545-29345-7

12 11 10 9 8 7 6 5 4 3 2 1          10 11 12 13 14 15/0

Printed in the U.S.A.          40

First Scholastic printing, September 2010

Typography by Amy Ryan

For Brian

"For we all must die, and are as water spilt upon the ground. . . ."

—2 Samuel, 14:14

# Prologue

I don't believe in ghosts. I don't believe in witchcraft either, or Ouija boards, levitation, tarot cards, astrology, curses, crystals, second sight, vampires—not any of the whole mumbo jumbo of the "other side." Of course I don't. I'm intelligent, sane, sensible Evie Johnson. Girls like me don't get mixed up in all that crazy paranormal trash.

At least, that's what I would have said before I arrived at Wyldcliffe Abbey School. But everything is different for me now. I have glimpsed *her* world, and I can never go back to being the girl I used to be.

Imagine a wild, lonely landscape where the moors rise in harsh folds of green and brown and purple. Sheep are dotted here and there on the hillsides, standing patiently in the bitter wind. A few trees have managed to grow, but they look bare and stunted. The moors encircle a bleak little village at the heart of the valley, like the walls of an ancient prison.

Welcome to Wyldcliffe.

This is the place that haunts my present, my past, and my future. That is, if I still have a future. If he will permit that. If he doesn't destroy me first.

She is by my side, as my sister, but he is in my soul.

He is my enemy, my tormentor, my demon.

He is my beloved.

# One

I never wanted to go to boarding school. Hanging out with a crowd of rich kids in a swanky school was never on my wish list. I was content with my old life, in a keeping-myself-to-myself kind of way. Not happy, perhaps, but content. And then, one soft blue September day, my grandmother—Frankie—became seriously ill.

She had never been Gran to me, only dearest Frankie, my surrogate mom, my best friend. I had stupidly expected her to go on unchanged forever. But no one is immortal, not even the people we love. And now Frankie was sick and I was forced to pack my bags for Wyldcliffe Abbey School for Young Ladies. Life really gives you a kick sometimes.

I was doing my best to think of it as a challenge.

The journey to Wyldcliffe seemed to last hours as the train headed north. I was traveling alone. Dad had wanted to come with me, but I'd convinced him that I would be okay going by myself. I knew he wanted to spend every possible moment of his leave with Frankie at the nursing home before he had to go back to his army posting overseas. So I told him I was quite capable of sitting on a train for a few hours without ending up on a missing persons poster. . . . *Honestly, Dad, I'm sixteen now, not a child anymore.* . . . It wasn't that difficult to persuade him.

The truth was that I guessed it would be easier saying good-bye to him at home. The last thing I wanted was for those snobby Wyldcliffe girls to see me sniveling as my dad drove away. No, there was going to be no "poor Evie" this time. I'd had enough of that over Mom. People whispering about me in the street. The pitying looks behind my back. It wasn't going to be like that again. I was going to show them that I didn't need anyone. I was strong, as strong as the deep green ocean. No one at Wyldcliffe would ever see me cry.

I transferred to a sleepy local train just as it was beginning to get dark. We chugged through an unfamiliar landscape of sloping hills covered with bracken and heather. In the depths of my misery I felt a twinge of curiosity. When I was little, Frankie had told me stories about Wyldcliffe, which she had heard from her mother, stories about the wild moors and the lonely farms and the harsh northern skies. I had never seen the place, but now I was almost there. I put away my magazine and my headphones and peered out of the window into the dusk.

Half an hour later, the train pulled into a little station at the head of a deep, shadowed valley. As I heaved my bags into a beat-up old taxi, a gust of wind whipped up a spatter of rain. I said, "Wyldcliffe, please," and we set off. I tried to make conversation with the bleary-eyed taxi driver, but he barely grunted in reply. We drove on in silence.

Between the clouds, I caught sight of the sun slipping behind the moors like a streak of blood. The leaden sky seemed to press down heavily on the land. I had lived all my life next to the open sea, and those dark hills made me feel strangely hemmed in. For all my brave talk, I suddenly felt very small and alone. How stupid I'd been not to let Dad come. . . . Then the car turned a corner, and the church tower and gray stone buildings of Wyldcliffe village finally came into sight.

The driver pulled up outside a tiny general store on the rain-blackened street. "Where to, then?" he growled.

"The Abbey," I replied. "You know, Wyldcliffe Abbey School."

He twisted his head around and glared at me. "I'll not take you to that cursed place," he spat. "You can get out and walk."

"Oh, but—" I protested. "I don't know where it is. And it's raining."

The man seemed to hesitate, but then he grunted again. "It's not so far to walk. Knock on the door of Jones's shop, if you like. He'll drive you, but I won't."

He got out of the car and dropped my suitcases onto the wet pavement. I scrambled after him. "But where's the school? Where do I go?"

"The Abbey is yonder," he said, pointing reluctantly to the church. "No more than half a mile from the graveyard. Tell Dan Jones that's where you're headed."

A second later his car roared out of the village, leaving me behind like an unwanted package. I couldn't believe that he had just dumped me there in the pouring rain. I knocked furiously on the door of the little shop, where the sign read, D. JONES, WYLDCLIFFE STORE AND POST OFFICE. There was no answer. It was a late, wet Sunday evening, and the whole village seemed to be shut down for the night. I swore under my breath. There was no choice but to walk.

The sun had set, and the pale moon was struggling

to break free from a rack of clouds. Tall black trees and slanting graves crowded the little church. As I walked past, I was startled by the sound of rooks screeching in the dusk.

I shook myself angrily. I wasn't going to be spooked by a few birds and a crummy churchyard. It looked like some ridiculously cheap set in a cheesy horror movie. Looking around, I saw an old sign marked ABBEY. I set off down the lane, hauling my suitcases over the mud. By now my long red hair was dripping with rain, and my hands were white with cold, but I felt boiling hot inside, raging against the unfairness of everything: first Mom, then Frankie, and now this godforsaken boarding school, the insane cab-driver, and the stupid, stupid rain. . . .

Lost in my bitter thoughts, I didn't see the horse—or its rider—until it was too late.

There was a great flurry of hooves and gleaming flanks and the swirl of a long coat. I looked up and froze, unable to get out of the way of a black horse that was hurtling toward me. Then it reared and screamed and something struck the side of my head. I just remember falling . . . falling into darkness.

When I opened my eyes again, the rider had dismounted and was hunched over me. He was only a boy, a few years older than me, but he looked as though he had come from a different world, a storybook land of knights and elves and princes. His long dark hair framed a pale, sensitive face with high cheekbones and brilliant blue eyes, and he was staring at me so intently that I felt uncomfortable.

This was unreal. I wasn't the kind of girl who crashed into good-looking guys. I scrambled shakily to my feet.

"I'm . . . sorry," I stammered. "I didn't see you."

"You weren't supposed to."

He looked tired and tense, and the shadows under his eyes were like soft bruises on a tender plum.

"I'm sorry," I repeated stupidly, waiting for him to apologize in return. But the boy simply stared at me.

"Did you stop my horse on purpose?"

"Did you ride into me on purpose?" I fumed back.

"There's no harm done to you," the boy replied. "But I cannot say as much for my horse." The great beast was trembling and sweating, tossing its head and rolling its eyes as though it had seen a ghost.

"Oh, I am sorry," I snapped. "Where I come from, humans are actually considered more important than horses."

"The world is overrun with humans, like rats, but I have

rarely found a horse that suits me so well." His expression was as cold as a winter sea. He murmured to the shivering animal, his long fingers searching its mud-spattered sides. Then he looked up at me, a fraction less hostile. "Fortunately there's no real damage."

"Oh, great," I said. "The horse is fine. Well, that's a relief. I thought it might be bruised and covered in mud after being knocked down, oh, and late for its first day at a hideous boarding school, that's all. But no, the horse is fine. Hallelujah!"

I scrambled furiously to collect the stuff that had spilled from my suitcases. Who did he think he was, this pretentious poser, with his long black hair and his long black coat? Some kind of romantic highwayman? Just some kind of jerk. I seethed, squashing everything back into the case as quickly as I could. A blue sweater lay in a puddle. I grabbed it, then yelped.

"Ouch!"

The sweater fell open to reveal my framed photo of Mom. She was beautiful in that picture, laughing into the camera on a long-lost summer's day. I had wrapped the precious keepsake in the sweater during my hasty packing, to keep it safe. But the glass in the little frame had broken and sliced into the palm of my hand, and now a drop of my blood oozed over Mom's face.

I rocked back on my heels. I just wanted to sit in the rain and howl. "Look what you've done!" I snapped angrily, trying to hold back my tears.

The boy threw his horse's reins over a low branch in the lane, then deftly folded the sweater around the broken frame. He whispered a few swift words before thrusting the bundle back into my suitcase.

"The picture was dear to you," the boy said abruptly. He looked at me in a strange, searching way, as though about to say something more. I caught my breath. He really was extraordinary, so pale and still and intense. "Don't cry," he said. "Please."

"I'm not crying." I gulped, standing up and sucking my hand where it bled. "I never cry."

"I can see that," he mocked. "But your cut should be covered, and it seems that I must do it for you." He quickly twisted a white handkerchief into a bandage and tied it around my hand to stop the bleeding. A weird shiver ran through me as his hand brushed against mine. "There," the boy said, looking at me more gently. "I have more than made up for any tangle with my horse by saving your life. I've just stopped you from bleeding to death."

A hint of a smile flickered over his lean face. I noticed

the curve of his lips, and the arch of his black eyebrows. He was still holding my hand in his, and I felt a tiny knot of attraction tugging under my rib cage.

"Don't be ridiculous!" I answered, dropping my hand with an effort. "A little cut like that isn't dangerous."

"Do you really know what dangers might lurk in this lane?" The boy moved closer to me and studied me with unnaturally bright eyes. I felt his cool breath on my cheek. Then he reached out and touched a strand of my wet hair and whispered, "How do you know what is waiting in this valley for a girl from the wild sea?"

I trembled under his touch, not knowing what to say. How did he know that I came from the sea? Who was he? And could he—would he—do me any harm out here in this lonely place? Stepping away from him, I tensed up and started to rack my brains for everything I had ever learned about self-defense. The boy seemed to read my mind.

"Don't worry; you'll get home safely tonight." He grinned and mounted his horse. "But we'll meet again, I promise you!"

He galloped away in the direction of the village. *We'll meet again.* I pushed the thought away into a secret place, unwilling to admit to myself that I hoped that he was right.

The pelting rain brought me back to my senses. I gathered up my things and carried on down the lane toward the Abbey. At last I reached some iron gates set in a stone wall. An old sign was fastened on one side of the gates. It read:

## WYLDCLIFFE
## BE   COOL
## OR YOU   DIE.

For a second I gazed in horror, then laughed weakly. I read the sign again, filling in the gaps where the painted letters had flaked away.

## WYLDCLIFFE
## ABBEY SCHOOL
## FOR YOUNG LADIES.

I had arrived at last.

# Two

I'll never forget my first sight of the Abbey. I made my way down the drive, turned a corner, and my new home rose up in front of me—gaunt, gray Wyldcliffe in all its Gothic splendor.

It was a brooding, heavy, secretive place. Towers and battlements jutted up crazily to the sky, and rows of hooded windows stared out like blank, blind eyes. A lamp swung in the wind above the massive front door. It was as though I had blundered back into a bygone age. I stood there, overwhelmed, then a group of girls dashed around the corner of the building and up the front steps, running to get out of the rain. They broke the spell, and I hurried after them.

Reaching the top step, I pushed open the carved oak door. There was no sign of the girls. They had vanished into the cavernous building. The dimly lit entrance hall stood empty and silent. Faded school trophies were displayed in cabinets, and firelight flickered in a huge hearth. At the far end of the hall a wide marble staircase wound upward. A landing ran around each of the upper floors, and it was almost dizzying to look up so high. The whole place was like nothing I had ever seen before, except in museums. I walked across the tiled floor to the fireplace and tried to get warm.

*This is it*, I thought. *My new life.* This was the famous Wyldcliffe Abbey School. It wasn't what I wanted, but I would try to make the most of it. I wouldn't complain, I would study hard and make Dad proud.

"You must be Evie Johnson," said an expensive-sounding voice. I spun around and saw a tall, elegant woman walking out of the shadows into the firelight.

"Yes, I am." I smiled, smoothing down my wet hair. I guessed that good manners would be a big thing at Wyldcliffe, so I held out my hand and said, "How do you do?"

The woman ignored my outstretched hand and my smile. She paused and scanned my face intently, then frowned.

"You're late. We don't tolerate unpunctuality at Wyldcliffe."

"Oh, I couldn't help . . . ," I began, but her look warned

to me to stop. I felt myself squirming under her cold gaze, as though she knew that I had been lingering in the rain with a stranger. "I'm sorry."

"Don't let it happen again," she replied coolly. "I am Celia Hartle, the High Mistress of Wyldcliffe. Now follow me. Leave your luggage here. The caretaker will deal with it."

So this was the principal. I hoped the other teachers would be slightly more human.

She led the way down a dark corridor to the left, then paused by a door that had a sign in black letters reading HIGH MISTRESS. We entered an elegant study with paneled walls, furnished with books and paintings and antique furniture. Mrs. Hartle sat behind an impressive desk, and I sat on a hard chair opposite her. She seemed to examine me again before announcing, "I was not in favor of accepting you into the school."

*Oh, great,* I thought. She didn't want me here. This was a perfect start.

"The term has already commenced," she went on, "and it will be difficult for you to catch up with the advanced level of work in the senior division of the school. It will be even more difficult for you to learn our ways, our traditions. Wyldcliffe is not like other schools. This establishment is not merely about academic success. It trains young women for a place in society. In recent years, the number of scholarship places has been very limited." She paused, and I knew she was expecting me to say how grateful I was, that I would be humble and good and meek, the perfect charity girl in a school full of young ladies. I wanted to snap back with red-headed fury, *I don't want to be in your crummy school either. I want to go home!* But I managed to keep quiet.

Mrs. Hartle sighed and continued, "The school governors, however, thought that in your circumstances they could not refuse assistance."

Dad had told me there was an old clause in the school's constitution "to make provision for the distressed daughters of the officers of Her Majesty's armed forces." In other words, free tuition for a motherless girl with a father in the army and not much money. *Well, I'm distressed, all right,* I thought with a grim smile.

"You have been fortunate to qualify for a scholarship. Make sure that you deserve it!" She looked me over with distaste, taking in my muddy clothes and my stringy wet hair. Her eyes rested for a fraction of a second on the blood-spotted handkerchief that was still tied around my hand, then darted to the silver chain around my neck.

"Jewelry is not permitted in school."

Instinctively I clasped the necklace that Frankie had

given to me during my last visit to the nursing home. She had pressed it into my hand, unable to speak, her face twisted by the stroke that had nearly killed her. It was an old-fashioned trinket of intricately worked silver, with a bright crystal at its heart. I didn't think it was valuable, but Frankie had wanted me to have it, and that made it precious.

"But Frankie, my grandmother, gave—"

"I am sure your grandmother would want you to obey the Wyldcliffe rules," Mrs. Hartle interrupted disapprovingly. I quickly pushed the necklace out of sight under my shirt.

"That's better. I might as well add that the use of personal phones, radios, and such is also forbidden. At Wyldcliffe we do not wish our girls to be overwhelmed by the gadgets of so-called popular culture, nor to be addicted to the mindless modern habit of communicating without meaning. You will give me any such devices for safekeeping, and they will be returned to you at the end of term."

Reluctantly I handed over my cell phone and my precious iPod. I was beginning to dislike Mrs. Hartle and her rules.

"Now, as you unfortunately arrived so late, the girls have already gone to supper. You do not have time to change before you join them. Come!"

She stood up abruptly, and I guessed that sending me

into supper looking like an absolute mess was punishment for being late. I shivered, and not from cold.

Mrs. Hartle led me through a confusing maze of paneled corridors hung with gloomy paintings, and we finally reached the dining hall. It was a chilly, vaulted room set up with long rows of tables and wooden benches. A high table ran across a raised platform, where the teachers sat. They were nearly all women, and most of them were wearing formal academic gowns. It all looked depressingly like something from a hundred years ago.

The murmur of conversation died instantly as Mrs. Hartle stepped forward. The students rose to attention, a mass of privileged girlhood from eleven to eighteen years old. They were all wearing the school uniform of dark gray and maroon—a sickly kind of bloodred color—and they all looked alike, with their shiny hair and clear complexions.

"Thank you, girls," said Mrs. Hartle. "Please be seated. But before you continue with your supper, I would like to introduce a new student. This is Evie Johnson, who joins us as a scholar."

She might as well have waved a placard saying, SHE'S NOT PAYING TO BE HERE; SHE'S NOT REALLY ONE OF US. I looked up at the rows of well-groomed girls, as my hair dripped onto the tiled floor.

"Hi."

My voice sounded like a lost echo. The students stared back in silence, all two hundred of them, judging, assessing, rejecting. The faintest snicker of laughter rippled around their polished ranks.

"I'm sure you'll do your best to welcome Miss Johnson," said the High Mistress smoothly. "Good night, ladies."

She marched out of the room. After what seemed like an eternity, a girl with curly brown hair stood up and said, "There's a place here." I walked down the long rows of watching girls and slipped gratefully into a seat opposite her. As I sat down, a rush of gossip broke out.

"Quiet, please!" scolded a low, harsh voice. I looked up at the teachers' table and saw a thin woman with a pinched face and tightly scraped-back hair. She was clapping her hands together to bring the room to order. "We do not eat like hooligans. Please continue your supper quietly."

The noise subsided into whispered conversations. I took a spoonful of something from a serving dish on the table, though I felt too tired to eat. The curly-haired girl who had called me over gave me an encouraging smile. I flashed a smile back at her and tried to force some food down.

"Hi, Evie," she said across the table. "I'm Sarah. Sarah Fitzalan."

"'Hi, Evie, I'm Sarah,'" mimicked the girl sitting next to her. She was the ice-princess type, with perfect features and smooth blond hair. An indefinable air of money hung about her. "Are you collecting another waif and stray to add to your collection, Sarah darling?"

"Oh, shut up, Celeste," Sarah retorted.

The girl called Celeste looked at me and said sweetly, "Do you always turn up to school covered in mud?" Two fair preppy girls on the other side of Celeste snickered as though she had said something funny.

"I got wet coming from the station," I said quietly.

"Oh, my God." Celeste gasped in mock horror. "You actually came on the train?"

"Some people do use public transportation, Celeste," said Sarah. "Not everyone goes around in gas-guzzling, chauffeur-driven cars."

Celeste turned her gaze on Sarah and said innocently, "Really? It must be awful. Remind me never to try it."

A bell rang out shrilly, making me jump. The girls quickly finished eating, then stood up. Sarah nodded to me to do the same. A long prayer was recited by the thin-faced teacher. After echoing, "Amen," dutifully, the girls began to file out of the room. I followed them, hoping that Sarah would show me where to go. Just as I got to the door a sharp voice called me back.

"Evie Johnson!"

I turned around. The teacher who had said the prayer was beckoning me over to her. Her black academic gown hung loosely from her narrow shoulders. It gave her the air of a severe nun, ready to pounce on the tiniest breach of discipline.

"Um . . . what is it . . . Miss . . . er . . . ?" I asked.

"My name is Miss Scratton," she answered. "I am in charge of the girls in the senior division. I'd like you to meet someone. Helen!"

I looked around and saw a tall, fair girl on the other side of the dining hall, setting out some little coffee cups on trays. She came over reluctantly when Miss Scratton called her name.

"Helen has been at Wyldcliffe for a year now and is our other scholarship student," explained Miss Scratton. "You will be in the same class and the same dormitory."

"Hi," I said, but Helen didn't reply.

"Perhaps you don't know yet, Evie, that scholarship girls are expected to perform some small duties as a token of gratitude and commitment to the school. You will help Helen set out the coffee trays for the mistresses after supper, tidy up the hymn books after choir practice, that sort of thing. Helen will show you what to do."

I looked at her in surprise. I hadn't expected to have to do chores. No wonder the girls had laughed. For one crazy second I was tempted to say, *Stuff your scholarship*, and walk out. But there was nothing waiting for me back at home. No Dad. No Frankie. No home. Nothing but the deep blue sea.

"Fine," I lied. "Sure. No problem."

"Excellent," said Miss Scratton crisply. "When you have finished here you will go straight to bed, as the bell is rung early on Sunday nights. So get on with your work now, Evie, and make sure you do it well. There's no place for slackers at Wyldcliffe."

Miss Scratton whisked away, her black gown billowing around her.

I glanced at Helen. Her hair was so fair it was almost silvery white, and she had delicate features and clear, light eyes. She looked delicate, as though a strong wind would blow her away, but her expression was heavy and sullen. Perhaps she was just shy, I thought. At least we were in the same boat—maybe we could be friends. "Thanks for helping me out, Helen." I smiled. "What do I do?"

She didn't smile back. "Set out the cups on the trays. The mistresses will collect them later. You need spoons, cream, and sugar. And don't break anything." Her voice was low and husky, as if she were not used to speaking much.

"So, I'm in the same dorm as you," I said. "That's great."

Silence.

I tried again: "Don't you think all this doing-chores stuff is a bit over the top?" I joked, rattling the cups and saucers carelessly onto my tray. "You know, like Cinderella, only with about two hundred ugly stepsisters. What else do they expect us to do? Sleep in the cellar?"

"I wish they did," Helen said with unexpected anger. "It would be better than . . ." She flashed me a strange look. Was it sympathy—or pity? But when she spoke, it was in an expressionless voice. "It's in the rules. Just deal with it."

I sighed. I guessed I was going to hear a lot more about the rules in the next few days. We finished up with the coffee things, and Helen began walking rapidly out of the dining hall. "Wait!" I called, chasing after her. "Aren't you going to show me the way to the dorm?"

"Oh, all right," she replied ungraciously. "Come with me."

She strode down the deserted passage. There was no sign of anyone, apart from a couple of teachers in their dark gowns. The passage wound its way back to the main hall and the marble stairs. These stairs intrigued me. The marble must have been incredibly heavy, yet the stairs seemed to float upward in an elegant curve. I placed my hand on the iron banister and looked up.

"Is that where the dorms are?" I asked.

"Yeah. Third floor."

Our feet echoed on the cold stone as we climbed higher. I was out of breath by the time we reached the top of the stairs. Yet another long corridor, lined with heavy doors, stretched away on both sides of the steps. I glanced back over the banister at the pattern of the black-and-white tiles in the hall below. How easy it would be to fall, and go crashing down like a doll.

"Come on," said Helen, striding ahead.

"So are we right at the top of the building now?"

"There's an attic above this floor, but it's shut up."

Muffled voices echoed behind the paneled doors. I read the signs on the doors: DRAKE, NELSON, CHURCHILL, WELLINGTON. . . . They were strangely warlike for a snooty girls' academy.

"Are these the names of the dorms?"

Helen nodded. "This is ours," she said. "Cromwell."

I was glad that the day was coming to an end at last. All I wanted to do was crawl into bed and sleep. I didn't know that there was still one more ordeal ahead of me.

# Three

I followed Helen into the room, looking over her shoulder to see if Sarah would be in the dorm too. She wasn't there, though, and my heart sank as I recognized Celeste lounging on one of the beds.

Helen walked over to her own bed and flung herself down. She dug a small book from under her pillow and began to read, ignoring everyone else.

I glanced around uncertainly, wondering which bed would be mine. The room was rather bare and cold, though it had obviously been quite grand once upon a time, with a big arched window and a fancy kind of window seat.

The two girls who had been sitting with Celeste at supper were curled up on it. One had baby blue eyes and a childish stare, and the other looked cold and unwelcoming.

"Meet Sophie and India," drawled Celeste, waving her hand lazily in their direction. "Did you have fun doing chores for the mistresses, Evie? How sweet that Helen has someone to help her to scrub the floors at last."

I noticed Helen hunch into a tighter ball on her bed.

"Yeah," I drawled back. "We had great fun. Now, which is my bed? I'd like to unpack."

"Oh, we did that for you already," Celeste said with an innocent smile. The girls by the window smirked at each other. "That's your bed in the corner."

There were five beds, with thin drapes that could be pulled around for a little privacy, like in a hospital ward. Someone had shut the drapes around the bed in the corner, so I walked over and pulled them open, then stepped back in horror.

The bed was shrouded in black silk and surrounded by tall, funereal candles. Rose petals lay scattered over the pillow, like drops of crimson blood, and a photograph of a wide-eyed teenage girl hung over the bed, staring out at me, watching me. My clothes had been dumped and kicked on the floor. I spun around to confront Celeste.

"What's this all about?"

Her smile had vanished. "It's about the fact that you aren't welcome. The last person who slept in that bed was my cousin Laura. She died. I don't suppose they told you that, did they?"

"N-no."

"You're only here because her place in the school became free. The idiots who are in charge wanted it to look like they were doing their Christian duty by letting you come to Wyldcliffe. But if Laura hadn't died, you wouldn't be here." Celeste's voice trembled with anger. "Just looking at you makes me feel sick."

"But it wasn't my fault," I protested. "I'm really sorry about your cousin, but I think—"

"I don't care what you think, Johnson. We don't want you here, and we're going to make sure you don't last long. Don't forget—you're sleeping in a dead girl's bed. And I hope she haunts your every breath."

Celeste marched out, followed by her little gang. I felt as though I had been slapped in the face. For a second I stood frozen with shock, then anger welled up inside me.

"What the—?"

A bell sounded in the corridor. Helen got up and made for the door, clutching a small bag of toiletries.

"You'd better get changed. The second bell will ring soon for lights-out." She avoided my eyes and hurried away.

Seething with fury, I snatched up the candlesticks and the yards of black stuff and threw them onto Celeste's bed. But I couldn't get the photograph down from the wall. *Oh, brilliant,* I thought, *now I have to sleep with a freaky picture of a dead girl staring down at me every night.* That was all I needed.

I couldn't believe that my first day at Wyldcliffe had been so disastrous. Celeste was being crazily unfair. Oh, I knew that grief did strange things to people, but it still hurt. I took a deep breath and tried to calm down. I could almost hear Frankie's voice in my head saying, *Poor Celeste, we should be very kind to her.*

Frankie knew all about grief. She had lost her only daughter, Clara, fifteen years ago, one cruelly bright spring morning. Clara Johnson. My mother.

She had drowned when I was a baby, swimming in the dark waves that rolled in from the Atlantic and pounded the shore at home. People who remembered Mom said that I was like her: long red hair, pale skin, and sea-gray eyes. I didn't have a single memory of her, not even the sound of her voice, so darling Frankie had done everything she could to replace her dead daughter for me. And now I might lose Frankie too. I guess I knew how Celeste felt.

"I promise," I said under my breath, "I'll try to be kind to her." But my words were empty. However much I might try to sympathize with Celeste, I knew we would never be friends.

I started to pick up my crumpled clothes. My old blue sweater was still rolled around the bits of glass from Mom's photo. I unwrapped the bundle, careful not to touch the shattered pieces and stared down in amazement.

The photograph was in an unbroken frame. The glass was completely flawless, as though it had never been damaged, and the bloodstain on my mother's face had vanished.

For one moment I thought I must have imagined the whole thing: the dark lane, the boy, the horse—but I couldn't have; I was still wearing his handkerchief as a bandage. I tore it off, and there it was: a thin mark of dried blood running across my right palm. That proved it. I really had cut myself. I had seen the broken glass. And now the glass wasn't broken anymore.

*Impossible.*

Helen walked back into the room. She pulled the drapes all the way around her bed, shutting me and everything else out. I decided to do the same.

I lay down and heard Celeste and her friends trooping back from the bathroom, giggling and whispering. Then a bell rang out and the lights snapped off. A few more whispers; then everyone settled down to go to sleep. But I couldn't rest.

*Impossible, impossible, impossible . . .*

Celeste's outburst faded into insignificance. It wasn't her threats that kept me awake, or the image of the dead girl, Laura, gazing down on me. It was thinking about the boy whose existence had briefly collided with mine. Had he mended the glass in some mysterious way? No, that was absurd, ridiculous.

I couldn't stop thinking about him, though. Who was he? Where had he come from? As I tried to fall asleep, I remembered his intense gaze, his smile, the shadows under his eyes. . . . I remembered the gentle touch of his hand as it brushed my face and the coolness of his breath on my skin. However much I tried to drive him from my thoughts, I seemed to hear his voice in my head, laughing. *We'll meet again . . . again . . . again. . . .*

Eventually I found sleep, but not rest. I dreamed lurid, fevered dreams, until one last dream came in which the terrible gray sea rose over the moors and smashed Wyldcliffe into oblivion with one mighty wave.

I awoke and bolted up, panting and sweating. For a second I struggled to remember where I was. Of course. The school. The dorm. The four other girls lying asleep so near me. I pushed back the white drape to try to get more air, then had to stop myself from crying aloud. Out of the corner of my eye I had seen a girl with long red hair and a pale, frightened face. I whipped around to look at her, then sank back, trembling. How stupid of me. It had only been my own unearthly reflection in a long mirror that was fixed to the opposite wall. I clamped my eyes shut, but there was no way I could get back to sleep.

The feeling crept over me, like rising fog, that I was being watched. There was someone else in the room apart from the five of us; I was sure of it. I strained to listen. There was the softest echo of someone singing a lullaby, as though long-ago and faraway. I heard light footsteps, a cough, and the pages of a book being turned. Someone was there, hidden by the deep shadows.

Another impossibility. I tried to shrug it off. I was just nervous, unsettled about being in a strange place. It was probably someone in the next dorm or on the floor below. Sounds got distorted in a big old house like this; that was all.

That first night I didn't know any better than to blame it on my imagination. On that first night I didn't know who was watching over me. I didn't know that her life was tangled with mine: my guardian, my sister, my other self.

I couldn't guess that I would get to know her, discover her secrets, and even read the pages of her private journal.

I lay awake all night long, until the pale sun emerged like a ghost from the grave.

# Four

*My news is that dearest S. is back from his travels at last, after months of wandering abroad with his tutor, Mr. Philips. We did not expect to see him again until Christmas, but he arrived at the Hall last night and came here in his father's carriage early this morning. This has been a wonderful surprise in our humdrum routine. I feel as though life has taken me by the shoulders and given me a thorough shaking and that now I am ready for any challenge.*

*It was so good to see my childhood friend again! At first, though, I was a little shy. He has grown remarkably tall and handsome, and made me feel quite babyish with his tales of Paris and Constantinople and Vienna—*

I who have scarcely been out of Wyldcliffe's lonely valley. But very soon we were chattering like magpies. He still has the same eager air, the same desire to share everything with me, the same intense blue gaze. Although our mothers are only very distantly related by marriage, he is closer to me than any cousin could be; truly the brother I never had.

He looked tired, however, underneath his smiles. I was not surprised to hear that he had suffered a fever in Morocco and had been dreadfully ill for many days. Now he is troubled by a wearisome cough and is thinner than he should be, with dark shadows under his eyes. His illness is the reason for his return home earlier than planned.

I cannot stop myself from being selfishly glad that he was forced to come back. This year of 1882 has been so very tedious, so long and dreary without him. I never realized before how much his talk and ideas, his books and poems enlivened my existence. Even rambling across the moors was not so keen a pleasure without him by my side. Miss Binns could not hope to fill his place, and I believe she is as delighted as I am that my companion has returned. He does not go to the university at Oxford until the New Year, so he will have every chance to recover his strength, and I will have him near me for many happy weeks.

Poor Miss B. has indeed been sadly puzzled by me of late. She does not understand my thirst for study, although she is a good creature, and I am grateful that Papa engaged such a kindly, gentle governess for me. But can a little French and music and the dates of the kings and queens of England add up to a real education in these modern times? If only I could go away to school! I asked Mama whether I could attend the Ladies' College in London that I have read about, now that I am sixteen, but she said it was out of the question for a young lady of my rank, and that I must remember that I am Lady Agnes Templeton, not some obscure girl forced to earn my bread by my wits.

I confess that I am driven to distraction by Mama's notions. What has worldly rank to do with the desire for knowledge? Today there are new ideas in every sphere, and I want to be part of this new world, not just a decorated doll.

Over these last months I have felt myself changing. Earlier in the summer my monthly bleeding began. Mama hugged me when I told her and cried a little, then dried her tears and said I would soon be a wife and mother. I am afraid that Mama will find some stammering young man whose only recommendation is that he is the son of a duke, and will force me down the aisle with him. But I could never marry anyone I do not truly love, not even a royal prince. However, my dear mother appears to think otherwise. I fear that if she knew my true thoughts, we should often quarrel. I must make sure that she never sees this journal.

I feel . . . I don't know how to express it . . . as though I am tingling with some unseen, unknown power, and I long to break free of everything that seems small and dull and superficial. My dreams are full of fire and color, both waking and asleep. There is one strange dream in particular that I have had many times recently. In it, I am standing in a deep underground cavern where a tall flame burns and twists. I walk over to this column of fire and scoop some of it in my hand. The flames dance like bright leaves in the wind, without scorching me. I am afraid, though exhilarated. . . .

Whenever I have this dream I wake feeling restless and head for the freedom of the moors. I lie on the grass, with the earth under my bones and the air on my face, and I still feel that flame burning and dancing inside me.

If only I had someone to talk to, a friend, or a sister. Sometimes I have imagined such a friend so strongly that I swear I could almost see her. But now at least darling S.

is back. I cannot be lonely with him only two miles away at the Hall. His father has given him a fine new black mare, so he has promised that we shall have many rides out together as soon as he is a little rested. I will have to be content with getting my education secondhand from him, and seeing the world through his stories. Yet I know in my heart that I am capable of doing something worthwhile, and I will not rest until I have discovered it.

I stand with my childhood behind me and my destiny ahead, as though I am poised on the crest of a wave that will send me hurtling to some distant, unknown shore.

# Five

The morning bell was clanging like a fire alarm. I dragged myself out of bed and found my way to the bathroom. There were two or three old-fashioned cubicles, each with an antiquated-looking shower and a tangle of copper pipes. I went into the nearest one and locked the door behind me.

My head ached with lack of sleep, and I couldn't shake off a feeling of nagging anxiety. As I undressed, I noticed that the cut on my hand had healed into a dark red line—the cut that had apparently come from nowhere. It didn't make any sense. If only there were someone I could talk to about it.

I missed Dad and Frankie so much it hurt.

Standing under the tepid shower, I tried to let the

water wash everything away. *Forget it,* I told myself. *I must have gotten it all wrong.* The glass had never been broken in the first place. I must have grazed myself on a corner of the brass frame; that was all. Or maybe something sharp had fallen into the sweater when I was packing it at home. There was no mystery. And there was no one watching me. There couldn't be.

*Impossible.*

I needed to concentrate on dealing with my new school, just ordinary stuff like finding my way around and doing my best in class and staying out of Celeste's way. I needed to forget the whole thing. Most of all, I needed to forget about the boy with the dark hair and the haunting eyes.

I got back to the dorm and put on my unfamiliar uniform: the dark gray skirt, the bloodred stockings, the old-fashioned tie. I looked in the mirror hanging on the wall and didn't quite recognize the girl who looked back at me.

Celeste, India, and Sophie came jostling back from the bathroom.

"Hey, how sweet," said Celeste. "She's admiring her uniform. Isn't it a shame that she won't be wearing it for long?"

I remembered my resolution to be tolerant and swallowed down the angry reply that I wanted to shoot back at her. It was a massive effort.

"Come on, Evie," said Helen. "Let's go to breakfast."

I looked at her in surprise. I hadn't expected Helen to show me any support. Gratefully I followed her out of the room, but she didn't go down the marble staircase, where girls were starting to make their way to the main hall. Instead she pulled me into an alcove partly hidden from the corridor by a curtain. At the back of the alcove was a plain wooden door. Helen drew back a bolt and pushed the door open.

I saw a dim, secret landing where some twisting wooden steps snaked down into total darkness. Helen groped behind the door, then picked up a flashlight and switched it on. "I keep this here. Come on," she said. "It's officially out-of-bounds, but I'll show you the way. Then we don't have to bump into Celeste and her crew."

"But . . . where are we going?"

"We can go down here. It's the old servants' staircase."

Helen shut the door behind us and pointed her light at the spiraling steps. They were so narrow they seemed to have been squeezed into a gap between the walls, like a ladder going down into a dark pit.

"You must be joking." I didn't really want to admit it to Helen, but I'd always been spooked by enclosed, dark spaces. "I'm not going down there."

"It's perfectly safe. Or would you rather hang out with Celeste?"

She set off, the light bobbing in front of her.

"Helen! Wait!"

I plunged down the crooked stairs after her, trying not to imagine that the walls were pressing in on me. After a few turns we came to another dark landing.

"That's the staff floor," said Helen. "Keep going."

We finally reached the bottom and stepped into a dank, deserted passage. Helen swept the light over the cobwebbed walls.

"So where are we now?" I asked, hoping that wherever it was, we'd get out of there as quickly as possible.

"This used to be the servants' quarters in the old days, when the Abbey was a private house. That door over there leads back into the main part of the school, near the marble steps, but if you go down this passage in the other direction you get to the old kitchens and out to the stables. I like it here. I'll show you, if you want."

The last thing I wanted was to go exploring some crummy back rooms that no one had used for more than a hundred years, but Helen seemed entranced by the place. I had no choice but to follow her as she headed farther into the old servants' wing. Everything was painted a depressing dark brown, and it was all thick with dust. I was sure I heard the rustle of mice in the walls. I'd had enough. I was just about to ask Helen to turn back when I caught sight of a row of old bells in a mahogany frame. There were faded labels under them saying things like, DRAWING ROOM, BLUE SALON, and BILLIARDS ROOM.

"What were they for?"

"The bells rang when the servants were needed in all the different rooms. The maids would have run up and down the back steps a hundred times a day, some of them younger than us. They wouldn't have been allowed to use the marble staircase, of course. That was only for the Templetons."

"Who were they?"

"The people who owned this place."

Helen opened the door of an abandoned kitchen. "This is where the servants would have worked." She gazed around. "Can't you hear their voices?"

She was really beginning to freak me out now. I had no desire to hear the voices of some dead Victorian maids, however much Helen was into all that. My heart seemed to slow down, and the weird feeling of being watched pressed in on me again. Whispers and secrets seemed to vibrate in my head. . . .

Just then a bell sounded in the distance, and I jumped. Helen blinked.

"That's the breakfast bell. We mustn't be late!" She darted back down the passage toward the main house. "Come on! Hurry!"

I struggled to keep up with her long legs, and in a few minutes we were back at the old servants' staircase. Then Helen pushed open a door that led into the main corridor, near the marble steps. The sound of footsteps trooping down to the dining room echoed away to our left. We raced to catch up with them, but it was too late. As we entered the dining hall, flushed and out of breath, the girls were already standing in their long rows by the tables. Mrs. Hartle was at the high table, saying grace. Helen looked agonized and waited nervously by the door. I caught sight of Celeste, smooth and pure as an angel, her mouth curved in a secret smile.

The High Mistress finished her prayer, then glanced at me coolly.

"So, Evie Johnson is late again? We'll have to help you and your friend Helen to remember that unpunctuality is against the rules at Wyldcliffe. Miss Scratton, two demerit cards, please."

Miss Scratton walked over and gave us each a printed red card. She frowned as we took them, and I gathered from Helen's miserable expression that this was a deep disgrace. Another of Wyldcliffe's dumb traditions.

"This is to remind you that the rules must be kept," said Miss Scratton. "And perhaps I should explain, Evie, that when a girl has been given three demerits, she must report to the High Mistress for a detention."

It all seemed a fuss about nothing, but Helen flinched as she held the card. I realized with astonishment that she was absolutely terrified of Mrs. Hartle. Helen was kind of strange, I thought uneasily. I couldn't help being annoyed with her for landing me in trouble on my first morning. Yet she had tried, in her own way, to protect me from Celeste. I was still trying to work her out when the bell sounded for the end of breakfast and the beginning of class. We filed out of the dining hall, and I found Celeste at my side.

"You've made a great start, Johnson. A demerit on your very first day. Must be a record. Just shows what happens when you hang around with a loser like Helen."

I tried to keep my temper. "It wasn't Helen's fault."

"Are you sticking up for her? That's so sweet," she mocked. "But don't expect Helen to be a real friend. She's completely crazy."

"She's not," I said stubbornly, though I had been pretty much thinking the same thing. "She's just . . . high-strung; that's all."

"Is that what you call it?" Celeste's face suddenly looked sickly white under her tan. "Was she too high-strung to talk to the police, even though she was the last person to see Laura alive? Was she too high-strung to tell us the truth about what happened that night?" Her eyes filled with tears. "Don't talk to me about Helen Black, or get involved in things you know nothing about."

She walked away, her blond hair swinging.

"Come along, Evie," said a brusque voice behind me in the corridor. It was Miss Scratton. "You don't want to be late again today. I will be teaching you this morning. Follow me."

She kept up a monotonous flow of information about my schedule and where to find the various classrooms, but I could hardly take it in. Why would Helen have needed to talk to the police about Laura? I suppose I had assumed that she'd been killed in some awful car accident, but it seemed as though she had died here, at Wyldcliffe. Had

45

she been ill? And why were the police involved? Even more bizarrely, Celeste seemed to be suggesting that Helen knew something about it.

"You can see from the thickness of the walls and the low ceilings that this part of the building is much older than the rest. . . ." Miss Scratton was saying as we marched side by side down yet another corridor. "It's part of the original medieval nunnery, possibly once used as a hospital wing."

I dragged my mind back into focus, murmuring, "Yes. Very interesting."

She led the way into a classroom. It had white walls, rows of desks, and a tall bookcase. A large framed poster of the witches in a production of *Macbeth* hung behind Miss Scratton's desk.

"Find yourself a seat."

There were about twenty girls in the class. I was pleased to see Sarah sitting at the back. At least that was one friendly face. She gave me a quick smile, but the other girls seemed to flick their eyes over the scarlet punishment card I was still holding, then turn away as though they didn't want to be associated with my disgrace. There was an empty desk next to Helen. I sat down and pretended to busy myself with my notebook and pens.

The atmosphere was hardworking and studious, quite different from the free and easy ways I was used to at home. Miss Scratton taught English and history, and despite her dull, dry voice, she was an excellent teacher. After a while I found myself actually enjoying trying to keep up with the arguments and theories she put forward. It was a relief to lose myself in the work and forget about everything else. I bent over my books, absorbed by what I was reading. And when I looked up, I got the biggest shock of my life.

The room had changed.

Oh, I don't mean the whitewashed walls and the latticed windows—they were exactly as they had been before. And the room was still set up as a schoolroom, but instead of rows of wooden desks and girls in dark uniforms, I saw a large polished table scattered with papers and heavy books. Old-fashioned furniture crowded the room, and a large globe was displayed on a stand. A plump, middle-aged woman with flushed cheeks and a fussy dress was pointing something out on the globe to her only pupil, a girl dressed in white.

The girl's gray eyes were alive with concentration, and her auburn curls were caught in a black ribbon. The image of the shadowy girl I had seen the night before in the mirror swam into my mind. This girl was real, though, not a reflection like a vision of a long-lost sister in a half-remembered life. But I didn't have a sister; I'd never had a sister. . . . As I watched her, I heard the sudden roar of fire and saw the blinding light of clear white flames. I cried out, then felt myself dissolving into nothingness.

When I came to I was slumped across my desk, and Helen was bending over me. The other girls pushed her out of the way.

"What's the matter? Has she hurt herself? Why did she scream like that?"

A low voice cut across their eager questions.

"Evie fainted for a few seconds, that's all," said Miss Scratton. "Please don't crowd around her. Back to your places, girls, and start reading quietly." Miss Scratton frowned at me as she felt my pulse. "Have you ever fainted before?"

I thought confusedly of my encounter with the boy and his horse, but I shook my head. I couldn't tell what was real anymore and what was just a daydream.

"I felt dizzy, that's all," I mumbled.

"Well, you'd better go outside. It is rather stuffy in here." She glanced at Helen, hesitated for a fraction of a second, then said, "Sarah, take Evie and show her the grounds. She'll soon feel better in the fresh air."

"Come on, Evie," said Sarah. "Let's go for a walk."

Her simple friendliness touched me and tears stung my eyes. I blinked them away. As I followed Sarah out of the classroom, I remembered the vow I had made. No one, absolutely no one at Wyldcliffe would ever see me cry.

# Six

We sat on a bale of straw in the dusty, warm stable. Sarah smiled and offered me a bag of apples. "I keep these here for Bonny, but they're perfectly okay, especially if you haven't had much breakfast."

I bit into one of the yellow apples. It was sweet and good. That exactly described Sarah too, I thought, with her rich brown hair and freckled complexion. She looked as though she belonged outside, in the fields and woods. As I munched my apple, Bonny, her sturdy little pony, tried to steal it with snuffling lips. Sarah laughed, then looked at me curiously. "So what happened to you just now?"

I avoided her eyes. I wasn't really sure myself. All I knew was that it wasn't the first weird thing that had happened to me since arriving at Wyldcliffe. But how could

I tell Sarah all that nonsense about a handsome guy on horseback, and broken glass that wasn't broken, and a red-headed girl who couldn't possibly have been there? Sarah seemed the first normal person I had met so far, and I didn't want her to think I was totally crazy. I was just stressed, I decided. Nothing like that would happen again.

"Just a dizzy spell." I shrugged and jumped to my feet, wanting to change the subject. "What about you taking me around the grounds, like Miss Scratton said? I haven't seen them yet."

"Okay." She smiled. "Bye, Bonny, darling. See you later. You wouldn't believe that she was a skinny wreck a few months ago, would you? My parents helped me to rescue her from some people who knew nothing about horses and were mistreating her. Now she's as fat as butter. My other pony is called Starlight. Come and see him first, Evie; then I'll show you everything." I followed Sarah to another stall, where a handsome gray pony nuzzled her hand and graciously accepted an apple. "Thank goodness Wyldcliffe allows us to bring horses to school. I spend every spare minute with them. I'd be lost without some of my animals around me. At home I have three dogs, two cats, and a donkey, and they've all been rescued from one place or another. . . ."

Sarah chattered on, and I remembered what Celeste had said about her collection of "waifs and strays." Well, I really was one of them now.

We wandered around the stable yard, which was attached to the side of the main house. I noticed a faded green door that looked as though it was hardly used. I guessed that it led into the old servants' quarters where Helen and I had been that morning. A black cat crossed the yard. We followed it and came to a walled kitchen garden set out with rows of beans and black currants.

"We can have our own little garden plots here," Sarah said. "I like growing things, digging in the earth and watching new life spring up. And I love the stables too. The grand parts of the Abbey can seem cold and gloomy, but out here I can really see what it must have been like when the whole place belonged to a proper family, with their gardeners and carriages and horses and dogs. But that was over a hundred years ago, when Lady Agnes was alive." She looked at me and frowned, as though she was trying to remember something.

"Who was this Lady Agnes?" I asked, trying to sound interested.

"She was the daughter of Lord Charles Templeton, who rebuilt Wyldcliffe in the middle of the nineteenth century. The original Abbey, from the days when the nuns lived here in medieval times, was mostly destroyed long ago, but Lord Charles thought the ruins were romantic, so when he built his new house for his wife and daughter, he kept every last stone. Come and look!"

We walked out of the kitchen garden to a graveled terrace behind the main house. From the terrace, a wide lawn sloped away to a lake. The lower stretches of the grounds were thickly covered with dense green shrubs, and beyond them, marching like sentinels around the Abbey's grounds, were the wild moors. It was an impressive sight, but there was something else about the view that took my breath away.

Next to the lake, the ruins of the ancient Abbey's chapel soared up into the air. Gaunt, broken arches hung like petrified lace against the gray sky. Tumbled piles of stone were heaped about the base of the medieval walls, and where the high altar once stood there was a smooth green mound. Everything was reflected in the lake, as though an underwater cathedral lay dreaming beneath its glassy surface.

"It's amazing, isn't it?" said Sarah.

"It's . . . beyond words." A strange shiver ran down my neck. "But it all seems so sad, somehow."

"So, you know about Laura, then?"

"Celeste told me." I didn't know why, but my heart began to thud.

"Laura was found here in the lake. She had drowned."

Just like my mother. I felt sick, and swayed slightly.

"Hey, are you okay, Evie? I don't want you fainting again." She half dragged, half supported me to a seat that looked out over the lake.

"Sorry. It's nothing. Let's talk about something else. Tell me about this Lady Agnes."

"It's not a happy story either," Sarah replied reluctantly. "There was some kind of accident and she died young. I read about it once. That's how this place became a school. After Agnes's death her parents shut up the Abbey and went abroad."

"Why?"

"I guess they couldn't bear to see anything that reminded them of her. When they died there was no one left to inherit Wyldcliffe. The building was empty for a while before the school took it over, and the local people told all sorts of stories about it being haunted. It was easy to imagine, I suppose. A big empty house with a ruined chapel—it doesn't take much imagination to concoct something out of that, does it?"

"I guess not," I replied, staring up at the ruins. Sarah's story explained the cabdriver's behavior the night I arrived. *That cursed place.* I couldn't blame him, really. My own imagination seemed to be spinning out of control at Wyldcliffe. But looking at those tumbled stones, I found it easy to see why people wove stories about this place. It *was* haunted—haunted by the many lives it had known. And those same dark hills had looked down on this place during each and every drama, and the same bitter wind had sung through the grass. . . .

"Do you like it here?" I asked.

Sarah burst into peals of earthy laughter. "How can you like anyplace that's full of stuck-up snobs like Celeste? I'm not sure how much longer the school and its traditions will survive, to be honest. The world has changed, but Wyldcliffe hasn't."

"So why do people still send their kids here?"

"'Wyldcliffe prepares young women for a place in Society, not just for academic success,'" Sarah parroted. "I'm the fourth generation of my family to come here."

"But did you actually want to come?"

"I suppose so. The place itself is really special—you know, the ruins and the moors and the old house. I guess I love Wyldcliffe and loathe it at the same time. How about you? Do you like it?

"Mmm. I'm not sure."

"So why did you come here, Evie?"

"My mother is dead, and Dad is in the army. He's stationed abroad right now," I said, trying to sound as unemotional as possible. "My grandmother, Frankie, always looked after me. But she's ill."

"I'm sorry. I sensed . . . I mean, I thought you seemed unhappy."

"Yeah, well, it's just the way it is." I didn't want any pity. But this unthreatening girl somehow made me want to talk. I swallowed hard and carried on. "Dad had heard of this school because Frankie's family actually came from around here, ages and ages ago. He found out about the scholarship, and it was all arranged in a rush. I know I'm very lucky really." Then I burst out, "But I don't think I'll ever fit in. My family hasn't been coming to schools like this for generations."

"That doesn't matter, not to me anyway," Sarah said. "Besides, my family only made it here by the skin of their teeth."

"What do you mean?"

"My great-grandmother Maria had been adopted from a traveling Romany family when she was a baby.

If it hadn't been for that, everything would have been different."

"Why? What happened?" I asked.

"Her adoptive parents were rich landowners and desperate for a child. Apparently they had helped Maria's father when he was wrongly accused of poaching from a neighboring estate, and when Maria's mother died giving birth to her, they persuaded him to let them bring the baby up. It was a pretty unusual arrangement on both sides, but they adored Maria and wanted to give her the best of everything—clothes, travel, education—which meant Wyldcliffe, of course."

"Why? What's so special about Wyldcliffe?"

"It's always been regarded as the most exclusive school in England. In other words, incredibly snobby and expensive." Sarah laughed. "The school's High Mistress made a stink about poor Maria and said she wouldn't let a filthy gypsy child pollute the hallowed grounds of Wyldcliffe. But her adoptive parents donated a huge sum of money to the school, which did the trick, so here I am." She looked thoughtful. "I often think about her. It's funny to think she once walked on these same grounds that we're on now. I sometimes feel—it probably sounds stupid—that she's watching over me."

"You mean . . . like a ghost?" I tried to joke, but there was a catch in my voice.

"Oh, I don't know, really. But I do wonder about her. I mean, I wonder if she ever thought about her real family, or regretted not being part of the old Romany way of life. I sometimes think I would have liked those ways, living outside, close to their horses, close to the land, in touch with the old knowledge—" Sarah broke off and smiled. "My family still has tons of money, which is kind of useful. But don't go thinking I'm anything like Celeste and her crowd, because I'm not, okay?"

"Okay," I said. "I don't think you're like that one bit; I promise."

"Glad we've cleared that up." She grinned. "Come on; we'd better get back to class if you're feeling better, or Miss Scratton will be handing out more demerits."

She pulled me to my feet. I felt reluctant to leave the lake somehow. It was the only expanse of water I had seen since leaving my home by the sea, and I felt drawn to its green depths. And yet it was a place of terrible tragedy—a girl had drowned.

I didn't want to think about it. I turned away from the lake and glanced up at the moors. Perhaps the boy I had met would be out there, riding over the hills. Then a cloud blotted out the sun and a gust of wind tore across the lawn, making me shiver with cold. I started to run.

"Hey, wait for me!" called Sarah. But I didn't stop until I was safe inside the shelter of the brooding house.

# Seven

*I do not know what to make of this latest enthusiasm that seems to have cast a brooding spell over my dearest, my only friend. All I know is that I am disturbed, even afraid for him. Somehow I no longer feel quite safe.*

*Yesterday S. brought me a great heap of gifts from his travels. The doctor had ordered him to rest completely, but he said he could not stay in bed a minute longer and had walked over from the Hall without letting anyone know. Walked! But then, he has always been stubborn when his mind is made up, and he was so eager to show me his parcel of presents. There were scarves and shawls and carvings and trinkets, so I scolded him for his extravagance, but he laughed and said they had cost only pennies* in the bazaars. Then he held out a parcel wrapped in silver tissue paper.

"This is the best gift of all," he whispered. "The gift of knowledge."

It was an ancient-looking book bound in dark green leather. In faint letters much worn by time I traced the words The Mysticke Way. I undid the silver clasp and opened the book. A dry, stale smell rose from its pages. The printing was thick and black and cramped. Some of it was in Latin, and the rest in an old form of English. I read aloud:

"Reader, if you bee not pure
Stay your hande and reade no more;
The Mysteries Ancient here proclaimed
Must not bee by Evil stained."

I looked up and laughed. "What fairy tale is this that you have brought me? Don't you think we are too old for such nonsense?"

"It isn't nonsense, Agnes; it's the most important thing I have come across in all my travels! You must read it!"

He looked strained and flushed, and I wondered if he

*was still feverish. Hurriedly, he took the book from me and began to read:*

"The Philosophers do tell us that the Four Eternal Elements of Fire, Air, Water, and Earth are the stuff of Life. And the greatest of them is Fire, which is an offspring of the Sacred Flame of Creation. Ye must also knowe that these Elements are the Key to our Mysteries. It is a grave error to think that such Elements are mere physical matter or bodily substance. The Great Creator made no body but that doth have its essence or spirit. For what is a body without the spirit? It is nothing, for the body doth corrupt and decay; but the spirit doth live for ever. And so it is also true that all physical matter hath an invisible spirit within. Thus the Air, Earth, Water, and Fire contain their own spirits, in which lie hid their great power."

*He looked at me, his eyes shining. "Do you hear that, Agnes? Great power. Isn't that what we all seek in this world?"*

*"I don't know," I said cautiously. "What else does the book say?"*

"We in our Human condition are made of these four Elements—the Earth being our Flesh, the Air being our Breath, the Water being our Bloode, and lastly the Fire being our Passions and Desires. And so it doth stand to reason that we are by subtle means connected with the everlasting Spirits of the Elements. Now, herein lies our great purpose, which is thus: Those persons who truly and righteously devote themselves to the study of the Mysticke Way may learn to summon the Power of the Elements. . . ."

S. stared at me again, and his eyes glittered like blue fire. "What if we learned to summon that power, Agnes? Imagine what we could do."

"I think 'imagine' is the right word," I replied. "It is a fable, that's all, no more real than the tales of The Arabian Nights that we read together as children."

"No, you're wrong. I have looked through these pages, and what I have read has amazed me. There are rituals here, teachings that unlock the sacred mysteries—"

"Sacred?" I interrupted. "Aren't they more likely to be full of unholy superstition? Let me see."

He passed me the book with trembling hands, and I

glanced over its pages. My eyes were drawn to the following words:

Yet let the unwary bee warned; it is no light matter to trifle with Earth and Air, Fire and Water. The four Great Elements of life may nourishe and protecte, but they may also destroy.

"That is surely warning enough," I said. "Where did you find this book?"

"I will tell you, but you must keep this as our secret." He drew me next to him on the sofa. "I was wandering in the bazaar in Marrakesh with Philips when we came across a stall draped all around with embroidered hangings and piled high with musty, antique volumes. The bookseller, an old man with long robes and hardly a tooth in his head, beckoned us over and showed us his goods. There were scrolls and books in every possible language, all jostled together in a great heap. We were about to walk on when the old man caught me by the sleeve and cried, 'English! Young English master! English!' He kept repeating this and wouldn't let me go, signing urgently for me to pass into the depths of his little shop, which was hidden away like Aladdin's cave behind the stall. Philips didn't much like the look of it, but I was determined to enter and see what the old man was so insistent upon.

"When we entered the back part of the shop, the bookseller unlocked a chest made of black wood, carved with strange emblems. With an air of great reverence, he lifted out this book and said, 'This is what you seek, young master; this is for you.' I asked him how much it was, but he pressed it on me and said, 'Nothing, nothing. This is the moment; take your destiny.' So, Agnes, what do you say to that?"

"It is a good story." I smiled. "I'm surprised he gave it to you for nothing. I suppose you gave him a handsome present for his trouble?"

"I told you," he replied impatiently, coughing a little before he could go on. "He wouldn't take anything. He wanted me to have it for a reason; I'm convinced of that. I believe that if we follow these ancient rites, we could work marvels together. Haven't you always said you wish to learn new things, to break out of the world of your mother and Miss Binns and all the petty restraints that hem you in like the walls of a prison?" His eyes became soft and pleading, and he laid his hand gently on my arm. A shiver ran through me, whether of pleasure or pain I couldn't tell. "So here is something new. Please, Agnes. Give it a chance."

I looked down at the heavy volume on my lap. Almost of its own accord it fell open in the middle. Each page was closely decorated with strange symbols, and my blood began to race as I read the different headings printed in faded red ink: For conjuring Rain. To calme the Winds. To make an Amulet against Lightning. To enriche the Earth before planting crops.

"Think of all the good we could do," he urged.

I carried on reading, entranced. Healing for a Dangerous Maladie. For easing the mind of Darknesse and Sorrowe. To find your Heart's Desire. To Summon the Sacred Fire.

In that instant my old familiar dream came back to me, but more vividly than ever before. I was standing as usual before a column of white-hot flame. But now the fire seemed instead to be burning inside me, and I had only to reach out my hand to grasp whatever I wanted.

"No!" I slammed the book shut. "I don't want anything to do with it. It's dangerous. It's wrong."

"You mean that Miss Binns wouldn't approve, and that fussing old vicar down in the village church, and the whole plague of reactionaries who have palpitations at any new discovery? I thought you had more ambition than to sit sewing with your governess like a stuffed doll that dares not think or breathe or live."

"It's not that," I said unsteadily. "I am happy to embrace all that is new and good in our modern age. But this is not progress. It is going backward into darkness."

"'There is in God, some say, a deep but dazzling darkness . . . ,'" he murmured. "Don't you remember that poem? Do you think the All Powerful is limited to what we know and approve of here in this little land, in this particular moment of time? Of course not! And neither are we." He snatched my hands in his and pulled me closer to him. "Don't turn your back on this adventure. We could create something good that would last forever. Share this with me, Agnes."

"But it's just a confusion of nonsense," I protested.

Laughing suddenly, he let me go, the passion cleared from his face.

"In that case we can do no harm except to make ourselves look foolish. Besides, our intentions are pure, like the book says. What harm can come from this game to pass the time of my convalescence? Why shouldn't we play once more, as we did when we were children?"

He smiled at me as though I were the only person on the earth who mattered to him. A tiny knot of attraction tugged under my ribs. I looked away, suddenly self-conscious and tongue-tied.

"Very well," I said. "Let us play."

And so it is to be a game. That is all. And I hope with all my soul that, as in our old childhood games, it may lead to a happy ending. But if it were up to me, I would fling this book into the lake and let it sink into those deep waters, never to be seen again.

# Eight

I am swimming in the deep waves at home, at sunrise. The light on the sea is like mother-of-pearl, and I am full of surging joy, as though I could swim on and on without ever getting tired. Then I feel something brush against my ankle. I kick out, thinking it is just a drift of seaweed, but it's a cold hand pulling me under the surface, down, down, too far down. Twisting in panic, I see Laura, dead and ghastly, her hair floating around her lifeless face, her eyes hollow sockets. She is dragging me with her into the black depths. I want to scream, but I am fighting desperately for breath. I can't breathe; I'm in danger . . . what dangers are waiting for a girl from the sea . . . I can't breathe. . . .

I opened my eyes and threw the smothering blankets aside. Fumbling for my watch, I saw that it was three o'clock in the morning. My heart was pounding and I had to get out of bed to shake off the nightmare. I crept over to the window seat and looked out at the grounds below patterned with moonlight and sharp black shadows. Each tree and bush seemed to stand out artificially, like something in a theater set. I laid my head against the cool glass of the window and tried to get my breathing back under control. I didn't dare look at Laura's picture on the wall. *I hope she haunts you*, Celeste had taunted me. *I hope she haunts your every breath.*

*Please let Laura be at peace, please, please. . . .* I begged in some sort of jumbled prayer. It made me sick to think of her struggling all alone in the lake, terrified, fighting for her life—choking for breath under the cold black water would be such a dreadful way to die.

I had always refused to think about what had happened to Mom, until now. Despite her death I had been drawn to the sea, as though I could cancel out the past by defying the waves myself. Every time I had gotten out of the stinging salt water and dried myself on the beach, I felt that I had cheated death as though I were immortal. But in that dark Wyldcliffe dorm, the absolute certainty of my own death rose up and terrified me. It would really happen one day, and then there would be no cheating. In a flash of memory I thought of an inscription on the harbor wall at home, put up in honor of the sailors who had lost their lives over the many centuries: *For we all must die, and are as water spilt upon the ground. . . .*

We all must die. Peering out of the window, I could see the ruins in the moonlight and the quiet lake next to them. How had Laura managed to come to harm in such a peaceful-looking place?

"We all must die," I murmured to myself. Then I seemed to hear, from somewhere in my memories, Frankie's warm, comforting voice, as though she were reading aloud in the little church at home: *We all must die . . . yet God doth not take away life. . . . Whosoever believeth in Him shall have life everlasting.*

I got back into bed and went to sleep.

It seemed only a minute later that the morning bell was dragging us from our beds. Another relentless Wyldcliffe day was beginning.

I got dressed quickly and set off down the marble stairs before Helen came back from the bathroom. I didn't mean to be ungrateful, but I really didn't want to wander around in the dark with her, communing with the spirits of long-lost kitchen maids. Besides, I didn't dare turn up late for breakfast again. I decided that I would count this as my first real day at Wyldcliffe. I wouldn't be late, I wouldn't get into trouble, and I definitely wouldn't faint.

Simple.

Little knots of girls were making their way down the stairs, their skirts and shirts and hair all smooth and clean and neat for the new day.

"Hi," I said brightly, but they just ignored me. Total silence. It was as though I didn't exist.

"No talking on the stairs," said a low voice behind me. I swung around and was grateful to see Sarah's friendly face. She put her finger on her lips. Now I understood— another rule. I grinned back at her in relief and clattered down the cold white steps.

When we reached the bottom, the High Mistress was standing there, elegant and aloof. She watched me with expressionless eyes.

"I thought I told you that jewelry is not permitted in school."

I had forgotten all about it, and the heavy links of Frankie's necklace showed at the top of my shirt.

"I'm sorry . . . I forgot. . . ."

"Please be aware that when I tell a student to do something I do not expect her to forget."

"I'll take it off." I fled back up the stairs before she had time to say anything more. There was something about her that gave me the creeps—those fathomless dark eyes, that ultracontrolled way of speaking, and yet the flicker of rage that was visible just under the surface.

"Be careful, you idiot!"

Celeste glared at me furiously as I almost knocked into her at the top of the stairs.

"Oh . . . yeah, sorry," I panted, dashing past. I wasn't going to give her—or Mrs. Hartle—the satisfaction of seeing me late for breakfast again. I raced into the dorm, unfastening the necklace as I ran, then pulled open the drawer by the side of my bed.

I paused. I felt strangely reluctant to drop the necklace into the drawer. How did I know it would be safe? Celeste would probably have no qualms about trashing my stuff, and I couldn't bear the idea of her touching it. This was too personal, too private. The silvery pendant gleamed hypnotically in my hand. This was my last link with Frankie. Her face flashed into my mind, and it suddenly seemed incredibly important not to be parted from her little keepsake.

Scrambling in the drawer, I grabbed hold of a nightgown that had a fine thread of white ribbon running around the neck. I tore the ribbon off. Then I slipped the pendant from its chain and strung it on the ribbon instead. In a couple of seconds I had tied it around my neck, tucking the whole thing under my shirt. I checked the mirror. Nothing could be seen of the necklace now. Mrs. Hartle would never know that I was still wearing it.

Running down the stairs again, I reached the dining hall just as the last few girls were taking their places, and managed to get a seat next to Sarah. I had to stop myself from grinning at her idiotically. Defying Mrs. Hartle, even over something as trivial as this, made me feel good.

After breakfast, Miss Scratton stopped me on the way out of the dining hall. "I hope you'll have a more successful day today, Evie," she said in her dry, harsh voice.

"Oh, I'm sure I'll be fine."

She stepped closer.

"Who knows what is waiting for us in each new day? Try to stay out of trouble." Her beady eyes darted all over me, and I wondered crazily if she could see Frankie's necklace hanging under my shirt. But that would be absurd.

"You will quickly get used to our ways," Miss Scratton continued. "I hope that you will soon feel at home at Wyldcliffe. It has been home to many wanderers over the years." I didn't know what she was talking about. I had lost sight of Sarah, and I needed to get to class. I sort of smiled at Miss Scratton, hoping that she had finished with me, and dashed out.

There didn't seem to be anyone from my class in the crowd of girls in the corridor, so I examined the printed schedule that I had been given. It was Tuesday, so the first class was gym. A map of the school was printed on the back of the schedule. After a few wrong turns in the endless passageways, I managed to find the changing room. The rest of my class was already getting ready for gym—lacrosse, I guessed by the look of the equipment.

"Hey, Evie, have you got your gym clothes?" asked Sarah. I shook my head.

"Dad ordered everything, but it hadn't arrived by the time I had to leave home. The store said they would send the stuff here."

"You'd better explain to Miss Schofield when we get down to the field. Come on; hurry up. You don't want to be—"

"In trouble again." I smiled. "Yeah, I know."

We trooped out of a side door with the others and followed a path that led away from the school building and down to the grounds.

It was a dull day with a dirty gray sky. In the distance,

the moors lay like a drab blanket on the horizon. On our right, the ruins of the chapel soared up to the heavens, fractured and broken, yet even in this sluggish light they were extraordinary. But the others ignored them, chattering to one another until we arrived at the fields and tennis courts that were tucked away behind a belt of trees.

The gym teacher, Miss Schofield, was waiting for us impatiently.

"Come on, come on, no dawdling!" she yelled. "Start warming up by jogging around the field." At least she looked younger than some of the other teachers—or mistresses, as Sarah had told me to call them—but she sounded irritable. "You, the new girl—come here. Why aren't you wearing your gym clothes?"

I explained what had happened. For an instant I thought she was going to explode with annoyance, but she just barked, "Run up to the housekeeper's room. She'll know if they have arrived."

"Um . . . where?"

"Second floor, corridor on the right, third door on the left. Ask for Mrs. Edwards. And hurry! Or the period will be over by the time you've gotten changed."

I didn't wait for her to tell me twice. I jogged back to the school, slowing down only as I passed the ruins again.

As soon as I could, I promised myself, I would come and explore them properly. First I had to find the housekeeper's room. Second floor, corridor on the left, third door on the right, she had said. Or was it the other way around? I consulted my printed map, but only the main teaching rooms were named: geography, French, art, music, and the rest. They were on the ground floor. A series of rooms on the second floor was marked, STAFF OFFICES AND LIVING QUARTERS, but that was all. There was no mention of the housekeeper's room.

"Drat!"

I followed the map back to the marble staircase and ran up to the second floor. The landing was decorated with granite pillars and carved paneling. Looking down over the edge of the banister, I could see the pattern made by the black and white tiles on the floor in the entrance hall. How easy it would be to fall and go crashing down below. The thought made me feel slightly sick, and I turned down the corridor to the left.

There were no signs on any of the doors. Hovering outside the nearest one, I listened for voices, then knocked timidly, but there was no answer. I moved on to the next. This seemed more promising. I thought I heard a soft noise coming from the room. I tapped on the door. There was no reply, so I grasped the heavy handle and pushed the door open.

Six or seven mistresses were huddled around a circular table, poring over an old book that looked like an ancient Bible. They were reciting under their breath as though they were reading aloud. I coughed and the women swung around to stare at me. One of them quickly shut the book and covered it with a purple cloth. A slightly overweight blond woman snatched something up from the table and slipped it in her pocket.

"How dare you come in here without permission!" snapped the tall, gray-haired woman who had hidden the book away. Her face was red and mottled with annoyance. "Don't you know the rules, girl? This is the mistresses' private common room."

"I'm sorry; I'm new," I apologized. "I did knock."

The plump blond mistress bustled up to the door. She had a reassuring, smiling face, but her teeth looked slightly too big and uncomfortable in her mouth, and for one absurd moment I thought of the wolf in "Little Red Riding Hood."

"Don't worry, dear," she cooed. "Let's have a look at you. I'm Miss Dalrymple, and you're Evie Johnson, of course. This is your first week, isn't it? Now, Miss Raglan, don't snap the poor girl's head off." The gray-haired woman glared at me, but Miss Dalrymple seemed determined to be friendly. "Come in, come in; don't be shy."

She hustled me into the room, and six pairs of eyes latched on to me.

"Look, ladies, at all that lovely red hair."

"I hardly think we need to get carried away by the color of Miss Johnson's hair," Miss Raglan replied coldly. "What were you doing up here?"

"Looking for the housekeeper," I said. Why were they all staring at me?

"That's the third door on the other side of the stairs," she snapped. "And remember—this room is out-of-bounds."

"Yes . . . sorry . . ."

"Good-bye, Evie, for now. I do hope you'll be in my class." Miss Dalrymple smiled another flash of teeth. "Geography, dear. Don't forget."

I backed out of the room, stammering more apologies, and then fled to the housekeeper's door. I collected my gym clothes and ran back down the marble staircase. I was suddenly not looking forward to geography. It had been plump, fussy Miss Dalrymple who had hidden something in her pocket. And I could have sworn that it was a silver dagger.

# Nine

*Yesterday we drew the Sacred Circle for the first time. For the ceremony, S. used a black-handled silver dagger that he had brought back from his travels, cutting the air in deft patterns to mark out a space in which to work the Mystic Rites.*

*I was so afraid that we were doing wrong, and would have begged him to stop, but he bade me to be patient. We were in a rough cave up on the moors lit only by a candle. We stood in our Circle, waiting. A deep silence fell over us. The candle burned without wavering, like a single bright eye. Then S. spoke the incantation written in the Book. It seemed to echo through me like the sound of a bell. But nothing happened. Then he called upon the spirits of the* four Elements to reveal themselves to us. Again there was no response. He turned the pages of the Book impatiently, calling out the words and prayers and charms written on them, growing frustrated as nothing had any effect.

A small voice in my head said, I knew nothing would happen. I felt my body relax. We had tried and failed, and now S. would forget all about this nonsense. Yet, if I must tell the truth, in some secret part of me I was also disappointed. What had I hoped for? A thrill of excitement from defying the rules set out by Mama and Miss Binns? Or was it to please him that I wanted something to happen? Suddenly he turned to me and pushed the Book into my hands.

"You do it."

"Oh . . . but—"

"Please, Agnes. Just once. Please do this for me. Call the Sacred Fire."

A strange shudder went through me, and I knew that I wanted to do this. I had to, and so I began.

I heard my voice tremble as I read the incantation to summon the elemental spirits. Then it grew in power, and the strange words rolled from my lips as though I had been speaking them all my life. The earth beneath my feet began to shake, and there was a flash of lightning. A blustering wind that sounded like the hungry sea swept through the cave. I dropped the Book and stretched out my arms. Tiny white flames danced in my cupped hands. I felt no pain or fear, and in that moment I felt more myself than I ever had before.

I saw him stagger away from me with a cry, and the Circle was broken. The white fire vanished, the wind dropped, and the earth was still. We stood eyeing each other warily, panting for breath, overcome with wonder.

"The Elements answered your call, Agnes," he said slowly. "You have called their spirits and they have answered. The Fire has spoken to you."

We walked back to the Abbey in silence, trying to believe it, trying to understand. And I knew that nothing would ever be the same again.

Since then I have felt transformed. I am indeed on fire with hopes and dreams. Everything shimmers and glitters around me. Life is overflowing; I see tiny insects crawling, I see fish in the lake and birds swooping over the chapel ruins—and I crawl and swim and fly with them.

And there are other things that I see too: strange ghosts glimmering in the shadows. This morning, as I left the schoolroom to fetch some new embroidery silk for Miss Binns that my aunt Marchmont had sent from Paris, I had an odd feeling that I was being watched. I turned and saw the faintest image of a young girl walking in the corridor behind me. I thought at first that it was a trick of the light, but it was as though the curtain between this world and another had been lifted. She wore a short tunic, and her legs were covered only by stockings, and like me, she had flame-colored hair. When I saw her shimmering there, half hidden by the gulf that lay between us, I seemed to hear the sound of the waves and smell the salt tang of the sea. . . .

Our "game" has proved to be gloriously, unimaginably real. Now I am burning to know more and discover every secret.

I have never felt so alive.

# Ten

I had never felt so depressed. It was as though part of me had died. Everything about Wyldcliffe seemed strange and uncomfortable—no, more than uncomfortable—threatening. Every shadow made me jump; every night brought disturbing dreams; every morning I woke with a sinking feeling in my stomach.

I told myself that it was just because the school was so different from everything I had ever known. I would soon get used to it. I would soon toughen up. *Be sensible, Evie; of course that teacher didn't have a dagger in her pocket. It was simply a letter opener shaped like a knife.* Of course I hadn't really seen Laura drown. It was only a dream. And the girl with the flame-colored hair was imaginary. There was nothing to worry about. I was just anxious and homesick.

But somehow I couldn't quite convince myself.

When I had been at Wyldcliffe about a week, I finally got a letter from Dad. It was set out with the rest of the students' mail on a long table in the entrance hall. My heart skipped as I recognized his neat handwriting. I stuffed the letter in my pocket and counted the seconds until the bell rang for morning break. When it did, I followed the class out onto the terrace overlooking the grounds. The other students hung around Celeste as she went on about the marvelous vacation she'd had in some exclusive island paradise. Helen had stayed in the classroom, reading, and there was no sign of Sarah either. I hadn't seen much of her, as she spent all her spare time in the stables.

No one offered to talk to me, or to share the cookies and hot chocolate that were always served at this time of the day. It was as though Celeste's dislike of me had made me untouchable. I told myself I didn't care, and ran down to the ruins to open my letter in peace.

*Dearest E.,*
*I hope by now you are getting used to your new school and making friends. What do you think of Wyldcliffe? It is fine countryside around there. Your mother and I visited the area when we were first married. Clara wanted*

*to see the old farm where her family had once lived. We walked for miles over the moors without meeting another soul, I remember, though perhaps it has changed since then. I can't tell you how pleased I am that you have been lucky enough to get a scholarship to Wyldcliffe. It is such a weight off my mind to know that you are being looked after so well.*

*I return overseas tomorrow. It will be good to get back to my men and the job we have to do, but I will be thinking of you every day. I saw Frankie at the nursing home this morning; I'm afraid there's no change. She didn't really know me. But never forget how much she loves you. And so do I, my chicken.*

*Be brave, study hard, and make your old dad proud.*

I fought the lump that came into my throat. I didn't feel brave at all. A crow screeched overhead. I glanced up. The ruins and the moors and the threatening sky seemed so incredibly lonely and desolate. *What do you think of Wyldcliffe? Actually, Dad, I'm beginning to hate the place. . . .* But I would never tell him that. I had to deal with it, as Helen had said.

Blowing my nose, I jumped up, then noticed with horror that the other girls had disappeared from the terrace.

They must have all gone inside for the next class. I raced over the damp grass and slipped into the building through one of the side doors. There was no one around. I searched my pockets for the schedule and map I had been carrying everywhere.

It was gone. I couldn't find it. I would be late, I would get into trouble again, and Dad would find out. . . .

Math. That was it—I was sure we had math next with Miss Raglan, the gray-haired teacher who had been so annoyed with me. And I remembered that the math room was at the front of the building, in one of the grand old rooms near the library. All I had to do was to get to the marble staircase and I would be nearly there. I had to be quick, though. Miss Raglan would be just the kind of mistress to dish out a demerit if I turned up late.

I tore along the deserted corridors. Everyone was in class but me. The whole house seemed still and hushed. At last I reached the right place. Yes, this was it, thank goodness. I opened the door.

But it wasn't Miss Raglan's room. It wasn't even a classroom. It was some kind of jumbled parlor stuffed with heavy furniture and vases and gold-framed pictures. A skinny young girl with a smudged face and a black dress was sweeping the fireplace. I slammed the door shut and looked around wildly. Suddenly I didn't recognize the ornate paintings on the walls of the corridor, or the red carpet on the floor. Now I was completely lost.

*Okay, okay,* I thought, *just make your way to Miss Scratton's room; you must remember how to get there. Just explain to her that you couldn't find your way and ask for another map.*

Before I could move, I heard a soft noise behind me. Then I saw her again, the girl in white, walking away from me down the corridor. She held a bundle of rainbow-colored silks in her hands. Without thinking I followed her down the corridor, as if in a dream, and all the time I could hear the *swish-swish-swish* of her long skirt.

"Hi, stop!" I tried to shout. She paused and turned, looking over her shoulder with a puzzled frown. The ground under my feet seemed to collapse, and the colors of the silks in her hand swirled into a strange kaleidoscope, as if the whole world had started to spin. I saw her pale face in the streaming shadows; then it turned into the dreadful dead stare of poor drowned Laura. I began to struggle for breath as the darkness came over me once again. I was falling and no one could save me, no one except a dark-haired boy laughing under the stars. I felt his cool breath on my cheek; I saw the fierce blue of his eyes; I heard his voice: *I saved your life. . . . We'll meet again.* The fading scar on my hand throbbed faintly, like a pulse. I cried out, "Where are you? Who are you?" But he just laughed and murmured, *Evie . . . Evie . . .*

"Evie! Evie!" A stranger was calling me. My head was bursting with pain, and I felt sick. I struggled to open my eyes. A man with gold-rimmed glasses was bending over me. I panicked and tried to push him away.

"This is Dr. Harrison, Evie." Miss Scratton's pinched face came into focus, hovering behind the doctor. She was watching me intently. "You fainted again. We're concerned about you."

I made an effort to sit up. I was in a bare white room that I hadn't seen before.

"Where . . . ?"

"You're in the nurse's room, in the infirmary," explained Miss Scratton. "One of the junior girls found you lying in the corridor outside the math room. What happened?"

I hesitated, then looked away. "I don't know."

"Well, we can't have you fainting all over the place," she said curtly. "There must be some explanation."

"I don't think there's anything terribly wrong, Miss Scratton," the doctor intervened. "Her blood pressure is normal. But this young lady's had a bit of an upheaval in her life, by all accounts, and no doubt is working hard and missing home. She needs fresh air and exercise." He turned to me and asked, "Do you ride? That would bring some roses to your cheeks."

I shook my head and croaked, "I like swimming."

"Swimming? Excellent! I'm sure that can be arranged. There's a pool on the school grounds, isn't there, Miss Scratton?"

"It's only filled with water in the summer term."

Dr. Harrison grunted, dissatisfied, but stood up to go. "I'll leave some vitamin tablets for you to take, young lady. And no skipping meals!"

He gave me a smile and left, followed by Miss Scratton. I lay back down, resting my head thankfully on the cool pillow. What had really happened in that corridor? Who was the girl in white? Was she connected with Laura in some way? And the boy—he had been there, next to me, close enough to touch.

A wave of nausea swept over me. I turned my face to the wall and closed my eyes. It was ridiculous to get worked up about people I would never see again.

Who were they, after all? A boy I had met only once and would probably never meet again. A dead girl from a photograph. A nonexistent redheaded girl I had dreamed up out of my imagination. It was pathetic. I was acting like some sad, demented kid, so desperate for someone to talk to that I'd invented crazy invisible friends. It was stupid, stupid, stupid. I didn't need anyone.

But however much I might say it, I knew in my heart that it wasn't true. I did need some kind of human contact, even if it was only with dreams and illusions. For the first time in my life I admitted to myself that I was painfully lonely. Celeste and the other confident, self-satisfied Wyldcliffe girls had made it clear that they didn't want me around. Perhaps I could have made more of an effort to be friends with Helen, but there was something about her that sort of scared me. And there was Sarah. I really liked Sarah, but she seemed quite happy with her horses and her garden. She didn't need me. No one did. I was alone.

As I clutched the doctor's little bottle of pills, I knew it would take more than a few vitamins to heal my troubled heart.

# Eleven

Let the reader beware that the Mysticke Way
is a path of healing, not darkeness. Although
there be those who, through ignorance and vul-
gar prejudice, have miscalled it common witchcraft, it is no such thing. But all true followers
of the Way must not seeke power for its own
sake, nor harm any living creature. . . .

*This is what the Book says. Now I know what I am
destined to do. I shall devote myself to the Mystic Way
and become a great healer. As S. said on that first day,
what great good could we achieve? There is so much dirt*

and disease and ignorance in this world to be cured and conquered. Even I, in my sheltered valley, know of the terrible hardship of some of the poor wretches in London and Manchester and our other so-called "great" cities. I am determined to use our discoveries to alleviate such suffering, and I have made a very small beginning.

There is a pear tree in the corner of the kitchen garden that is blighted, and the gardener had told me that he planned to cut it down next week. So when both Miss B. and Mama were resting after luncheon a few days ago, I locked the door of my room and closed the curtains and consulted the Book.

First, I made an altar on my dressing table, draping it in white silk, lighting pure wax candles, and invoking the secret words of blessing. On the floor in front of the altar I drew a Circle all around me for protection and strength. Then I spoke the incantations, burning the oil and herbs as described in the Book. As I did so, I emptied my mind and concentrated until I seemed to see stars of fire and light all around me.

When the mixture had cooled, I crept into the kitchen garden, making sure that no one saw me, and anointed the tree with it. Then I bound a single strand of my hair around one of the branches. When I placed my hand on the tree, I felt the life force within it answering my call. Today the canker on the stem is shriveling and the blight is fading from the leaves. And I know I can do more, much more. As some have been given the gift to sing or dance or paint in a way that I could never hope to imitate, so I too have been given a miraculous gift: to know and serve the Secret Fire and its great Creator. Oh, my words seem wild, yet I know what I have seen and done.

I can snuff candles with a blink of my eye, and light the fire in my grate with the flick of my wrist and the strength of my thought. I can see through the shadows into the light, where a girl with bright hair and strange clothes walks by the lake, alone and lonely. I want to experience all this and more, and to understand every deep mystery that the Book contains. But S. troubles me. Already I feel that we are walking in different directions, and that makes me afraid for this great adventure. Yes, he troubles me, though it is hard to explain exactly why.

It began the day after our first attempt to cast the Circle in the cave on the moor. He called at the Abbey after breakfast, as usual, but was sullen with me, even angry.

"Why did the spirits answer you and not me?" he asked again and again, as though I had done this on purpose to spite him.

"I do not know; perhaps you should try again. . . ."

"Yes, let us go back to the cave now, immediately." He hurried me out of the house, and we rode recklessly over the hills. Once in the cave again, he repeated the ritual with a ferocious intensity, following the instructions with great care, omitting nothing of the strange rites. With all his strength and passion, he summoned the powers and called on the immortal fire. But again, the flames sprang to life in my hands, not his. He wouldn't give up, however, and he called out every word of incantation that he could muster, until his eyes burned with despair. I could not bear to see him so abandoned and distressed, and I secretly wished that he would be granted what he desired.

As the white flames flickered on my hands like laughing children, I seemed to be given a choice. It seemed as though I could allow S. to be included in the Mysteries or not. And I hesitated. All my life I have been in his shadow: younger, ignorant, a mere girl. For one fleeting moment I was tempted to keep this new power to myself.

I could not do it. "Let it happen," I breathed, "let it be as he would desire. . . ."

There was a fearful rumbling in the cave, like an earthquake, and I thought the walls must fall in on us. Dark coils of smoke, crackling with tongues of green fire, rose at his feet and wound themselves around his body until he was clothed in darkness. I reached out for him, but I was thrown down on the rocky floor. A silver light exploded in my mind. Then a long line of women's faces passed in front of my eyes, all calling his name, screeching and gibbering and weeping, until the last one was the strange girl whose face has begun to haunt my dreams. She looked so sad. An almighty crash of thunder sounded as I shut my eyes and covered my ears in terror.

Later—I don't know how much later—I opened my eyes again and saw S. standing over me. He bent down and helped me to my feet. A deep crack had appeared on the floor of the cave where our Circle had been.

"It has happened," he said simply. "I have been reborn."

And so he is satisfied, and I must be too. It is what I wished for, after all. But I cannot help wondering whether I made the right choice.

This thought has haunted me for days, like the cry of the gulls by the sea.

# Twelve

I was pining for the sea. It actually hurt, a raw physical pain in my chest. I couldn't forget what the doctor had said about going swimming. My body ached for the stinging waters and the dip and roll of the great waves. I began to feel that if I couldn't swim, I would crack up.

"Evie Johnson, are you working, or daydreaming?" asked Miss Scratton.

The words on the page I was supposed to be studying danced in front of my eyes like a foreign language. I felt as though another tiny bit of me was dying. And then, suddenly, I knew what to do.

I would swim in the lake. *That's it,* I thought. *I'll creep out at night, and no one will ever know.* Then the rising flutter of excitement inside me was suddenly checked.

Laura.

What about the nightmares I'd had about her—wouldn't they be a hundred times worse if I actually swam in the waters where she had drowned? My heart plummeted again. It was impossible, a stupid, sick idea. *Forget it.*

I tried to. I really did. But one night I couldn't sleep. Celeste had fussed about being cold and had turned up the heat until the room was sweltering. I was tired, but restless, lying awake for what seemed hours while the others slept, feeling anxious and hot and stifled. Eventually I flung off the covers and got up to open the window, but it was bolted shut. I could see the lake, pale and silver in the moonlight. It looked so cool and pure and inviting.

I couldn't resist. I had to feel the air on my skin; I had to get outside; I had to be by the lake. I wouldn't swim there, but if I could only look at it and feel the cool night breeze across the water . . .

Did I know, or guess, what would happen if I went out that night? And if I had known, would I have gone? All I know is that I persuaded myself that what I was doing was perfectly rational as I crept out of the dorm.

I decided to use the old servants' staircase that Helen had shown me. There was less chance of being seen that way. Pushing aside the velvet curtain, I drew back the bolts and opened the door. I groped for Helen's flashlight, then switched it on, my heart hammering away. The thin beam of light was comforting, though I hated the shadows that flickered all around me, and the dark cracks of those narrow steps.

*Just get on with it,* I told myself. All I had to do was walk calmly down them, and I would be free. *One step at a time, one step at a time . . .*

I reached the bottom and realized I had been holding my breath the whole way down. The door to the main hallway was ahead, and behind me was the desolate servants' wing. I stepped forward and pressed my ear to the door. There were voices outside in the corridor. I caught the words ". . . another attempt . . . soon." It sounded like Mrs. Hartle. Her voice sank too low to hear. Another voice—Miss Scratton?—protested, "No, not yet. We should wait."

Then Mrs. Hartle cut in icily, "Am I the High Mistress, or you?"

A late-night teachers' quarrel. It would be impossible to go that way. I would have to sneak through the servants' wing and find my way to the green door that led to the stable yard. It was either that or give up and go back, and I couldn't bear the thought of giving up. I had to go on.

I forced myself to walk down the musty passage, holding up the flashlight and trying to imagine that Helen was with me as I tiptoed past the deserted rooms and storage areas, past the row of old bells, past the door to the ghostly kitchen, on and on until I reached a cobwebbed green door. I tugged at the bolts and chains, and then I was outside in the cold night air.

The moon was huge and low and yellow in the autumn sky. A horse stamped restlessly nearby. I had made it. I took a few deep gulps of air and grinned. It had been worth it. I was free.

I tucked the flashlight behind the green door and ran lightly out of the stable yard to the terrace at the back of the house. Checking to make sure that no one was watching from the tall windows, I flitted across the lawns and under the shadows of the trees. The dark ruins on the other side of the water seemed to loom taller than in the daytime, and for an instant I thought I could see something fluttering between the broken archways. An owl hooted. *Go back, go back* . . . it seemed to screech. I ignored its warnings and made my way down to the silent lake.

I stooped over the water, feeling wildly happy. I was myself again, not a zombie in a Wyldcliffe uniform. My hair fell over my shoulders as I trailed my hands in the shallows, and the breeze ruffled my clothes. I closed my eyes in ecstasy, imagining that I was sitting on the beach at home, with the wind blowing and the waves racing and the water calling me.

Then I heard a footstep and I knew someone was behind me, watching me, waiting for me. I forgot to breathe, and cursed myself for being so stupid. *What dangers might be waiting?*

I opened my eyes and saw my wavering reflection in the dark water, and behind it a familiar figure in a long black coat.

"I told you we would meet again."

I whipped around. He was standing there in the moonlight, the boy with the haunting eyes.

"You terrified me!"

"And you enchanted me." He smiled teasingly. "You looked like a water nymph saying her prayers. What were you dreaming about?"

I blushed scarlet and tried to summon a brusque tone. "It's none of your business."

"I want to make it my business. I want to know everything about you."

"What makes you think I want to have anything to

do with you?" I snapped. I had secretly hoped I would see him again, but now I wanted to get away and hide, as though he already knew too much about me. "I have to go, and so should you. You'll be in terrible trouble if Mrs. Hartle catches you here."

"So will you," he replied. "What is the punishment for girls who wander by the lake at night?"

"I don't know, and I don't want to find out." I began to walk away.

"Don't go yet," he said. His voice was soft and pleading and I hesitated. "I'm not used to asking for things. But I'm asking now. Please stay. I just want to talk to you." He came up behind me and wrapped his thick coat around my shoulders. The warmth of his body still clung to the heavy fabric. The strangest feeling that I had known him before, long ago, swept over me. For one crazy moment I wanted to sink into his arms and lose myself totally in him. But I pulled away and turned around to face him, trying to ignore his strange, compelling beauty.

"What happened that night when I cut my hand?" I demanded. "Who are you? Why are you here?"

"To see you," he replied. "I've been waiting for you, girl from the sea. I think I've been waiting for you all my life."

"How . . . how do you know I come from the sea?"

"I saw it in your face; that's all." His eyes held mine in their gaze, like a magician.

"What do you mean?"

"Haven't you ever seen something that other people can't?"

"Of course not," I began, then stopped, remembering my "vision" of the old schoolroom and the girl in white. "I don't know," I said, confused. "Maybe in dreams."

"One person's dream is another's reality."

"But I cut myself. You touched the glass, and then it was mended. That wasn't a dream."

He walked abruptly to the edge of the lake. "It was nothing."

"But—"

"Honestly, it was nothing. I just pulled an old trick on you, a stunt; that's all. I wanted to impress you. To please you."

"Why?"

"I behaved like an arrogant idiot when we first met. Then you were so upset over that photograph and I wanted to do something for you." His voice sank low. "I know what it's like to lose someone you care for and have nothing left but their image." He began to cough, a hoarse sound that seemed to rack his whole body.

"Are you ill?" I asked, stepping closer to him.

"No . . . no . . . I'm getting better." The coughing fit subsided. "I'm not ill. I'm just tired. I'm tired of being alone, Evie."

"So am I," I said blankly. The silence hung between us, and our eyes met. I felt as though he could see right into me, as though we could look at each other forever and not get tired of it. . . . I dropped my gaze and moved away.

"How do you know my name?"

"It was easy. I've been hanging around the school since we met, hoping to catch sight of you, trying to find out all about you." He suddenly caught hold of my hands and drew me to him. A thousand pinpricks swept up and down my spine as he begged, "Let me get to know you. I'm sorry if I frightened you; I never meant to. Please promise you'll see me again."

A voice in my head, a million miles away, was saying, *Don't be silly, Evie; you don't know anything about him. He might be crazy. Be sensible. . . .*

I didn't want to be sensible Evie any longer. Being sensible, not making a fuss, putting on a brave face—where had it gotten me? Stuck all alone in this dreary wilderness, miles from everything and everyone I cared about. But this boy wanted to get to know me. No one else at

Wyldcliffe did. I looked up at him, trying to see into his mind.

"What's your name?"

He hesitated, as if searching for something from far away.

"My name is Sebastian." He held my hand even tighter. "Please say yes."

"Yes," I said simply. "Yes, I promise."

His pale face flooded with a smile as joyful as sunshine. Gently he turned my hand over and pressed his lips on the almost invisible scar.

"Tomorrow night, then."

I didn't reply. His coat fell from my shoulders and I fled, not knowing how I got back into my bed, knowing only that my heart sang with every step I took.

The next day flew by. Everything in school was just as dull as before, but now I had a secret, like a delightful dream. Now there was a voice in my head keeping me company, the voice of a hollow-cheeked boy with mocking blue eyes. He seemed to be with me wherever I went that day, talking to me, teasing me, guiding me. When I hesitated over the way back to the classroom from the school library, I heard him say, *It's the left turn, Evie.* For the first time since arriving at Wyldcliffe I didn't feel alone.

It couldn't last. When I got into bed that night, the impossibility of seeing Sebastian again crowded in on me. I had gotten away with one reckless hour of wandering about on the school grounds, but it wasn't safe to do it again.

*But you said you would meet him tonight. You promised. Just one more time,* I argued with myself.

*It's too risky,* my rational self answered back. *You'll get caught; you'll get expelled.*

*I won't! I'll be so careful.*

*He might not even be there.*

I knew he would. All I had to do was slip down the back stairs and I could be with him again.

*Don't do it, Evie. Be sensible.*

My sensible side won the argument, of course. I wasn't the kind of girl who broke the rules for the sake of a handsome face. Bashing my pillow into shape, I closed my eyes and drifted into an uneasy sleep.

In my dream, Miss Scratton was furiously angry with me for something that I had done, but I wasn't sure what it was. She was pacing up and down in her classroom while I waited miserably for her to pronounce my punishment. Suddenly the sound of thunder rumbled all around us, and the walls began to shake. Then I knew that it wasn't thunder, but horses galloping. The white walls cracked and crumbled, and I saw an army of horsemen pouring across the grass outside like a dark shadow. One of them wheeled around and it was Sebastian. I leaped up behind him on his black horse, and we sprang away, leaving Miss Scratton behind. She screamed, "Your necklace, Evie! Give me your necklace!" But I laughed at her and held on to Sebastian's taut body as we galloped freely over the moonlit moors. I laid my head against his shoulder, and our hair streamed out and mingled in the wind. Then the dream changed. We were all alone under the stars, and he breathed my name as he bent down to kiss me.

I woke and didn't recognize where I was. Slowly I remembered and knew what I had to do. Pulling the thin drape to one side, I felt carefully for my shoes. Then I headed straight for the narrow stairs that would lead me to freedom.

# Thirteen

THE JOURNAL OF LADY AGNES, OCTOBER 19, 1882
*I am like a bird that has been set free. The Mystic Way is beautiful, like something from a long-forgotten story of stars and fire and ice. We are both making new discoveries every day, and although for some reason S. still cannot reach out to the Sacred Fire, he astonishes me with what he has so quickly mastered. Yesterday he startled me by taking my little mirror and breaking it to pieces, then returning it to me as new, appearing to control the very atoms with his mind.*

*I would have not believed this if I had not seen it with my own eyes, but now my ideas of what is possible have been overturned. I cannot explain this strange magic. It is enough for me to be able to see it and do it. I spend hours studying the pages of the Book, and S. is translating those* passages of Latin and Greek that hide further mysteries. But one chapter I could read easily enough myself: "To Bring Light into a Darke Place." I could not resist this and had to try my skill.

Late last night, when Mama believed me to be in bed, I locked the door of my room and prepared my altar once more. Then I drew the Circle and made the signs, whispering the secret words from the Book. All at once the candles guttered out, and I was surrounded by darkness so black and thick that I could almost taste it in my throat. I began to be afraid that I had done something wrong, for this was not what I had expected at all, but I persevered, chanting the incantations and focusing my mind. I heard the wind blowing over the moors and the sound of the distant sea, and finally a light blazed out in the blackness. This would have been astonishing enough, but there was more to it than that.

The light seemed to be totally at my command. It took whatever form my fancy gave it, at first like a star, but then it became a brilliant bird with glowing blue wings, then a fiery flower with vivid petals, then a pale round moon of silver. I laughed and caught the light in my hand, then released it like a cloud of shimmering yellow butterflies. . . .

There can be no harm, surely, in something so beautiful?

# Fourteen

Sebastian was beautiful, just as I had remembered.

"Have you always lived in Wyldcliffe?" I asked as we sat by the lake, with the ruins tall and dark behind us.

"All my life. Nineteen years." A shadow flickered across his face. "But you have no idea how long it really seems."

"Where do you live? In one of those cottages in the village?"

"My family has an old house on the other side of the valley," he said evasively. I guessed that he didn't get along with his parents and didn't want to talk about them. He stood up and walked about restlessly. "I know every inch of this valley, every hill, and every path to the top of the moors. Oh, Evie, I long to see something new!"

"But you said that you've been traveling in India and

Morocco," I said. "You've seen lots of places."

"Not enough."

"But you'll be doing new things when you go to college." He had told me he had a place to study philosophy the following year.

"Oxford! A whole lot of eager schoolboys showing off about who can make clever remarks and drink the most beer. That's not what I want." He flung himself back onto the ground, then made an effort to speak more calmly. "The only thing I ever wanted was to study the very heart of things, to know the immortal truths."

"You don't want much, then," I teased. "To know the truth, the meaning of life . . . aren't you being a bit ambitious?"

He stared into the water's depths. "I won't go to Oxford."

"But won't your parents be disappointed if you drop out?"

"No," he replied. "Maybe. I don't know. Let's not talk about it." He gave me a dazzling smile. "I want to talk about you. I want to hear all about your life: what you do, what you think, what you eat for breakfast, what you were like when you were five years old."

I laughed. "Plump and bossy, with crazy red curls."

"Irresistible."

"Yeah, pretty much."

It was good to see him laugh. "Oh, Evie," he said, "you make me feel well again." It was true that he didn't seem quite as pale and tired as before. He looked at me wonderingly, as though trying to memorize my face. "I can't believe you're really here, talking to me. You're so . . . different. . . ."

"From what?"

"Different from all the other girls I know." He smiled. Then the light faded from his eyes. "I am not very good with . . . relationships."

I didn't want to admit that I had never even had a relationship. I knew nothing about boys or dating. There had been boys at school and at the beach, of course, noisy and scruffy, only into surfing and loud music and motorcycles. They had never interested me. But Sebastian wasn't like them. His idiosyncratic way of dressing, his intense gaze, his precise manner of speaking—everything about him fascinated me.

"What do you mean, not very good at relationships?" I asked. "Why not?"

"I spoil things." He frowned. "If something is less than perfect, I destroy it."

"Is that what happened—I mean, you said you had lost someone. . . ." I searched for the right words. "Someone you cared about, you said. Did it go wrong because of that?"

"You could say that."

I made myself ask the question: "So, who was she?"

"Let's forget it. It is all over." He got up and walked to the edge of the lake, then turned and looked at me, his eyes as blue and bright as a summer's day. "I just want to think about being here with you. Come on; I want to show you something."

I couldn't help wondering about the girl he didn't want to discuss as he led me away from the lake. I wondered if she'd been heartbroken when they had split up. And where was she now? I tried to let go of it. It wasn't important. Nothing mattered but this moment.

We walked under the arches of the ruined chapel. At the far side of the chapel, beyond a smooth lawn, was an overgrown thicket of shrubs. A low sign had been set up, which read, NO TRESPASSING.

"Another rule for you to break." Sebastian grinned. "Are you willing?"

I had a faint pang of conscience about what Dad would say if he could see me. I could almost hear Mrs. Hartle's voice sneering, *Wandering in the grounds at night with a local boy, Evie? This is hardly what we expect from our Wyldcliffe girls.* But the last person I wanted to listen to was Mrs. Hartle.

"Sure." I grinned back.

We crashed through the tangled growth, snapping twigs and scratching ourselves on the brambles. I was just thinking that it was like the prince arriving to wake Sleeping Beauty, when I saw a mass of rock looming over me in the darkness. A gaping black slit in the rock looked like the mouth of a tomb.

"We're not going in there, are we?"

Sebastian saw the anxious look on my face. "There's nothing to worry about, Evie. I'll be with you." He took my hand and suddenly all the world seemed safe. I had never felt so right, so wonderfully alive.

We entered the gloomy cavern. I heard the sound of running water; then Sebastian let go of my hand and fumbled to strike a match. A gleam of light flickered over the damp, shining walls.

"Look!"

I lifted my eyes in wonder. The walls of the cave were not bare and rough, as I had expected. They were embedded with shells and crystals and pieces of colored stone arranged in intricate patterns and shapes.

The match went out and for a moment we were in total darkness. Sebastian struck another match, then groped in an alcove at the side of the cave, found a candle end, and lit it. The wavering yellow light fell on fantastical mosaics of flowers and fruit and wicked-looking fauns, all glittering darkly on the walls. In the farthest part of the cave a little spring gurgled around a statue of Pan, or some other ancient god.

"I love this place," Sebastian said. "Don't you?"

He seemed enchanted, like a little boy who runs onto the beach and claims the whole sea for his own. I didn't want to admit it, but the cavern gave me the creeps, as though the glistening shells were hundreds of leering eyes.

"It's . . . um . . . interesting. But what on earth is it?"

"It was Lord Charles's grotto. The stones and shells were all sent over from Italy for him. This was his little indulgence when he built his house on the ruins of the old nunnery. It was the latest fashion in those days, an expensive hideaway, and now none of the young ladies up at the school probably even knows that it exists."

"So, what was it used for?"

"There were picnics and musical parties. And there were other meetings here, darker and more secret."

His eyes blazed in the candlelight. I couldn't tell whether he was sad or angry, but he looked lost somewhere faraway.

"How do you know about the old days at Wyldcliffe?" I asked. "Sarah told me that Lord Charles and his family lived here more than a hundred years ago."

"I sometimes feel as though it is all still happening. Can't you see Lord Charles and his silly, snobby wife sitting here right now, admiring their expensive folly? And can't you see *her*—Agnes? Can't you hear her?"

He reminded me of Helen. *Can't you hear their voices?* Why was everyone at Wyldcliffe so obsessed with the past? It seemed more real to them than the present.

"But I want to live now," I heard myself saying.

Sebastian smiled sadly, and the knot under my ribs tugged again. He seemed locked into his own private unhappiness. I wanted desperately to be able to chase away the shadows that hovered over him. "You are right." He sighed. "Now is all we have." He looked at me as though waking from a dream. "I'm glad you're here, Evie."

"Good." I smiled awkwardly. "At least someone appreciates me."

"No, I mean it. You make me want to live again."

Sebastian moved closer to me, touching the side of my

cheek as gently as a feather falling on snow. He looked at me, yearning and unsure.

"Oh, Evie," he began, "if only . . ."

"What?" I breathed.

"Nothing." He hesitated. I thought he was going to kiss me and my heart seemed to fly on wings. Then he suddenly stepped away.

"Will you see me again, Evie? Please?"

I wanted to hold him, to comfort him, to tell him I wanted to see him every night for the rest of my life. But I didn't, of course. I wasn't that crazy.

"Sure. Why not? I'll meet you by the lake tomorrow."

For one moment Sebastian smiled his most glorious smile. "Tomorrow night. I'll be there."

It was only afterward, as I lay restlessly in bed, that I remembered that he hadn't answered my question. How did he know so much about the Templetons? It didn't matter, I thought sleepily. I would see Sebastian the next night. Tomorrow and the next night and the next . . . Helen sighed and turned over in the bed next to mine. I closed my eyes and tried to settle down. Tomorrow would soon be here. There would be time to find out everything.

I fell asleep, still feeling the touch of his hand on mine.

# Fifteen

*I need to find out everything. I need to know how to make
S. truly happy without destroying my own happiness, how
to raise him up without degrading myself. He is restless
and dissatisfied, and this casts a shadow over everything.*

*I fear he has not forgiven me for being the first to touch
the elemental world. That moment still seems to disturb
him, and he is searching for a way to be the leader in our
"game" once again. For instance, he was pleased by a por-
tion of the Book's teaching that he came across, and read
the passage aloud with great relish.*

"You must heede that it is only the Females of
our Way who align themselves with the forces

of their chosen Element and thus become
Mystic Sisters. . . .

*"So this explains it, Agnes,"* he said eagerly. *"I must
reach the Elements by other means. Listen!*

"Yet Men may also achieve muche knowledge
and wisdome by following the Mysteries and
the Rites. A Male of our kind, who is called
to a deep and subtle Power, may build around
him a Coven of Sisters who will serve him as
their Master. Through the energy of his Aura,
he may reach out to their Elemental Powers. In
this way the traditional rule of the stronger sex
may bee restored, but all must be used for the
Common Goode.

*"That is what I must do, Agnes; don't you see?"*
*I laughed and said I would not serve him and that he
would have to look elsewhere for his throng of sisters to
obey his every whim. "You are spoiled enough with everyone's attention," I teased. "And besides, I do not wish to
have a master."*
*"But one day you will marry, Agnes, and maybe soon.*

You know that your mother has plans to take you to London next year to make a great match. Will you not promise, according to your church, to obey your husband? Will he not become your master and your lord?"

"Then I shall not marry," I said lightly.

"Are you sure? Is there no one you could give your heart to?" He moved closer to me and touched my face gently, so gently that it was like a feather falling on snow. My heart was beating like the wings of a trapped bird, and I half wished that he would kiss me, and yet part of me was afraid. I forced myself to laugh.

"I told you, I wish to be free."

But perhaps deep down I was not telling the whole truth. We have been so much together these past weeks, yet we are not the same as we used to be. We are no longer children. When he studies the Book with hungry eyes and is not aware of me, I secretly watch him, trying to understand what has changed in him since he went abroad. The angle of his pale cheek, the dark silk of his hair, the line of his shoulders—all this moves me in some strange way that I barely understand. I feel that I would do anything for him, whether it is right or wrong, good or evil. I am afraid that if I allowed myself, I would be swept away by the force of his presence and I would lose myself in him.

*Papa has been so good to let me see S. without a chaperone, allowing him this privilege as an old friend of the family. But I confess that I no longer see him simply as a brother. When we are apart it is his face that I see in my mind; it is his voice that calls to me on the wind over the moors; it is his touch that I crave.*

*What would my dear father say if he knew the truth about what we are doing with our time? Or if he could guess what thoughts are swirling through my head like a storm?*

# Sixteen

I replied to Dad's letter with false cheerfulness. *Yes, I'm fine; Wyldcliffe is amazing; I'm working hard.* I conveniently forgot to mention roaming around the grounds at midnight, although my conscience told me that Dad would not be happy if he knew the truth. I kidded myself that my meetings with Sebastian were only a bit of fun, not worth making a fuss about.

Although I knew I wouldn't get another letter back from Dad for ages, I couldn't help waiting for the mail each morning, hoping for some sign that the outside world hadn't completely forgotten me. I got a scribbled postcard from a girl who had been at my old school, but that was all. Nothing from Frankie, of course.

But one morning, when the October mist hung over

the lake, there was a letter. The writing on the cover was thin and curved, and I knew in a flash that it was from Sebastian. It couldn't be from anyone else. We had been meeting nearly every night, talking endlessly about . . . oh, everything—nature and history and philosophy and the places we wanted to see and the books we had read. But I noticed that he never talked about his family.

Books, stars, journeys, sonnets . . . One night Sebastian had laughingly promised to write me a poem. Perhaps that was what the letter contained. My heart seemed to bang about inside my chest as I reached for the envelope. But someone else put a hand on it first.

It was Helen.

"Hey, that's my letter!"

"Do you like poetry, Evie?" she asked, with that unnerving blank look on her face.

"I . . . What?" Surely she couldn't know about Sebastian?

"They say words can be dangerous. I'd take care if I were you."

Then she walked off, and Celeste pushed in front of me.

"Evie Johnson's got a letter? Who on earth would want to write to you, Johnson?" She snatched the envelope from my hands. I tried to grab it back from her, but she quickly passed it to Sophie, who tossed it India, and soon a whole crowd of laughing girls was throwing it about among them, twisting and dodging out of my reach.

"What is all this noise?"

At the sound of Miss Scratton's voice they broke away and stood in a circle around me. I was red-faced and furious.

"They're trying to take my letter!" I sounded like a sulky ten-year-old.

"It was only a bit of fun, Miss Scratton." Celeste smiled, handing her the envelope. "Mrs. Hartle always says it's important to be a good sport."

Miss Scratton beckoned me over to her. She glanced down at the curling black writing. "Who is this letter from, Evie?" she asked.

"I . . . I don't know. A friend."

"A friend you don't know? How very odd."

"A friend from home," I lied.

"Very well, Evie, here it is." She seemed reluctant to hand me the envelope. "Try not to make such a scene in the future. You would do well not to draw attention to yourself."

I was too angry to listen. I was getting the blame for making a scene when it had been Celeste's fault. I stormed out and stomped down the corridor to our classroom.

It was empty. I threw myself down in my seat and tore the letter open.

> *My dearest Evie,*
> *It was so good to see you last night. Well, you asked for a*
> *poem, and here it is. Read it, and forgive me for not being*
> *able to express myself better.*
> *Sebastian.*

On the other side were some verses. I began to scan them eagerly.

> *My Lady Eve,*
> *Whose heart is kind,*
> *Can soothe and heal*
> *This restless mind . . .*

"Hey, Evie, are you okay?" I jumped and looked up. It was Sarah. For once I wasn't pleased to see her. I quickly folded the letter away. "I heard Celeste was being a pain."

"It was nothing."

Sarah looked at me searchingly, just as Miss Scratton had.

"Evie . . ." She hesitated as she sat down next to me. "I know this sounds a bit odd, but I get the feeling that something's going on with you. Are you in any kind of trouble?"

"I'm perfectly okay. I just want to be left alone for five minutes without everyone prying and staring like I'm some kind of freak."

"You're not alone, though, are you? I can tell."

"You can't tell anything about me! None of you!" My frustration with Wyldcliffe blazed out of control. "Life's great for you, with your horses and your family and your money and your 'I'm not like them.' Well, you're not like me either! You don't really know anything about me or my life, so just leave me alone!"

As soon as I had spat out the words, I regretted them. Sarah looked hurt, and gathered up her books to sit at another desk. The rest of the class began to come in. I flashed a pleading look at Sarah, trying to show I was sorry, but she deliberately turned the other way and started to talk to a girl called Rosie.

Everything I did at Wyldcliffe seemed to go wrong.

# Seventeen

Sarah didn't bother to come near me after that. I felt bad, but I was getting good at hiding my feelings. I ignored her and she ignored me. I told myself that I was finished trying to make friends at Wyldcliffe. Instead I got through the days like a zombie. Gym, assignments, choir, grades—none of it mattered. My life was at night, in those precious moments with Sebastian.

I no longer dreamed of Laura. I didn't have any more fainting attacks, or weird "visions" of the redheaded girl either. It seemed as though now that I had someone real in my life I could live without fantasies.

"Wait for me!"

We raced across the wet grass in the moonlight. Sebastian ran effortlessly ahead and reached the ivy-covered wall that marched around the Abbey's grounds.

"Cheat!" I panted as I caught up with him.

"How was that cheating?" He laughed.

"Your legs are longer than mine."

"You can hardly blame me for that!"

"Anyway, why are we here?" I asked, trying to get my breath back.

"We're running away. We have to climb over the wall."

He grasped hold of a thick vine of ivy and pulled himself to the top of the wall. Then he reached down to help me up.

"I'm not sure about this," I said in a sudden fit of conscience. It was bad enough to be out at night, but if anyone caught me leaving the grounds . . .

"Please, Evie." He was suddenly serious. "I need to talk to you about something important, but I have to get away from here first. I swear you won't get into trouble. I'll take care of you."

He whistled softly, and his black mare appeared like a shadow from farther down the lane. A few moments later I was perched nervously on the horse's bare back.

"You'll have to hold on to me."

I slipped my arms around Sebastian's waist, acutely conscious of his lithe body next to mine. The horse began to pick its way delicately down the lane. I closed my eyes and breathed in Sebastian's presence, trying to convince myself that this was actually happening. Everything seemed like a dream: the great black horse, the stars, the shiver that ran through me when a strand of Sebastian's dark hair blew across my face. *I'll always remember this*, I thought. *Whatever happens to me, I'll never forget this moment.*

We began to climb the sloping moor.

"Where are we going?"

"To the old watch tower. They say it was part of a fort in Saxon times. It's even older than the Abbey's ruins."

We rode on farther, passing a couple of lonely farmhouses in the dark. Everything was empty and still. It was as though we were the only two people left on earth, immortal wanderers in a silent land. Finally Sebastian came to a halt at the top of a rough mound circled with stones.

"Here we are."

I was disappointed. I had been expecting a high tower with walls and arrow slits, like a castle from a fairy tale, not just a bare hill and tumbled rocks.

"But there's nothing here," I said as Sebastian helped me to dismount.

"The fort would have been built in wood, so it disappeared long ago. But before that this was probably a temple, or a holy place." He threw himself down onto the heather and looked out over the sleeping valley. "In ancient times people worshiped the sun and moon and the elements. A hilltop like this would have allowed them to get closer to their gods. It was a place of power."

"I've never thought about all that stuff before," I said. "It's as if you can't get away from the past at Wyldcliffe."

"You can never get away from the past, wherever you go," he said bitterly.

"Sebastian, what's wrong?"

"Nothing." He smiled up at me, his eyes clear and bright again. "Nothing's wrong when you're with me." He patted the ground invitingly. "Come here."

I sat down. Slowly, questioningly, he put his arm around me and drew me to him. The most wonderful sense of warmth and peace stole over me. I leaned my head on his shoulder, my heart dancing like a newborn creature.

"Oh, Evie," he breathed. "My Lady Eve. Now, at this moment, I am happy."

"So am I," I whispered.

He held me tighter, and murmured, "I want to remember it like this: you and me, far away from the Abbey and its past. Just one moment to remember . . . whatever happens next."

I don't know how long we sat there in silence. There was no need for words. I was with Sebastian, and it was enough just being together, looking up at the stars, like the people from thousands of years ago. As we sat there, a wind blew up and the clouds changed and eventually it began to rain.

"I could have stayed like that forever." I sighed.

To my surprise, Sebastian's face darkened. "Have you really thought about being stuck in one place forever? It would be like being in prison." He stood up and walked away and began to speak in a low voice, stilted and unnatural, as though he had rehearsed what to say. "I said that I needed to talk to you, Evie. You've been such a good friend. I'll never forget it. But after tonight—after tonight I don't think we should go on seeing each other. It's too much of a risk for you."

The ground seemed to slip underneath me.

"But if I'm careful they'll never find out at school. . . ."

"It's not just the school. This whole thing—it could be dangerous for you."

"You mean you've had your fun, and now I can go back to my dreary little life," I exploded. "Is that it?"

"No! I'm trying to think of what's best for you. Please believe that. But there are things in the past, things I've done that I regret."

"I don't care!"

"But I do." He groaned. "And you would if you knew."

"Then tell me," I pleaded. "At least tell me the truth."

Sebastian's face was sickly white in the starlight. "I can't."

I had been so happy just a few minutes ago. Now I felt like an outcast. Sebastian had shut me out, and the pain was almost physical. The rain lashed down. I started to run over the moor.

"Where are you going?" Sebastian called after me. "You'll get lost."

"What do you care?"

"Evie!" he cried. He caught up with me. "Don't go like this, Evie. Let me take you back to the school."

"So that we can shake hands at the gates and say it's all been great fun? If you really don't want to see me again, it's easier if I just go now."

"I do want to see you. Of course I do. I just don't want to mess up again. Not with you. I want to keep this as something perfect. And I'm trying—for once—not to be selfish, not to just take what I want without thinking about the consequences. I'm trying to do the right thing, but it hurts so much!"

My anger melted like spring frost.

"Sebastian," I said gently, "I'm not like you. I don't expect things to be perfect. And I'm not obsessed with the past. This is a new day, a new life. You can't go around burdened by old mistakes forever."

"It wasn't just a mistake. I hurt someone very badly." He spoke in an expressionless voice.

"Was it that girl you told me about?"

He nodded.

"These things happen. Don't make it worse by hurting me as well."

"I don't ever want to hurt you," he whispered. "I care for you more than . . . more than I could ever say."

My heart lifted. He cared for me. That was something.

"Then don't say that we can't see each other," I pleaded. "Nothing bad will happen. I trust you, Sebastian."

"But perhaps you shouldn't. Sometimes I think you've been sent to me, and sometimes I think I am just telling myself what I want to hear. I don't know anymore. I just know that I am trying to do the right thing for you, Evie."

"How can you be sure what that is? Didn't you say to me that we can't see what's going to happen in the future? Every single day is a risk. Being alive is a risk. Well, I'm willing to take the risk if you are."

He hesitated, then looked at me gratefully. "Are you sure? Do you really mean that?"

"Of course I do."

"So we can still be friends?"

I took his cold hand in mine. "Sebastian, I'll always be your friend."

But as we rode back to the school in the wind and rain, I knew that I wasn't quite telling the truth. I wanted to be more than Sebastian's friend. Oh, I wanted so much more.

# Eighteen

"This is not up to your usual standards." Miss Scratton frowned, handing back my report on William Blake. "I want you to go to the library after supper and do it again. And you really must stop yawning, Evie! It's extremely impolite. You'll have to go to bed early, at the same time as the younger girls, if you carry on like this."

"I'm sorry, Miss Scratton," I said meekly. The truth was that I was incredibly tired. Missing two or three hours' sleep every night to see Sebastian didn't exactly make me feel eager for academic work. Trying to concentrate on the book of poems in front of me, I read, *In what distant deeps or skies / Burnt the fire of thine eyes.* But the only eyes that burned in my memory were Sebastian's.

Eventually, the lesson crawled to a close.

"Put your books away, girls. I have something to tell you. We will be visiting Fairfax Hall next week as part of our research on the nineteenth century. Some of you may have been there already, but for most of you I imagine it will be a new experience."

Everyone looked up eagerly.

"What is it like, Miss Scratton?" asked Celeste, looking primly enthusiastic.

"Fairfax Hall is a perfectly preserved example of a Victorian country house. It is not as big or imposing as Wyldcliffe, but fortunately the Fairfax family kept the house largely untouched since it was built. The Hall was passed down through various cousins and distant relations until the Second World War, when such large houses became no longer practical. When the last owner died the house stood empty. It has only recently been opened as a museum, thanks to the splendid efforts of our local historical society."

"How will we get there?" asked a girl called Katherine Thomas.

"The Hall is only about two miles across the moors, to the east of Wyldcliffe. I have arranged for you to have lunch over there, and a private bus will collect us to return to school. If the weather is good, I propose that we set off early in the morning and walk to the Hall."

A buzz of excitement broke out all around the classroom. I guessed that the idea of getting out of school and roaming the moors was what appealed to most of the girls, rather than actually looking at the museum.

"That will do, girls; quiet down," said Miss Scratton. For once she smiled. "You'll need to bring your notebooks and sketch pads with you. Everyone should assemble by the main door promptly after breakfast on the day of the visit."

The bell rang for lunch, and the class jostled into the corridor, chatting excitedly. I found Sarah at my side, looking self-conscious but determined.

"You could sit next to me on the bus, if you like," she said quietly.

I looked at her freckled face and wondered how I had ever been angry with her.

"I'd really like that. Thanks. And I'm so sorry, Sarah; I never meant to—"

"It doesn't matter."

She smiled, and I knew we were friends again.

"Have you been to this place before?" I asked.

"I've ridden past it on Starlight," said Sarah. "You can't see much, as it's surrounded by enormous trees. To be perfectly honest it just looked like an old house to me, but if it perks Miss Scratton up to go see it, that can't be a bad thing."

The prospect of spending the day out of the school in the company of Sarah was like a breath of fresh air blowing through Wyldcliffe's corridors. That evening, when I was tidying up the music room with Helen, I asked her cheerfully if she was looking forward to our visit to the Hall.

"I wouldn't go there if you paid me," she said, looking more awkward than ever.

"Don't be silly." I laughed. "We won't get lost on the moors."

"I wish I could get lost out there," she exclaimed passionately. "I'd like to walk on the moors forever and never come back."

I didn't understand her. Was she just odd, or was she ill in some way?

"Are you feeling okay, Helen? You seem really stressed. Don't you think you should tell Mrs. Hartle—"

"No!" Helen burst out. "Don't you dare say anything to her!"

"Sorry," I said, taken aback. "I was only trying to help."

"Well, don't." She glared, starting to stack a pile of crumpled music. "Concentrate on helping yourself. You'll need it."

I finished my chores without trying to make any more small talk. I was looking forward to the day at Fairfax Hall, even if crazy Helen Black wasn't.

# Nineteen

THE JOURNAL OF LADY AGNES, NOVEMBER 4, 1882
*I am almost crazy with worry.*

*I wish I could heal S. as easily as I did Martha. My old nurse has long been troubled by a cataract in her eye that clouded her vision, but now she cries and laughs and declares that it is a miracle that she can see perfectly well again. Only I know what has brought about this change—it was the power of the living Fire, which I called upon in my Circle of healing.*

*I cannot rejoice in this as I should, for I am so concerned about my beloved friend. It is as though he is ill with some strange depression, and he is as pale and thin as when he first came home from his travels. He cannot relax, and pushes himself to work harder and study* deeper, without allowing himself to rest.

Although I do not like to think this, I believe that S. envies my achievements, despite the fact that his powers increase by the day. His long white fingers can bend metal, or shatter a glass or cup, then reassemble their atoms as easily as liquid flows from one shape to another. But he dismisses what he has learned and wants more. Yesterday he was in a particularly black mood.

"Magic tricks, that's all I know, Agnes. And my knowledge does not seem to produce anything good or useful. I am no healer."

It is true. He does not have this gift. I did not know what to say to him.

"Perhaps it will come later, as you study more."

"Perhaps! I am already weary with study. And perhaps I will never achieve anything at all. I have no insight into the deep elemental powers. But you have been touched by the Fire, the greatest of them all."

He brooded for a while, then spoke hesitantly.

"You remember that the Book said that men . . . males should have followers . . . a group of females? Maybe that is what I need to go further—" In that instant, I seemed to see him surrounded by a group of women shrouded in dark cloaks.

"No!" For some reason this idea was distasteful to me. Then the vision changed and I saw him with one girl—the girl I have seen before—and he looked at her with such tenderness that my heart twisted with pain. . . . "No," I repeated more calmly. "This is our secret, for the two of us. Let's keep it that way."

"The two of us?" His eyes glittered brilliantly, and he took my hand. "Agnes, you and I could do so much together, if only you would really help me."

"I do help you," I protested. "You know I would do anything for you."

"Then tell me what you know, Agnes," he urged. "Teach me your secrets."

"I don't have any secrets, especially not from you. Everything I know has come from the Book."

"That's not true, and you know it's not. You do more than is set out in its pages. How do you do it? Tell me!"

"I don't know, truly. I carry out the Rites as instructed, and then I think, I feel, I desire. And then . . ."

"Then what?" he asked eagerly.

I shook my head. How could I describe the dazzling images in my head, the tingle in my hands, the surge of power through my body when I carry out the Mystic Rites?

"I can't explain. But does it matter how it happens if good comes of it? Look how happy Martha is now, and there are so many others I can help."

He threw my hand aside. "You have the power of Fire, Agnes, and yet you will not share it with me. I have seen what you can do, and you could teach me your secrets if you chose."

I shook my head dumbly, thinking of how I'd first willed the spirits to answer when he called them. Perhaps he was right: Perhaps I could help him further. But something in his desperation held me back.

"I can't explain," I said slowly. "It is something given to me and me alone."

Was I wrong to say this? Was I wrong to deny him? How could I refuse him, when his happiness means more to me than my own? I barely understand myself, yet I know that I did right.

Now silences that were never there before fall between us. From time to time I catch him staring at me, yet seeing nothing, as though he wanders far in his thoughts. I cannot describe how this grieves me. I would do anything for him . . . anything but this.

I fear we no longer entirely trust each other.

# Twenty

"I thought you said you trusted me," teased Sebastian.

"I do trust you," I replied with a laugh. "I'm just not sure about the boat."

Sebastian had somehow produced an old rowing boat, which floated sluggishly at the edge of the lake, and he was as excited as a kid at the idea of taking it on the water. I prayed that no one would spot us, but it was good to see him fool around, as though he had managed to throw off his worries for a while.

Despite my laughter, I didn't feel that great. It was the night before the class trip to Fairfax Hall, clear and windless and bitingly cold. I had put on a thick sweatshirt over my nightclothes, but I still shivered, as if I were getting sick. I hadn't forgotten my desire to swim, but tonight the lake looked uninviting, its black waters still and sullen. I felt uneasy. This was no innocent swimming pool, I reminded myself. Laura had died here, on this very spot.

I was sick of shadows and secrets.

I wished that Sebastian and I could meet like other people did, in coffee bars and at the movies and parties. Just do regular stuff. I was getting tired of hiding in the dark.

"If the boat springs a leak we'll get a dip in the lake; that's all," Sebastian said, untying the ropes. Then he glanced up at me. "Evie, are you all right? You're not scared, are you?"

"I'm not scared of anything," I said, stepping into the boat and trying to shake off my strange mood. It rocked from side to side. There was a faint smell of mildew from its damp timbers.

"Where did you find this?" I asked.

"Oh, there are all sorts of things that have been abandoned at Wyldcliffe that people don't value anymore. This fine vessel was rotting in an old boathouse, covered with laurel bushes. . . ."

"Rotting!" I exclaimed. I liked the idea of our expedition even less.

"It will last for one more outing." He smiled coaxingly.

"Don't worry. Just lie back and enjoy the trip. Here, Evie, wrap my coat around you."

Sebastian looked so happy as he passed me the thick coat that I couldn't resist. He began to row skillfully across the lake. His cheeks were flushed, and the dark shadows under his eyes seemed to have faded. My stomach tightened at the sight of him as he pulled and stretched in his white linen shirt. I wanted to reach out and touch him.

But I didn't know whether he would want that. *Dearest Evie, sweet Evie, wonderful Evie . . .* Since our ride out to the old fort, Sebastian had been kind and attentive and affectionate, but he hadn't touched me again or put his arms around me. And he had never kissed me, not even a peck on the cheek.

Why not? I kept asking myself. Was I unattractive to him? And what had really happened with that other girl? As we glided farther out onto the deep lake, a horrible thought flashed across my mind.

The girl Sebastian had once known might have been poor dead Laura.

Laura. Of course. That would explain why he had been hanging around on the night I had first come down to the lake. He must have been keeping vigil over the spot where Laura had died. It was Laura who had drawn Sebastian to the lake, not me. It all made sense now. I had been sleeping in Laura's bed, taking her place at the school, and now I was with the boy she had left behind. *I hope she haunts your every step.*

So that was why he was determined to view me only as a friend. After all, how could I compete with the idealized memory of a tragic victim? But what had he meant about hurting the girl he had known? How would that fit in with Laura? Maybe they had quarreled before she died; maybe he blamed himself somehow.

"You're very quiet," said Sebastian, letting the oars hang motionless over the edge of the boat. "Do you want to go back?"

"No, I'm fine," I lied. "I was just thinking."

"What? Tell me."

I struck out randomly at the first thing that came into my head.

"I miss my home. This lake and the gardens and the hills, they all seem—I don't know—too still. Stifling, somehow. I wish we could walk by the sea when the waves are angry and the wind is racing. I can't really explain, but I feel different there . . . free."

"I'd like that." He smiled. "I'd love to walk on the beach with you."

"We could walk and sail and swim." My voice cracked with longing. My mind was on fire, and my body ached with restless, unnamed desires. I tried to pull myself together, to be sensible Evie again. "At least I have one day of freedom tomorrow," I said. "My class is going for a walk over the moors."

"So Mrs. Hartle's prisoners are going to be let out, are they? And where is she letting her poor captives wander?"

"We're going to visit an old house—Fairfax Hall. Do you know it?"

Sebastian began to row back to the overhanging laurels at the side of the lake.

"Sure," he said, almost too carelessly. "Everyone around here knows the place. Poor Evie, if that's tomorrow's big excitement you'll be disappointed. It's a dull old house full of other people's memories, that's all."

He tied the rope around a thick branch and jumped out of the boat, splashing his boots in the mud at the edge of the lake. Then he turned and lifted me onto the grass. For one moment we clung to each other like lovers.

"Evie," he said urgently. "Promise me something."

"Of course, what is it?"

"If you hear anything . . . in the village . . . anything bad about me, you'd still trust me, wouldn't you? You'd still come to see me like this? Promise?" He held me even tighter. My heart thudded against his.

"I promise," I said. "I promise."

Sebastian stepped back, pale and tense. "I have to go now."

"Why?" I asked. "Don't go yet."

"I must," he repeated. "I'm sorry, Evie." He began to stride away over the dark lawns.

"Sebastian, wait! When will I see you?"

"Tomorrow night," he called back. "And remember— you gave me your promise!"

I felt chilled right through to the bone. Why would anyone try to turn me against Sebastian? Perhaps he really had done something to hurt Laura. Perhaps it was common knowledge among his friends in the village, and he was worried that I would find out. Perhaps I was an absolute idiot to have anything to do with him at all. I set off wearily, anxious to get back to the dorm.

When I reached the stable yard, something looked different. I paused. The green door that led into the servants' quarters had swung open. Strange, I thought. I was sure I had closed it carefully.

Everything in the yard was quiet, apart from the occasional swish of a horse's tail. I crept across the cobblestones and slipped though the door. Then it banged shut behind me, and I heard a key grate in the lock. I whipped around and tugged at the handle, but the door wouldn't budge. Someone had locked me in.

Panic leaped up in me like a sheet of fire.

"Who's there?" I called. "Open the door!" But there was no answer, only the soft sound of footsteps outside. Fumbling wildly on the floor, I felt for Helen's flashlight. It was gone. Of course it was gone, and I knew who had taken it—Celeste. She must have set up this stunt; it would be so like her. . . .

*Think, Evie, think.*

I had to get back to the dorm before Celeste got hold of one of the mistresses. The faintest gleam of light spilled through a skylight above the door into the old passageway. It would have to be enough.

It was easy to tell myself to keep calm, but the farther I went, the darker it got. Soon I was groping along in dense blackness, feeling the wall as my only guide. I could hear rustling noises, scampering and whispering in the dark. There was the faint swish of a skirt and the clatter of boots as I passed the old kitchens. *Can't you hear their voices?* I dreaded to feel the touch of a long-dead hand on my arm. *Don't be stupid*, I kept saying to myself. *It's only your imagination; the dark can't hurt you . . . it can't.*

I found the narrow entrance to the servants' stairs and climbed them in total blindness. As I counted the steps with sobbing breaths, I was convinced that another girl's light footsteps were following me. *Swish-swish-swish:* The sound of her skirt was getting nearer.

At last I could see a crack of light ahead, the outline of the door to the dormitory corridor. I fell upon the handle just in time to hear the bolt being pushed home on the other side. Celeste must have run unseen up the main stairs and cut me off.

My efforts had been for nothing. I was locked inside the old servants' wing, trapped, just as she had intended. I sank to the floor, my back against the door, trying to breathe. There was no one following me, I told myself frantically. I was alone. All I had to do was wait until morning, when Helen would surely unbolt the door and find me here.

*Breathe . . . just breathe.*

I remembered the words of an old song that Frankie had sung when I was a little girl.

> *The night is dark, but day is near,*
> *Hush, little baby, do not fear. . . .*

*The night is dark,* I repeated over and over again, *the night is dark,* until I thought I would scream. Then the door behind me rattled, and someone opened it. I fell into the corridor, expecting to see Celeste. But it wasn't Celeste who had opened the door.

It was Miss Scratton. And standing next to her was Helen.

# Twenty-one

I had been totally wrong about Celeste. She'd had nothing to do with what had happened on the stairs. It was Helen who had betrayed me to Miss Scratton.

After we had finally gotten to bed, I had whispered to her angrily, "Why did you do that?" She had mumbled that I would understand one day. I was furious, but for once I agreed with Celeste: Helen Black was completely nuts. And now, thanks to her, I was in disgrace.

"I cannot express how disappointed I am in you, Evie," Miss Scratton declared the next day. The whole class was waiting by the Abbey's imposing front door, coats and hats tugged by the November wind. Miss Dalrymple was there too, decked out in walking boots and holding a map. "It was very silly of you to go wandering down those old stairs in the middle of the night. You could easily have fallen and broken an ankle. The High Mistress will not be pleased when she hears about this."

Celeste shot a look of triumph at India and Sophie.

"This is the second demerit you have acquired in your short time at Wyldcliffe. Let it be the last!" I took the crimson card that Miss Scratton gave me and stuffed it in my pocket. "The other girls will not speak to you today, and you will walk to Fairfax Hall at my side. Think yourself lucky that you are allowed to come on the outing at all."

I hung back from the others. Sarah shrugged sympathetically but didn't dare speak to me.

"Now, girls," said Miss Scratton, "it's a long walk, and we don't want to be late. Miss Dalrymple, if you would kindly lead the way." The class began to head down the drive.

"Oh, wait!" Sarah exclaimed. "Where's Helen?"

"Helen is not well. She will not be joining us."

I glanced up. The infirmary was on the second floor, overlooking the drive.

I thought I caught a glimpse of Helen's fragile features at the window. But I was distracted by Miss Scratton hovering at my side, looking sterner than ever.

"Listen, Evie," she said. "This is really important. You can't get another demerit. Is that clear?" Then she stiffened and looked over her shoulder. The High Mistress, Mrs. Hartle, was standing on the top step by the front door, watching us silently. I felt as though someone had poured ice water down my neck.

"Your behavior has been quite disgraceful, Evie Johnson," Miss Scratton announced in a loud voice. "Now keep up with me."

We followed the others to the school gates. Instead of turning down to the village and the gloomy church, as we did on Sundays, we took the path that led up to the moors. Miss Dalrymple went on ahead, pointing out the site of the old fort where I had ridden with Sebastian. I didn't listen. I was puzzling over what Miss Scratton had just said. Had she simply been telling me off—or was there some other warning behind her words?

I looked up at her fiercely plain face, and it struck me that there was some kind of tension between her and Mrs. Hartle. Perhaps Miss Scratton had wanted the job of High Mistress herself? That wasn't any of my concern, though. All I cared about was that Miss Scratton had accepted my garbled explanation the night before about feeling faint and wanting to get some fresh air in the yard.

I'd pretended that I'd used the back stairs so I wouldn't disturb anybody, then got shut in by accident.

As we started to climb higher over rough ground, I wondered if Helen knew why I had been out on the grounds at night. And if she did know about Sebastian, would she tell Mrs. Hartle? Then I would be in real trouble. I could imagine the frost in Mrs. Hartle's voice, the quiet triumph. *I never wanted to accept you into the school.*

Dad would be so upset if they kicked me out. I couldn't let him down like that. Secretly, I felt slightly ashamed. After all, I had come to Wyldcliffe to help Dad, not add to his troubles. I was in school to learn, not to chase after a boy with blue eyes. Something would have to change. I couldn't bear to stop seeing Sebastian, but there had to be some other way of meeting that wouldn't break any more rules.

The path began to snake down the other side of the ridge to a wooded hollow below. Miss Dalrymple trotted out facts about limestone outcrops and the ancient mines that had left a honeycomb of tunnels and shafts under the hills. The girls crowded around her, asking questions and admiring the view. Miss Dalrymple turned and smiled rather unpleasantly, her cheeks pink and plump in the wind.

"Miss Scratton, don't you think dear Evie could join the rest of us? It would be a pity for her not to enjoy the day's adventure."

"Evie had enough adventures last night," said Miss Scratton icily. "She will stay under my supervision."

Strangely enough, I was glad of her reply. Miss Dalrymple looked annoyed for a fraction of a second, then shooed the class along, lecturing them enthusiastically about our surroundings. But Miss Scratton and I walked behind them in silence.

# Twenty-two

airfax Hall was not what I had expected. I had grown used to the somber gray buildings of the Abbey, but the Hall, behind its thick screen of laurels, was a gracious house made of light stone, with an elegant pillared facade. It looked out of place on the side of the rugged moors. But that wasn't the main surprise. As we trooped down the driveway, we saw two police cars parked outside the door. The museum director came rushing out to meet us.

"Oh, it's such a shame," she began hurriedly. "I tried to call you, Miss Scratton, but the school said you had already set off, so it was too late to let you know."

"Let us know what?" replied Miss Scratton.

"About this terrible break-in. I can't quite believe it yet. The whole place has been ransacked." The poor woman looked on the verge of tears, and kept pushing her glasses nervously into place.

"Oh, dear, has anything been stolen?" asked Miss Dalrymple.

"That's the strange thing," said the museum lady. "Everything has been turned upside down, but we think that only one item has actually been stolen."

"And what was that?" asked Miss Scratton sharply. "If you don't mind my asking."

"Not at all. I suppose it will all be in the local paper anyway. It was a portrait, not terribly valuable, but of great interest: a member of the Fairfax family, a fascinating character. Oh, dear . . . I'd better get back to the police—and you've walked all this way for nothing. I'm afraid no one is allowed to come in while the police are examining everything."

A few of the girls let out groans at the news.

"But we can't go back to school right away, can we, Miss Scratton?" asked Sophie.

"No," agreed Miss Scratton. "It's too far to walk back without a rest, and the bus I have arranged for us won't arrive for a couple of hours. We'll just have to wait here until it comes."

The woman from the Hall looked heartbroken at the

idea that we were being deprived of the chance to see her beloved museum.

"Oh, dear, oh, dear," she said. "Of course, I'll have to check with the police, but perhaps you could at least walk around the gardens. Even at this time of the year they are full of interesting specimens. They were laid out in the nineteenth century by Sir Edward Fairfax and are considered a very fine example . . . Oh, dear, please excuse me."

She rushed back into the house, appearing again a few minutes later.

"The sergeant says that your girls can walk in the lower gardens, down by the lake."

The lake. I looked up with interest.

"Excellent. You can all make some sketches, girls. There'll be a prize for the best one," said Miss Scratton.

The class flocked behind the mistresses, cheered up by the idea of a little competition. We reached the formal gardens behind the house, with their walkways and patterns and stately flower beds. But the lake turned out to be a disappointment. It was a sterile, man-made affair, a glorified pond with a fancy fountain stuck in the middle of it.

I found a stone bench to sit on and made a feeble attempt to draw the fountain. Sebastian had been right:

Our visit to Fairfax Hall had been a complete letdown. I wondered when he had been here—he had seemed to know all about the place. I imagined him being dragged around the museum by his parents when he was a kid. No, that couldn't have been right, I remembered, because Miss Scratton said the house had been opened only recently. Perhaps he had sneaked in at night, like he sneaked into Wyldcliffe. That would be more like Sebastian. I grinned to myself, and suddenly ached to be with him.

Without being consciously aware of it, I had drawn a figure in a long dark coat next to my sketch of the lake. I looked around, half expecting to see Sebastian lounging against one of the trees, with that mocking smile on his lips.

He wasn't there, of course. On the far side of the lawn dark shrubs had been clipped into tall shapes. Beyond them the garden ended and the moors began. Then I noticed something. High on the slope that rose up from the edge of the garden, behind a tangle of thorn trees, there was a dark block of stone. A girl was standing next to it, her pale hair blown about by the wind.

"Helen!" I cried, and jumped up, letting my sketch book fall to the ground. "Helen! Wait!"

Large, splashy drops of rain began to fall. The girls by

the lake snatched up their things and ran, half grumbling, half laughing, toward the Hall. But I was running in the opposite direction, trying to get a better view of the girl. Then Miss Dalrymple stepped out in front of me, barring my way. I let out a yelp of surprise.

"Whatever is the matter?" she asked smoothly. "You're going the wrong way—you'll get soaked."

"But . . . but I saw Helen up there on the hill!"

She laughed a little tinkling laugh. "There's no one there. You're imagining things, my dear."

It was true. There was nothing to see. There was no girl there, only the thorn trees and the dark stone, and the rain falling like tears.

"Evie!"

I turned to see Miss Scratton standing tall and thin in her flapping black raincoat. "Run over to the Hall and out of this rain! We'll have to shelter there until the bus arrives, whether the police like it or not. Quickly!"

She shooed me in the direction of the house, but I wasn't sure whether she wanted to get me away from the rain or from Miss Dalrymple.

When we finally arrived back at school we were told to change into dry clothes. I flew up to the dorm for a clean

162

shirt, then found my way to the infirmary. I tapped on the door.

"Come in." The nurse looked up from her desk. "Yes, what is it?"

"Um . . . I came to ask about Helen. How is she?"

"She's not been at all well today. It looks as though she's in for a nasty dose of the flu."

"So, she hasn't been outside all day?" I asked, trying to peer past her for any sign of her patient. "She didn't manage to go out for some fresh air?"

"I hardly think so, with the temperature she's been running. And she's tucked up in bed now."

"Well . . . um . . . tell her I came," I finished lamely, and walked away. The girl I had seen must have been someone from the local village. The truth was, I told myself, I was light-headed with exhaustion. I half envied Helen her bed in the quiet infirmary. I longed to sleep and sleep and sleep.

But not yet. I had promised Sebastian to be there that night, and I would never break a promise to him.

I made my plans like a thief. Helen would be staying in the infirmary, so I knew she couldn't possibly interfere. After supper, when it was getting dark, I quietly raided a gardener's shed and "borrowed" a flashlight, so that I wouldn't have to face that utter blackness on the stairs again. Oh, I had it all planned out. I promised myself one more stolen hour of happiness with Sebastian; then I would be sensible and get some sleep at last.

# Twenty-three

"But why not, Sebastian?" I said, staring sulkily over the lake. Nothing was turning out as I had imagined.

"I've told you." He sighed. "I can't see you in the daytime. This is the only way we can see each other."

"I could meet you on a Sunday afternoon. Some of the girls are allowed out then to go riding, or for walks."

"So you are going to tell the High Mistress that you're going down to the woods to meet a boy from the village?" he asked. "Do you really think she'll allow that?"

"Well, no . . ." I admitted. "But if we told her that you're a family friend." I needed to say what had been on my mind for some time. "You know, if your parents actually invited me to your house for tea or something, Mrs. Hartle couldn't object to that. Jessica Armstrong has some cousins who live a few miles away, and she goes to visit them."

"I cannot ask my parents to meet you. I'm really sorry."

"Why not?" I fumed. "Are you ashamed of me?"

"It's not that!"

"Is it because I don't really belong at Wyldcliffe? Would you rather take Celeste or India or someone like that to meet them? Is that it?"

"I have no idea what you're talking about," he said, bewildered by my fury. "Please, Evie, it's just impossible. Don't drag my parents into this. They . . . they wouldn't understand; they are old-fashioned; they can't . . . Evie, please don't look like that."

"Did your parents meet that other girl?" I blurted out. My lingering jealousy over the girl from his past—whether it had been Laura or someone else—flared up like a white-hot flame. "Did you invite *her* to your house?"

"I'm not going to lie to you. Yes, they met her."

"It's not fair." I was horrified by the whining tone of my voice and tried to pull myself together. "It's just that I'm so tired," I pleaded, staring into the rippling black water.

"Do you mean you are tired of me?"

"You know I don't mean that. But I'm in so much trouble already, and if I get another of those blasted demerits I don't know what will happen. Whatever you think of your parents, I don't want to upset my dad by getting thrown out of Wyldcliffe. And if I do get kicked out," I carried on miserably, "then I really will never see you again."

"But you said you wanted to keep meeting, that you didn't mind the risks."

"I just don't see why we have to creep around like this every night. It's getting ridiculous. I'm putting myself in a really bad position with the school, as well as being exhausted, and I don't even know . . ." I looked up at his troubled face. I wanted to say, *And I don't even know how you really feel about me.*

The words wouldn't come. I dreaded getting an answer I didn't want to hear. I knew in my heart that there was a barrier between us, something holding Sebastian back. Yes, I was his dearest Evie, but I needed more. I couldn't go on just wondering and hoping, waiting for a sign that never came. I kicked an old laurel root that grew near the water's edge and growled, "I don't even know your full name."

"Sebastian James," he said with a mocking bow. "Delighted to make your acquaintance. There, does that satisfy you?"

"And where do you live?" I persisted.

"I told you, Evie, up on the moors."

"But where? What's your address? What's your telephone number?"

"What is wrong with you tonight?" he exploded. "You sound like . . . like a police inquiry."

"Maybe that's what I need to get some answers from you," I said, my temper blazing up in an instant.

"I'll give you answers when I can," Sebastian blazed back. "But not now."

I stared up at the dark horizon. It was hard to see where the moors ended and the sky began. Tears blurred my sight.

"Let's not fight," I begged. "All I want is to find some other way to see each other. Something normal. You don't seem to realize how hard this is for me." *Hard because I'm crazy about you . . . because I don't know if you are still dreaming of the girl you lost . . . because I don't know where any of this is leading.*

"Hard? You want to know what is hard? Do you think it's easy for me to spend every day alone, wondering what you're doing, waiting to see you for a few snatched moments? I *have* to see you, Evie. I . . . I need you."

"Then invite me to your house," I argued. "Introduce

me to your family, your friends. Treat me like someone you care for, not just some midnight prank."

The demand I had made seemed to echo in the night. At last, Sebastian spoke.

"I can't."

"Then I can't keep on seeing you," I replied bitterly.

I turned away from him, but he caught hold of my arm.

"Don't go like this," he pleaded. "I would do as you ask if I could. Please trust me."

"How can I trust you after this? Let go of me!"

He stepped back, his face a mask of misery. "I'll be waiting for you, Evie."

"Don't bother," I cried. "I never want to see you again!"

I stumbled back to school, sobbing all the way.

# Twenty-four

THE JOURNAL OF LADY AGNES, NOVEMBER 13, 1882

*I have sobbed my heart dry, and now I can cry no more. My old happiness with S. is over. I am shaking even as I write this.*

*The torrential rain had prevented us from riding over the moors together for several days. I was feeling uneasy that I had not heard from him in all that time, but two days ago he sent me a note asking me to meet him in the grotto. "Come toward midnight, when everyone will be asleep. That way there will be no danger of being overheard." I did not like the idea but hated to disappoint him. At least in this one small thing I could do as he asked.*

*When I guessed that most of the household had retired to bed, I threw some clothes on and crept from my room* to the servants' staircase. I thought this would keep my excursion a secret if Papa happened to be sitting up late.

A single candle was sufficient to give me a little light on those narrow steps. I was ashamed to think that I had never set foot there before. It was cold and bare. I thought of the maids, Nellie and Mary, who run up and down those stairs fifty times a day to serve us, and wondered if people in years to come will look back and wonder at our lives: rich and poor side by side and yet hardly knowing anything of each other's worlds. When I am of age I would like to have my own little house, where I could learn to manage for myself, and have no servant, unless it was poor Martha, who would be welcome as a faithful friend.

I reached the ground floor and made my way past the kitchen and out through the stable yard. Then I ran as swiftly as I could across the lawns to the lake. How the shadowy ruins seemed to glare over me in the darkness! I had never felt afraid of them before, but now it seemed that they stood like a broken crown, guarding the entrance to some awful dungeon. My heart pounding, I hurried past them into the shrubbery. I heard S. call my name softly, and I entered the grotto.

A lamp was burning at the base of the statue of Pan,

and the little god seemed to dance in the flickering light. S. was sitting slumped against the wall. His face was half in darkness, but I could tell, with a sinking heart, that he was in one of his bitter, willful moods. It struck me that he looked terribly ill, and I knew at that moment that I loved him, that I had always loved him. I wanted to hold him, comfort him, take him in my arms. But I didn't know how.

"What is wrong?" I asked. "Are you ill?"

"No, it is nothing," he answered, coughing impatiently and scrambling to his feet. "Let's begin the Rites."

I started to make the Sacred Circle, but he stopped me, catching my arm roughly.

"What's the matter?"

"I don't feel in the mood."

"Then shall I go back?" I asked, but he gave no answer. His eyes were dull and tinged with red. The gurgle of the spring echoed in the darkness. Still he did not speak, and still he clutched my arm in a tight grip.

"Should I go back to the house?" I repeated. "If Mama finds me out of my bed there'll be a great fuss."

"Mama! Mama!" he said with a savage scowl. "You still speak like a little girl, Agnes. Do you not understand what we have here? Soon no one will be able to tell us,

'Do this, do that, go to bed, eat your supper.' That old life will be over! Instead we will command them. We will command all!"

"Why would we want to command anyone but ourselves?"

"Do not talk like a fool. Do you really want to go through all this secret labor just so that you can cure your cook's toothache and such trifles?"

"If that is all I can do, it is better than nothing," I replied stubbornly. "Why should you be angry that I want to help other people?"

"Because you are not helping me! I should be the one to whom you offer your talents, not the clinging crowds of humanity. Aren't I dearer than anyone else to you? Agnes, do you not care for me at all?" He slowly pulled me toward him until I could feel his warm breath on my lips. His mouth rested on mine, and a fire sprang to life inside my body as he kissed me. I had been dreaming of this moment, and I wanted to cling to him and never let him go. But he pushed me away.

"Stop! What use are your kisses to me when you will not give me the one thing I really want?"

"What?" I gasped. "What do you want?"

He was silent for a long time. Our heartbeats seemed

to echo through the little chamber.

"I want to go beyond these . . . these tricks that we have learned. The book tells us that the Mystic Way is a path of healing and power." His voice was stilted and strange, as though he had been rehearsing a speech. "You are a healer, Agnes. I have seen what you are capable of, and I know you could work yet greater marvels. I want you to heal me."

"Heal you of what? So you are ill? Tell me!"

He avoided my gaze and spoke very softly. "Yes, Agnes, I am ill. I have a condition that will kill me if you do not save me."

I stifled a sob. I could not believe what I was hearing.

"Is it . . . was it brought on by your fever?" I asked, forcing myself to speak.

"Yes," he repeated strangely. "I have a fever burning in me. The fever of life."

"I don't understand you."

"We are all sick, Agnes. What is this life but a long, slow death sentence? The seeds of our destruction are within us from the second we are born. I need you to cure me of my humanity so that I will not die."

"But—"

"You must!" He gripped my arms again. "These

studies are exhausting me. I feel them as a burden in my mind. And what is the point of carving out this hard-won knowledge if it will die with us? Maybe not in ten years, or twenty, but eventually. We will die, Agnes, when our time runs out. So why not use this great gift that has been thrown in our path to transcend time? Power and healing, Agnes! Think of it!" He looked at me eagerly, the blue of his eyes dimmed to steely gray by the cavern's gloom. "Why not heal me so completely that I could transcend death itself? Why not search the Mystic Way for the key to eternal life?"

"No, stop it. You're frightening me."

"But why not, Agnes? What is there to prevent us standing side by side forever: unchanging, untouchable, immortal?"

I couldn't speak or think. He tried to clasp me to him, but I broke free from him.

"Because it is wrong. It is madness."

"It is madness not to do it, and I won't let you stop me." His voice was harsh, and he panted slightly, as though he were running a fever.

I tried to speak reasonably. "Have you forgotten that eternal life has already been promised to all mankind?"

His face hardened. "And to reach it I must grow old

and die and be punished for my sins? Who can be sure that eternal paradise waits for them and not eternal damnation? Besides, I want to live here, in this world, to be young and strong forever, not fade into some other world that might not even exist." He fell to his knees in front of me. "Please, Agnes, please help me," he begged. "I cannot continue like this, in this torment, knowing that everything I desire is so close and yet so out of reach. You must help me! I know you have the power to do this. I know you touch the Sacred Fire in your mind, and I could reach it through you, if only you would let me. One spark would be enough!"

I longed to help him with all my heart, but not by listening to his ravings. For the first time in my life I wanted to get away from him. I tore my skirt from his hands and ran, slipping in the darkness, hardly knowing what I was doing. When I got back to my room I was shaking. I turned the key in the lock and dragged a chair against the door. I was afraid of him. I was afraid of myself.

Surely the limitations on our human life have been placed to keep us safe, to stop us from falling into the void of chaos? What will happen if S. tries to step over those limits? There was a wild look in his eyes, a desperation that torments me. I know, in the secret places of my heart, that I could learn to do what he asks. For some unknown reason I have been blessed—or cursed—with the ability to call upon the Fire. But being able to do something does not make it right. I would have to bend my powers to darkness and despair and know that it would lead to misery. "The four great Elements can heal and protect, but they can also destroy." Now I know I was right to be fearful when we first dared to explore their mysteries.

Since this dreadful quarrel, I have pleaded that I am unwell and have seen no one. I cannot sleep; I cannot lie still; I cannot sit down. I pace my room with restless energy, and I feel his kisses burning on my lips once more. I am longing to show him my love, but not by doing what is wrong.

Last night I got up and sat on the window seat, looking out across the gardens to the ruins, and I thought a caught a glimpse of him down by the lake. He was dressed in his riding coat and was talking to a girl, but they were both veiled by a strange mist. It was the girl with the short skirts that I have seen before in trancelike visions. I felt no longer jealous but oddly drawn to her; she pulled at my heart for some unknown reason, as though she were as dear to me as a sister. I opened the window, and their figures melted into the shadows. And then this morning

I was walking in the gardens and I thought I saw her again. I tried to call out, to warn her, but she faded into the air like a dream.

Today I have heard that he has gone to London. I believe he has taken the Book with him, as it has vanished from our hiding place in the grotto. I hate to think what dark places he might be seeking out in that great city, and in his heart. Perhaps it is too late to save my beloved. But if nothing else, I must find out who the girl is and save her from him.

And from what he might become.

# Twenty-five

"Evie Johnson!" Miss Schofield yelled at me from the other side of the lacrosse field.

"That's the fourth pass you've dropped this morning. Stop daydreaming!"

I looked up, startled. I was so miserable about the row with Sebastian the night before that I hadn't even noticed that the ball was anywhere near me.

"Get it together, Johnson," called Celeste as she slyly dug me in the ribs with the end of her stick. Then India barged into me, a sneer spoiling her pretty face, but I didn't care. Nothing hurt compared to the pain of quarreling with Sebastian. *I never want to see you again. I never want to see you . . . never again.* The wind moaned through the trees, and I felt utterly alone.

"Come on! Get those tackles in!"

As I jogged up and down, pretending to look interested, the light suddenly dimmed as though someone had flicked a switch. The shouts of the game around me faded into the thin blue sky, until the only sound I could hear was my own heart, hammering out a message of fear. I stood paralyzed, rooted to the ground, unable to speak. The lacrosse stick fell useless from my hands. And then a girl in white walked out of the trees by the side of the field. Her long gown fluttered in the wind, her red hair hung loosely over her shoulders, and her gray eyes pierced mine. She called out, *Stay away from him . . . stay away . . . be careful.*

*What do you mean? Who are you?* I tried to call back, but my throat was dry and the words wouldn't form. Then she faded into the air like a dream.

*Bang!* The lacrosse ball hit me on the side of my head, and I reeled. I thought dizzily that Celeste had chucked it at me out of spite, but then I saw Sarah running up to me.

"Oh, I'm so sorry, Miss Schofield," she panted. "I messed up my shot. I'm sorry, Evie; you must be hurt." She looked at me significantly.

"No. I don't know," I mumbled.

Miss Schofield squared her heavy shoulders and glared

at me. "It's your own fault for not keeping your eye on the ball at all times, Evie. It's the first rule of the game."

"I'll take Evie to the nurse to lie down for a bit," said Sarah. "Just in case."

"I'm sure there's nothing wrong . . ." began Miss Schofield. Sarah squeezed my hand painfully.

"Ow! Yes . . . it hurts."

"All right," said Miss Schofield. "Off you go. Now, girls, back to the game. You two there, Becky and Sophie, you can come on as subs, but for heaven's sake, concentrate."

By now Sarah was already steering me down the path that led back to the main gardens and the chapel ruins. I felt sick and dazed. I thought I had cured myself of these weird visions, that Sebastian had chased them from my overheated imagination. But the girl had looked so real. *Stay away from him.* I looked around again in panic. Was I having some kind of breakdown?

"Come on, in here," Sarah said firmly.

The shattered remains of the ruins loomed over us, and Sarah ducked beneath a low archway. A damp stone staircase led underground.

"What's this?" I asked in alarm. The steps ended in a small, dank chamber slimed over with lichen and moss. It was just the kind of place that I hated. I tried to pull myself together, to think and speak rationally. "Where are we going?"

"I need to talk to you in private, where we won't be overheard," Sarah replied. "I'm sorry about chucking the ball at you, but I had no choice."

"You nearly knocked me out so that you could talk to me? Wasn't that a bit extreme?"

"I'm just trying to help you, Evie. I know you're in danger."

"Oh, come on, you're not going to give me that 'I'm a Gypsy with second sight' junk."

"It's not junk," Sarah replied earnestly. "It's real. I never thought of it as anything special," she continued, "because I've always been able to do it. Oh, nothing earth-shattering, just things like being able to tell whether people are happy or not, and knowing for certain what the weather is going to be like the next day. And once, when my grandmother fell and broke her arm, I knew it had happened before my mother told me. But since you arrived at Wyldcliffe it's been different. I keep getting these messages about you that someone is trying to reach you from far away. What did you really see just now?"

What did she mean? Had she seen the girl too? The words of the cabdriver suddenly echoed in my head. *That cursed place*, he had called Wyldcliffe. Why had I ever come here? I thought wildly. I was drowning in fear, going out of my mind, surrounded by crazy people. And now Sarah was one of them.

"Tell me what you saw," she urged.

"I didn't see anything! What's gotten into you? I thought you were the normal one around here, down-to-earth. . . ."

"The earth is full of secrets," Sarah said with a faint smile. "You've got a few secrets yourself, haven't you, Evie? Like, wandering the grounds at midnight."

"How do you know?" I gaped.

"There's no mystery about that," she replied. "I went to see Helen in the infirmary last night. She told me that you've been sneaking out night after night. She's been watching you. And she's worried about you."

"Oh, yeah, so worried that she told Miss Scratton! That was really friendly of her."

"Friends sometimes have to make difficult decisions."

"Listen, Helen Black is not my friend, and if she wants to spend her time spying on me, that's her problem."

"So what is your problem, Evie? Why were you staring into space just now, talking to the air? If I hadn't crashed the ball into you, everyone would have noticed. What's going on? Why do you leave the dorm every night?"

I couldn't fight it anymore. I was so tired, too tired to keep pretending. Sinking to the ground, I slumped against the cold stone wall and let the words slide out of me. "I've been seeing someone, a boy I met. And I've seen *her* again."

"Who?"

"The girl in white. I've seen her three times now. The first time was that day in Miss Scratton's room when I had just arrived and you looked after me."

"I knew something was going on," said Sarah. "I was sure of it. And so you saw her again just now?"

"Yes." I nodded. "But this time she was telling me to be careful—of him."

"This guy you've met?"

"I guess so," I said miserably. "Who else could she be talking about?"

"So who is he?" Sarah asked. "Why would some girl warn you about him?"

"I don't know! I don't even know if she really exists. I just feel that I'm going crazy."

"What is the girl like?"

The pale, ghostly image floated in front of my eyes again. "She has red hair and gray eyes."

"You mean she looks like you?"

I shrugged. "Maybe. I don't know who she is, or what it all means. And I'm scared."

"Come on. We've got to get to the library before anyone sees us."

A few minutes later we slipped into the ornate library, which was lined with dark mahogany bookcases. A couple of older girls were reading quietly at one of the large tables. One of them looked up and frowned at us. "Are you supposed to be in here?"

"Miss Scratton sent us to find something, Emily," Sarah lied, walking purposefully over to the history section. She glanced over the crowded shelves, pulling out books, searching for something.

"What are we doing in here?" I asked.

"Just wait a second. . . . Ah! Here it is." She began to flip through a small blue book. It was old and dull looking, hardly bigger than a pamphlet. *A Short History of Wyldcliffe Abbey School* by Rev. A. J. Flowerdew. "I found this when I was in my first year. I've always been interested in this kind of stuff. It was written by the local vicar—not the one we have; another guy years and years ago. Hang on—look!"

She pushed the open book into my hand. I looked down and read quietly:

*The only surviving portrait of Lady Agnes is kept at the Abbey. It is believed to have been commissioned by Lord Charles to mark his daughter's sixteenth birthday in 1882, two years before her fatal riding accident, which took place after a period of travel on the Continent. The artist is unknown.*

The painting was reproduced on the opposite page, its colors blurred on the cheap paper. But there was no mistaking that familiar face, those gray eyes framed by that sweep of auburn hair, and the long, old-fashioned clothes.

"Is that the girl you saw?"

I nodded slowly. A riding accident, it said. I seemed to see it all so clearly. The girl lying in a broken heap on the purple heather. A chestnut horse nuzzling her bright hair, and her eyes staring blankly at the high blue sky as the larks swooped overhead.

"She died," I said idiotically. "She's dead."

But of course she was. Even if she had lived to be a hundred, she would have died long ago.

"She looks like you, Evie. I knew you reminded me of someone when I first met you." Sarah frowned over the faded pages. "You could be sisters."

"We don't look that much alike," I replied in a panic.

"Just because we've both got red hair . . ."

Emily glared at us and said, "Have you two found what you're looking for? I'm trying to concentrate."

Sarah slipped the book under her shirt, and we headed for the marble stairs.

"We have to go see the nurse," she said, "like we told Miss Schofield. Tell her that your head still hurts from being hit. If she lets you lie down for a couple of hours you can read the rest of this book and see if there's anything useful in it."

I let myself be told what to do. The nurse took my temperature, gave me an aspirin, and told me to rest on one of the beds in the infirmary. Helen was fast asleep at the far end of the room. I hid the blue book under my pillow. I didn't need to look at it again to know that the girl I had seen and the girl in the painting were the same.

Lady Agnes.

If Sarah was right, I was being contacted by the spirit of a dead Victorian girl who looked so much like me we could be mistaken for sisters. And she was warning me to stay away from Sebastian.

# Twenty-six

THE JOURNAL OF LADY AGNES, DECEMBER 21, 1882

*S. returned from London nearly three weeks ago. I have made myself stay away from him all this time. I longed to see him but I did not want to repeat our quarrel. Then, yesterday, he called unexpectedly at the Abbey and asked me to walk on the moors with him. It was there that he told me his news, half-proud and half-defiant.*

*"How could you do this?" I stormed. "And why did you not tell me?"*

*"I did it because you wouldn't help me. I had to find allies elsewhere. And I didn't tell you because I knew you would react like this."*

*I paced across the heather, hardly aware of where I went. The sun gleamed peacefully on the tops of the moors,* but between us all was turmoil and anger.

"Stop! Agnes, wait! Let me explain."

He caught my hand and made me sit down on the sweet turf. The breeze blew his dark hair from his forehead, and I caught my breath at the sight of his face, as open and eager as in the old days. If only I could stop loving him! Then it would all be so much simpler.

"So, what explanation can you give?"

"I had no choice, Agnes," he replied with a strange light in his eyes. "You know as well as I that the Book says that to become a Master of our craft I must have a coven of Sisters around me. You have made it quite clear that you will not serve me, so I had to look elsewhere. I have found what I need here in Wyldcliffe."

"What? A few simple village girls flattered by your attentions? How will they help you achieve anything great or good?"

"I am teaching them. They are stronger than you think. And they are eager to learn, to please me." His eyes lingered on me, and I blushed, hardly knowing why. Then he laughed cruelly. "Why, Agnes, I believe you are jealous of my new Sisters. But you cannot refuse to stand by my side and then complain if others choose to fill the place that you have left empty."

"I would never have left that place had you not driven me away!"

"How? How have I driven you away?"

"By delving too deep and too dark," I said. "I cannot follow you down the road you are set upon."

He came and sat next to me, gentle for a moment, like a tamed hawk.

"Yes, you can, Agnes. It is not too late." He took my hands in his. "If we join forces again, we can find the key to what I am seeking. I am so close, but I need you to help me. Think, Agnes, think! Eternal life—life without death, without failure, without sickness, without end. And it could be ours, if only you would agree. We would always be together, never to be parted. You have no need to fear my new servants. They are necessary to me, but they mean nothing; they are mere tools for me to use as I choose."

I struggled to resist him. "You should not speak like that. They are each one of them a precious life—a precious soul. And you are not teaching them the true Mysteries. You are turning an ancient art into sickening witchcraft. We should use our powers to live well in the time given to us, not try to steal time that is not ours to take. Tell these girls to go home to their mothers and their spinning

190

wheels. You do them no good."

"They are grateful that I am leading them on the path to immortality."

"You are leading them into danger and despair! There are worse things than death. To live forever is to be less than human. Let them go! Release them from your service."

"I have a better plan," he said. "My Sisters need a leader to guide them. They need you, Agnes. You would be the High Mistress of my coven, and I would be its Master. You and me—isn't that what you want?"

"No, not like this; it is wrong." I looked up at him, suddenly clear and calm. "Besides, there is another girl, far away. I have seen her with you. It is she whom you love, not me. You will put her in danger if you continue, you will put us all in danger—"

"What nonsense, Agnes." He laughed. "We will never know danger, only power and glory. And it's you that I care for. You know that." His eyes pierced me like a splinter of glass and I shuddered, helpless under his gaze. "Oh, Agnes," he breathed, "our life could be so beautiful. Don't you love me at all?"

He kissed my hair, my face, and my eyes. I felt the force of his will beating against me. I swayed dizzily, and he caught me in his embrace.

"Yes," I confessed. "I love you. I love you."

He kissed me, and I kissed him back again and again, until I was trembling with fever. Then he said: "We could have this moment forever. This and more, going on and on, and never growing weary of it. I have already traveled part of the way down that road. I have all that I need, except for one thing: One touch from your mind and will, Agnes, that is all I ask, one spark of the Fire. Heal me once and for all, I beg you. But if you refuse, you become my enemy forever."

I drew back. This was the moment to which everything else had been leading. And at that very moment I knew that I could not give him what he desired.

"I'm sorry. I cannot do as you ask."

"You can, Agnes; you must," he urged. "Share your power with me. Marry me so that we can have no more secrets, and we'll live in bliss for all eternity."

He began to kiss me again and I tried to push him away.

"I can't," I sobbed. "I will not! Leave me! Let me go, I beg you. . . ."

But he wouldn't. He gripped me cruelly, almost crushing me in his arms. "I need your powers. I will have them!"

In desperation I closed my eyes and saw the Sacred Circle in my mind, blazing with white fire in the darkest night. I repeated the incantations. Bursts of red and blue and orange exploded behind my eyes, and I spoke a word of Power.

The blast threw him across to the other side of the heather. A trickle of blood was on his face. I ran to him and laid his head on my lap, trying to soothe his pain. Over and over again I murmured, "I'm sorry, I'm sorry, I'm sorry. . . ."

At last he opened his eyes and staggered to his feet, wiping the blood on his sleeve.

"So, that is your answer. You will not join me. You are sorry."

"That is my answer."

The silence hung heavy between us. A lark swooped and soared overhead.

"Look, Agnes," he said. "It is so beautiful." He turned to me and paused. "So beautiful—and so out of reach."

Then he set off, walking down into the valley until he was out of sight.

I have not seen him for many days. I do not know whether I will ever see him again.

# Twenty-seven

I didn't know whether I would ever see Sebastian again, but I dreaded seeing any more visions. As I lay in the infirmary for two—or was it three?—days, a fire burned in my head, bringing confused thoughts and rambling dreams. The nurse called in Dr. Harrison, who raised his eyebrows at seeing me again. He said something about my having a virus and needing plenty of rest and hot drinks. I did what they told me to do, but I wasn't really there. I was reliving everything that had happened, going over every scrap of memory, trying to make sense of it all.

The girl. The warnings. Sebastian. *But she's dead*, I kept saying to myself, *she's dead. I don't believe in ghosts.... I don't believe ... I don't ...*

Yet it had happened. I had seen her, heard her voice.

However much I tried to fight it, there was something in me that knew she was real. She was somehow part of me.

That was it, I rationalized. The girl with the red hair was part of my subconscious, a version of me, a hidden part of my mind that was trying to tell me to be cautious about the relationship with Sebastian. His refusal to let me meet his family had spooked me, and this girl and her message were simply some kind of psychological reaction.

I had seen her on the very first day, though, I reminded myself, long before I had begun to have a relationship with Sebastian. A relationship. Such a clumsy, ugly word for something that was impossible to pin down, an intricate dance between two people, like the pull and tug of the waves.

*I'm not very good with relationships.*

Sebastian had said that. Was it his fault this time, or mine? It didn't really matter. Our relationship, whatever it had been, would be over now. I had walked out on him, and his pride wouldn't tolerate that. Why had I lost my temper so stupidly? I was already regretting it. Yet he had said that he would be waiting for me.

It was late Sunday evening. I was feeling better, at least physically. A cool drink stood on the bedside table. I sipped at it eagerly. There was no one else there. Helen had gone back to class, healed of whatever had brought her here. When I had been awake she had slept, or faked sleep, so I hadn't had the chance to talk to her. It didn't matter, though. I had nothing to say to Helen Black.

Slowly I got out of bed and walked to the little bathroom. I ran the tap and splashed my face with cold water. As I glanced at myself in the mirror, my skin looked paler than ever, as pale as a Victorian girl in an old painting.

The painting. That wasn't just some psychological manifestation. It was a portrait of Lady Agnes Templeton. Plain, solid fact. The painting looked like the girl I had seen. And it looked like me. Was all that just a coincidence?

"Evie!"

I jumped. The nurse was calling from the other side of the door. I dried my face and let myself out of the bathroom. She was holding a thermometer in her hand. "I've just come to check your temperature. Are you feeling any better?"

I wasn't ill, only heavy-limbed and tired. I climbed back into bed.

"Yes, I think so. What time is it?"

"Nearly nine o'clock. The girls have had supper." She took my temperature efficiently. "Quite normal. You'll be able to get up and join your classmates tomorrow. Speaking of which, your friend is dying to see you. She's waiting outside now. Shall I let her come in?"

I nodded. The nurse went out and talked to someone in her little office. I waited fearfully, half expecting the redheaded girl to come in, trailing her long white skirt behind her. But it was Sarah, cheerful and real.

"Sarah!" I gasped in relief.

"How are you feeling?" she asked. "I brought you this."

It was a delicate bit of greenery in a little pot, with flowers of palest blue.

"Thank you. It's beautiful."

"It's not from me. Helen found it growing wild near the ruins. She asked me to give it to you and say she's sorry."

"Sorry about what?"

"Telling Miss Scratton that you were out of bed that night. Helen wants you to know that she did it to stop you from getting into worse trouble. She said she hopes you'll understand."

"I don't understand anything. I certainly don't understand Helen."

"Helen is . . . different," said Sarah. "She's had a difficult life so far, from what I can make out. I've heard that before she came to Wyldcliffe she was in some kind of children's home."

"You mean, like an orphanage?" I couldn't imagine having no family at all.

"I guess so. She won't talk about it."

"Do you ever, you know, sense stuff about her?" I asked curiously.

"It doesn't take any special gift to tell that she's unhappy. But no, to be truthful, I can't make out anything more than that. It's as though she's wrapped herself in a swirling wind, protecting herself from any outsiders. She's always been a bit of a loner. Some of the other girls give her a hard time."

I knew she meant Celeste. "Did Helen . . . Was she friends with Laura?"

"Not really. Laura was totally influenced by Celeste in everything she did. She wouldn't have bothered to try to get to know Helen. Not many people do."

I felt uncomfortable. I had been quick enough to give up on Helen myself. Sarah went to make sure that the door was closed, then turned to me and asked, "Evie, have you thought any more about what you saw?"

"I've not thought about anything else. And I've been wondering whether the whole thing with Lady Agnes isn't some kind of message from my own feelings, telling me to slow down with Sebastian." I stumbled over the name. He had been my secret, and it seemed wrong to speak so casually of him.

"But you said that the girl you saw was just like Lady Agnes in the painting, and you'd never seen the painting before I showed you the book. So the first time you saw her—in the classroom—you couldn't just have been projecting her image from your subconscious or whatever."

"I'm not so sure. Reverend Flowerdew's book says the painting is kept at the Abbey. There are loads of old pictures on the walls. I might have walked past it without realizing it."

"Or you could actually have received a message from Lady Agnes."

"So why didn't you see her?" I asked. "I mean, you're the one with Romany blood and second sight and all that."

"I don't claim to have the Sight with all its powers. I'm just willing to be open to possibilities. Anyway, I guess Agnes would only appear to you, because it's you she needs to communicate with."

I didn't want to be convinced. "I just think we should try to stick to the facts," I said, "not get carried away with all this mumbo-jumbo stuff."

"All right, then, let's stick to the facts. The portrait of Lady Agnes looks weirdly like you. Well, there's usually a perfectly logical, scientific explanation for people looking alike."

"What do you mean?" I wondered aloud.

"Simple genetics, Evie," she said. "You and Lady Agnes could be related."

"That's impossible."

"Why?"

"Because she was rich and aristocratic," I tried to explain. "And I'm just . . . ordinary."

"I think you're anything but ordinary," Sarah said. "Even so, families change, lose their money, move to different areas. We know that Agnes didn't have any children, because she died in that accident. It says in the reverend's book that her parents died a few years later of some fever they picked up on their wanderings. They had no direct descendant to take over the Abbey, so it became a school."

"I don't get—"

"It's simple, Evie. Agnes might have had other relations, like cousins, and they might have had children. And you told me that your grandmother once had family in this area, didn't you? We could try to trace your family tree back to see if you're connected with the Templetons in any way. That wouldn't be messing with any old voodoo. That would be sticking to the facts, wouldn't it?"

I was fascinated by the idea, which seemed reassuringly practical. Perhaps there really was nothing more to all this than an old family blood tie and the workings of my unconscious mind. "But I wouldn't know where to start. And I can't ask Frankie. She's too ill to be able to help."

"You could write and ask your dad, though. He might remember something."

"Yeah, he might," I agreed. "Okay, I will."

Sarah smiled encouragingly, then hesitated. "Evie, who is this guy you've been seeing?" she asked.

It was a question I had been asking myself over and over again.

"He's called Sebastian James. He lives near here." I groped for the raw facts. "He rides a black horse. And he's going to college next year. To Oxford."

"I'm impressed. He must be clever. But why are you meeting at night?"

"Mrs. Hartle's hardly going to invite him for lunch, is she?"

"Okay, okay," said Sarah. "So, he's waiting to go to college, he knows he wouldn't get past the Wyldcliffe staff, he

201

obviously likes the romance of midnight meetings—what else?"

What else indeed. How could I describe the slant of his cheek and the light in his eyes and the warmth of his smile? How could I explain the sheer exhilaration of being with him, or the pain of our quarrel? I couldn't even try. I said nothing.

"I don't know whether you're planning to see this Sebastian again, but I don't think you should," Sarah went on. "Not until we've found out some more. And you definitely shouldn't meet him at night, Evie. It's too risky. He might be dangerous."

Sebastian's moods. Sebastian's secretiveness. The glitter in his eyes, the flash of his temper. Did that make him dangerous? Wasn't every human being potentially dangerous? A nagging voice in my head reminded me of something Sebastian had once said: *I don't want this to go any farther. It could be dangerous for you.*

"Are you saying he's an ax murderer?" I said defensively.

"No, I'm just asking you to be careful. If he's genuine he'll get in touch with you properly—you know, write a letter or something. And if you get caught going out at night again you might even be expelled."

"Yeah, well, I could have done without Helen landing me with another demerit," I grumbled.

"She was only trying—"

"I know, I know. Only trying to help."

"Please, Evie."

I didn't want to tell Sarah that it was probably all over with Sebastian anyway. Telling her would make it too real. I pretended to be persuaded by her arguments.

"All right," I agreed. "I'll wait. I won't see him until we know some more. Okay?"

"Okay." She looked relieved.

Just then the nurse put her head around the door. "Sarah, it's time you left. You look a lot brighter, Evie. Your friend has done you good." Then she hurried away.

Sarah squeezed my hand and smiled. "See you tomorrow."

"Yeah, see you tomorrow. And thanks so much, Sarah." I watched her go, feeling better. My friend *had* done me good. I glanced down at the little flower that Helen had given me. Perhaps Helen, in her own strange way, wanted to be friends too.

My friends. It seemed an eternity since I had been able to say that, and I rolled the words around in my head luxuriously: *my friends, my friends.* And from far away, an answering voice echoed: *my sisters, my sisters.*

I was tired. Closing my eyes, I wondered if Dad would know the answers to my questions when my letter reached him. All I could remember Frankie saying was that her own grandmother had been a northerner, a country woman, who had lived on a farm near Wyldcliffe. Oh, what was the name of the farm? I was sure Frankie had mentioned it to me. Then the farm had failed for some reason, and Frankie's grandmother had died, leaving a baby daughter behind. Her husband—Frankie's grandfather—had married again and moved away with his new wife and the little girl, finding his way down to the west and the sea. And the girl grew up to be Frankie's mother. It all seemed very complicated.

The clock in the white room struck ten. I yawned.

So Frankie had only ever known her stepgrandmother. I remembered seeing an old photograph of her—Sally? Molly?—sitting on an upturned boat and mending a fishing net. But that wasn't the right woman; I wasn't related to her. I began to drift, sinking into sleep. I had to go farther back. I had to go back to the farm, the name of the farm . . . the farm . . .

When I opened my eyes the next morning, the answer was ringing in my head like a bell.

# Twenty-eight

THE JOURNAL OF LADY AGNES, FEBRUARY 12, 1883
*I woke up yesterday morning with the answer to what I must do clear and bright in my mind's eye. But it is so very hard!*

*These past weeks have been dreadful. S. has been very ill. If only he had been able to go to Oxford in January, as he had planned—the new people and ideas he would have encountered there might have shaken him from his obsession. There is no hope of that now. He has fallen into a series of fits and fevers that make any such attempt impossible. His parents are in despair and have summoned a well-known physician from London to treat his melancholy.*

*Martha told me that the servants at the Hall are*

whispering about the terrible scenes that take place over there; how S. fights the doctor and destroys his instruments and raves like a lunatic until he has to be restrained by his father and the serving men. They imagine that the fever he suffered in Morocco is burning in him again, but I know what is really eating at him, body and soul. I know it is me whom he seeks in his delirium, and the precious "gift" he thinks I could give him if I chose.

I have to get away from here, out of his reach. I must.

Like many desperate wretches before me, I have decided to run away to London, where it is so easy to hide. It will tear my heart to leave Wyldcliffe, but more than anything it hurts me to think of the pain I will cause my parents. They will never know why I have to do it.

I have written a letter for them saying that I want freedom and a new life, and that it will be useless to search for me. I wrote that they must pretend to the gossiping world that I have gone abroad to stay with my aunt Marchmont in Paris. When I said good night to them just now, I told them that I love them. Will they believe that when they have read my letter in the morning? There is nothing else that I can do, though, and no other choices left to me.

Tomorrow I will get up before even the maids are

about, and take what little money I have and a small bundle of clothes. I have bribed the local carter, Daniel Jones, to meet me at the end of the lane and take me to the nearest railway station, and then I shall make the journey to the great city, dressed in some plain clothes I have secretly bought in the village.

Poor Papa had promised to take me to London on the railway this summer. How he would have enjoyed showing me the changing landscape as we sped toward the city. Now I shall be traveling alone. But I am sixteen, quite capable of sitting on a train for a few hours.

It is no use to pretend that I am not crying. My father has always been so kind to me, and even Mama, now that I know I must never see her again, is dearer to me than I thought possible. I see now that she only ever wanted my happiness, and if she could imagine no greater happiness than sitting in an elegant drawing room, that was not her fault.

I cannot write any more. My new life starts here. After tomorrow, it will be as though Lady Agnes Templeton does not exist. It is the end of everything.

And it is a beginning.

# Twenty-nine

It was a new beginning.

I left the infirmary and clattered down the marble stairs, hungry for breakfast, clutching my flower in its little pot. At the bottom step I turned carelessly into the corridor and ran straight into the High Mistress.

"Oh! I'm so sorry!"

Some of the rich black earth from the pot had spilled onto Mrs. Hartle's light silk sleeve. She calmly brushed it away, then stopped me by laying her hand on my arm. It gave me a strange sensation, like being touched by something dead.

"It is against the school rules to run on the stairs and in the corridors. You should know that by now."

"Sorry," I mumbled again.

"And what's this?" Her dark eyes rested on the plant. It looked so fragile and easily crushed next to her powerful presence. "Ah, *Campanula rotundifolia*." I must have looked confused, because she explained with a flicker of contempt, "In English, the common harebell. One of our native plants. It grows on the moors."

"Helen gave it to me. I'm going to plant it in the old kitchen garden."

"Helen?" she repeated with a faint arch of her eyebrow. "How very nice. Only you must remember that it's very difficult for a wildflower to survive once it is uprooted. I think you'll find that her gift to you won't live very long."

My skin crawled as her fingers dug deeper into my arm. Then the High Mistress seemed to lose interest in me, and swept down the corridor toward her study. I watched her go. I wouldn't like to see her really angry, I decided. I made my way to the dining room, taking good care not to run.

I slipped into a seat opposite Sarah, eager to tell her my news. An instant later someone shoved me in the back. Celeste was standing over me.

"Well, look who it is—our friend Evie, back from the dead. I thought that lacrosse ball had finished you off? Such a disappointment." She sashayed away, and Miss

Scratton called everyone to attention for prayers.

"Why does she hate me so much?" I asked Sarah as we ate our breakfast.

"Oh, Celeste's always been a bit of a drama queen. She adored Laura, and she's somehow gotten it into her head that you're taking Laura's place. It's totally unfair, of course, but I guess she's just still really upset. Try not to let her get to you." Sarah lowered her voice. "Have you written to your dad yet?"

"I don't need to," I said excitedly. "I've remembered the name of the place where Frankie's family lived. It was called Uppercliffe Farm. I'm sure that was it—Uppercliffe."

To my surprise, Sarah's face fell.

"I don't think we'll find much information there. I've ridden past Uppercliffe loads of times. It's in ruins. But we could still go and look," she added quickly, seeing my disappointment.

"Okay. When?"

"Let's go out that way for a ride on Sunday afternoon. We'll have to ask Miss Scratton's permission first. You can't afford to get another demerit, so we'll have to do it all by the rules. I'm sure she'll say yes, though. She's knows I've been riding for years, and she lets me go out on my own sometimes."

"I can't ride at all!" The only time I'd been on horse-back was with Sebastian, and then I had been able to cling to him. This would be different.

"I'll teach you. We've got a few days to practice. I'll ride Starlight, and you can ride Bonny. She's such an angel, all you have to do is sit there and not fall off."

But I could just see myself falling off. I could see myself lying twisted on the moors, my eyes staring sightlessly at the gray, gray sky, just as she had, long ago. BE COOL OR YOU DIE. I pushed the thought away.

"Okay," I said with an effort. "I'll do my best."

Miss Scratton made a sign, and the rows of girls began to file out. I looked around for Helen. She was still sitting on the other side of the room, crumbling a piece of bread and gazing into space. I walked over to her.

"Thanks for the flower, Helen; it was really nice of you." Without meaning to, I was using the voice people keep for the sick. The voice the nurses used when they spoke to Frankie. I tried again. "Sarah says I can plant it in her part of the walled garden."

"Things shouldn't be walled up," she murmured. *Oh, Lord*, I thought, *she really is completely loopy.* Then she looked up at me and gave me a rare, sweet smile. I saw for the first time how beautiful she was, with her white-gold hair and her delicate face. "I'm glad you like it, Evie. It's my favorite flower. And I'm really sorry about the demerit. I just wanted to stop you from going out at night."

"Why?"

She looked around nervously, then whispered, "Strange things happen at Wyldcliffe. Be careful."

I needed to know more.

"Helen, I thought I saw something strange over at Fairfax Hall. I know you were sick that day, but I saw someone just like you, with your color hair and everything. Was it . . . Could it have been you?"

Her expression changed, as though a shadow had fallen on her. Mrs. Hartle had walked into the room and was giving a message to Miss Scratton. Helen jumped up. "I don't want to talk about it."

"But—"

"Leave me alone!"

It looked as though we weren't going to be friends after all.

# Thirty

The Journal of Lady Agnes, March 2, 1883
*I have left all my friends behind. My parents, Martha, the village people—they are all lost to me. I would give anything to be able to wake from this dark dream of a city and walk again over the moors, with the harebells in bloom and him at my side. . . .*

*But I must not think like that. My life is here now. This is my home.*

*I have found a cheap place to stay, and even some work. I am paid to sew fine linen for rich women, together with a dozen other girls crowded into a shabby room over a shop in Covent Garden. We work late into the night to complete the orders, and our overseer, Mr. Carley, is very harsh. I feel ashamed that I once wore* such clothes without questioning how they had been produced, or at what cost. At least in my new life I earn my living honestly. I hope I can keep this job; otherwise I will very quickly run out of money. I have never had to think about money before. There is so much that I have to learn.

One of the other workers, a thin, dark girl called Polly, has been especially good to me, showing me around and helping me when she can. I think she has taken some kind of fancy to me because I can read and have promised to teach her. At first the other girls doubted my story and eyed me suspiciously, but they are beginning to accept me. I have told them that I am nineteen and an orphan, and that I was employed by a grand family as a governess, but was turned away without a reference after the master took too keen an interest in me. It is a poor and common enough tale, but they seem to find it believable, romantic even. They sigh and hope that I will be miraculously discovered by my parents, who will, according to them, be a rich lord and lady, ready to whisk me away in their carriage. If only they knew the truth.

But I must not think of the past. I must not look back. My only comfort is the girl with red hair who haunts my *dreams like another self. Last night I saw her again, walking by the restless sea. I know that my destiny is somehow connected with hers. Apart from her, I must forget everything that once linked me to Wyldcliffe.*

# Thirty-one

I didn't really know why, but it seemed important to find some link between me and Wyldcliffe, and I was excited about going to Uppercliffe Farm. The days passed quickly as I planned the outing with Sarah and practiced my riding. Underneath, despite these distractions, I was aching for Sebastian. *Please forgive me; please get in touch*, I prayed every night, and every morning I eagerly scanned the letters set out in the hall. He didn't write.

I had to get over it and forget him. But a voice inside me cried, *I can't. . . . I won't.*

That Sunday morning seemed the longest I had ever experienced. The late, leisurely breakfast. The walk to church, with the clouds threatening rain. The gloomy hymns, the long prayers, the reading from the Gospel. . . . *And men loved darkness rather than light because their deeds were evil. . . .* And then the cold walk back to school, before we were finally free.

I went up to the dorm and pulled on a pair of jeans and some riding boots I had borrowed from Sarah. An old sweatshirt hid Frankie's necklace from sight. I was glad that I was still wearing it on my ribbon, especially today, when I was going to see where Frankie's family had once lived. As I changed my clothes I wondered if she ever thought about me, and my heart stabbed with pain. I missed so much about her. How she always woke me in the morning with a big mug of tea and a bigger smile. How she loved the sea and the stars and her simple cottage flowers. How she made me feel important for all those years, just by loving me. *I'm doing this for you too*, I tried to tell her as I hurried down the marble steps.

When I got to the stables, Celeste and Sophie were there already, all done up in immaculate jodhpurs and tweed jackets. A teenage boy I had never seen before was holding the reins of their long-legged horses. He had corn-colored hair and quiet brown eyes. I guessed he must be a local boy helping out in the stables for the weekend.

"Thanks, Josh," said Celeste, swinging easily into the saddle. She and Sophie clattered off. I hoped we wouldn't come across them on the moors. The boy gave me a quick smile, then turned away, busy with the other horses.

"Hey, Evie," Sarah called, leading Bonny and Starlight across the cobblestones. I scrambled up onto Bonny's broad back, and soon we were riding down the lane outside the school gates. I breathed out and tried to trust the steady jog-trot of the strong little pony. I mustn't fall off. I mustn't end up like Agnes. . . .

"We turn off here," said Sarah. "There's a path that leads to Uppercliffe. It's quite high up on the moors. Apparently there was a hamlet there once, just the farm and a few cottages. But the people moved away years ago. Perhaps they couldn't make enough money from the land."

A bird—I didn't know what kind—cried mournfully, and the wind sighed over the bare hills. It must have been such a hard, lonely life in the old days, I thought. No wonder they had given up and moved away. We jogged along, and the sound of the wind seemed to be heavy with voices from the past. . . .

"I've found something else out about Agnes," said Sarah as she rode next to me. "I went to the library after supper last night to get a book for my French class, and I bumped into Miss Scratton. I thought she might know something, being a history teacher and all that. I told her that we were interested in finding out stuff about local history and had looked at that book about the school."

"So what did she say?"

"She said that Reverend Flowerdew wasn't exactly a reliable historian, and that it wasn't totally clear that Agnes had died in a riding accident. That was the official story that people like Flowerdew repeated, and that the family acknowledged. Agnes was found dead on the grounds, supposedly thrown from her horse, but the talk among the servants was that she had been killed by some kind of intruder at Wyldcliffe."

"You mean . . . murdered? That's so horrible."

"It's only a possibility, according to Miss Scratton."

"What else did Miss Scratton say?" I asked as we rode slowly side by side.

"She said the servants' stories about an attack were dismissed as gossip. The official coroner supported the riding accident theory."

"But why would there be two contradictory versions of her death?"

"I don't know. Perhaps the servants simply got it wrong. Miss Scratton said Agnes was really popular with the ordinary people. Her old nurse even had a kind of seizure when she heard that Agnes was dead. I suppose it would only take a couple of hysterical young maids to get carried away when the news broke and then the rumors would be all over a little place like Wyldcliffe. Perhaps the authorities and her parents just came forward later and told the truth—that it was an accident."

I hoped so. The idea that someone would deliberately kill a slim girl with starry eyes and bright hair was too awful. But these things happened, had always happened. *Strange things happen at Wyldcliffe. . . . That cursed place.*

No, it couldn't be true. Impossible.

"Do you really believe in ghosts, Sarah?" I said abruptly.

"Yes," she answered. "Yes, I think I do. I can't believe that the energy that makes a person's identity can just be destroyed and disappear into nothingness. I think that part of us lives on after death, whether you call it the spirit or the soul or whatever. So if our spirits do go on after death, isn't it possible that some spirits might get lost, or stuck between worlds, like a penny that has been dropped down a crack?"

"Is that what you think happened to Agnes?"

Sarah shrugged. "Don't they say that someone who has experienced something very traumatic—such as being murdered—could leave a kind of electrical energy behind them? A sort of shadow or a footprint? And people who are sensitive might be able to pick that up."

"You mean like a radio signal, but it's the actual person

you receive, instead of music?" I was half joking, but Sarah didn't laugh.

"Yeah, I think so. Besides," she added, "I'm still loyal to my Romany ancestors. The Romany people have always held that life for the dead continues, and that the dead can return to haunt the living."

"The dead can return," I repeated. My heart began to race, and I changed the subject. "Let's get going, or it will be dark before we get to Uppercliffe."

"Okay, then. Ready?"

We had reached a broad path across the heath, and Sarah cantered away smoothly. I tried to copy her. Bonny obediently pricked up her ears and set off after Starlight. At first I thought I would fall off; then I settled into the rhythm and clung on grimly as we sped across the moors.

Sarah had told me everything she had found out. I hadn't been equally honest with her. I'd also done some research, but I'd kept the results to myself.

Without telling her, I had sneaked into the little telephone room at school and looked up the name James in the directory. There had been two entries, and I had called them both. No, they didn't have a Sebastian James there. No, they didn't know of anyone of that name in the Wyldcliffe area. No—getting impatient now—they couldn't think of how I could contact him. But not finding his number didn't mean anything, I told myself. His family was probably unlisted; that was all. I imagined them living in a big house with a high wall around it, keeping everyone away. Just as Sebastian had wanted to keep me away from the rest of his life.

Sarah pulled Starlight up to a walk. "There it is," she said. "Uppercliffe Farm."

Lying in a dip in the moor were the tumbled remains of a farmhouse, hardly bigger than a cottage. Weeds grew in the wide cracks in the walls.

"What do you think happened to it?" I asked.

"I guess when the family abandoned the farm other people came and took some of the stones to repair their own cottages. It looks sad, doesn't it?"

"I'm going inside."

"Be careful. The roof doesn't look too safe. I have a weird feeling. I think we should start heading back." She glanced around anxiously.

"Oh, come on, Sarah," I pleaded. "We've come so far; we can't go back yet."

We dismounted and let the ponies crop the grass, then walked up to the abandoned house. The door had fallen off its hinges, and the staircase had rotted away. Sheep and rabbit droppings littered the ground. The whole place seemed on the point of collapse.

I felt so disappointed. There was nothing to see, nothing to connect me with the people who had once lived here. It was time to move on. Then I saw it.

"Look!" I pointed above the space where the door had once stood. "Look at that shape, up there. . . ."

Over the doorway there was a stone block crudely carved with a date. But underneath the lettering was another carved mark, a curious shape I felt sure I had seen before.

"What's that?" I asked. "Ordinary farmers like these wouldn't have a family crest or anything like that, would they?"

"I don't think so. I wonder what it means?"

Staring at the ruin, I tried to imagine the farmhouse as it might once have been, with solid stone walls and smoke drifting from its chimney. Where the weeds and grasses grew now, there would be onions and potatoes and a few bright flowers. I closed my eyes and concentrated, until a picture shimmered in the darkness behind my eyelids. I could smell wood smoke. Where the gaping doorway had been, a neat blue door stood open. A plump, red-cheeked little girl toddled out and sat on the step. She clutched an apple in her hand, and the sun glinted on her bronze curls. A slow, comfortable woman's voice called out from the house, "Effie? Effie, you mind and be a good girl out there, my chick."

Effie . . . Effie . . . Evie.

"*Evie!*" A high, thin wail reached us on the wind. I opened my eyes with a start. Something had happened.

"*Eveee . . . Saraaah . . . Eee-veee!*"

"Someone's shouting for us," said Sarah. "Come on!"

We ran over to Bonnie and Starlight and heaved ourselves up, then charged away in the direction of the cries. Soon we saw two horses wandering loose and two girls huddled in the bracken. One of them was lying awkwardly, her leg twisted beneath her. It was Celeste. Sophie was crouching next to her with a white, terrified face.

"Thank God," she moaned. "I thought you would never hear me."

"What's wrong? What happened?"

"A rabbit shot out and spooked Celeste's horse, and she fell off. She keeps fainting. I didn't want to leave her on her own to go and get help. We'd seen you riding up to that old cottage, so I knew you couldn't be far away. I've been calling and calling. I was so worried that Celeste might . . . like Laura . . ." She burst into noisy sobs.

Sarah tried to calm her down. "Listen, Sophie, she's certainly not going to die, but she has hurt herself. I'll gallop back to Wyldcliffe and get the doctor. Evie will stay here with you. I won't take long. Don't worry. Everything will be fine."

In a second Sarah had gone. It began to rain. Sophie stopped crying and started to shiver. I put my arm around her awkwardly.

"Th-thank you."

We sat in uncomfortable silence. Celeste groaned faintly, drifting in and out of consciousness. A bird sang high above us, unconcerned by the rain, oblivious to our presence. I tried to think of something to say. "Don't worry. It will be okay." It sounded so meaningless.

Sophie glanced sideways at me. After a long pause she said, "Celeste hasn't been very nice to you, has she? None of us have."

"It doesn't matter."

Sophie sniffed and wiped her face on her sleeve.

"It's just that she really loved Laura. You wouldn't think that Celeste would be that emotional, but they were like sisters."

"Oh."

She raised her eyes to mine. "I think love is the most important thing in the world, don't you?"

"Umm."

"I've got a puppy at home. He loves me. I miss him."

She huddled in the rain and fell silent. I had written her off as a dumb snob, and now I saw that she was just sad: packed off to boarding school by distant parents, clinging on to Celeste for friendship, missing her dog like a child would miss her teddy bear. But her trite words had opened my eyes like a profound revelation.

*Love is the most important thing in the world.*

I saw then that there was no point trying to dig up the past. I had allowed myself to be sidetracked by my imagination, searching for things that couldn't possibly be there, and all the time I had been turning my back on something real. Lady Agnes, the portrait, the people at the old farm—none of that mattered compared to how I felt about Sebastian.

Sitting on that damp hillside, I finally admitted to myself that I loved him. And I couldn't turn my back on him now, whatever I had promised Sarah. Love was the most important thing. I couldn't allow a silly fight, or neurotic visions, to destroy it.

*Stay away from him,* the girl in white had said. But I knew that I couldn't. I needed to see Sebastian again. I had to find out whether there was something real between us. And if there was, I would hold on to it and never let it go.

# Thirty-two

THE JOURNAL OF LADY AGNES, APRIL 15, 1883

*How could I have let him go so easily? How did I get onto that train to London and leave him behind?*

*When I first came here I had to put all my efforts into finding a way to carry on living; simply to feed and clothe myself and keep off the streets was an effort. My work seems to please Mr. Carley and I am making just enough money to survive. Now that I can look beyond the basics of survival, I am desperately unhappy. Without love, life is mere existence.*

*Yesterday I walked by the river. It is not like our bright streams at home, but a stinking, sluggish tide wrapped in fogs and foul stenches. How easy it would be, I thought, to fall into its depths and let it swallow me up. . . .*

*I came back to my lodging feeling sick and exhausted. As soon as I reached my room I bolted the door, shut the blinds, and drew the Circle, whispering the incantations as low as I could. It was the first time I had allowed myself to indulge in the Mysteries since arriving in the city, and it was for one purpose only: to see the faces of those I love.*

*The bright, cool flames sprang up, red and gold and white, like hothouse flowers. I cut them with a silver knife, carving his name on the air. Then the flames sank low, and in their gleaming heart I saw an image of my beloved, so far away. His face was full of pain and fever, and as he spoke my name he cursed me. Then I cast my mind to my parents' house and saw them too as tiny images in the flames, holding on to each other and weeping.*

*A wave of fury swept through me. Sparks shot from the Circle, and I created a whirlwind of phantoms; stars and planets seemed to spin above my head, waterfalls of light crashed to the ground from my outstretched hands, and a legion of fantastical creatures leaped around me: bronzed tigers and shimmering peacocks and galloping horses, all burnished with fire. I* cried out in my mind to the Powers, How is it that I can summon such wonders, yet I cannot be with those I love? Why have I been forced to cause them pain? Why was I chosen for this?

There was no answer. I flung myself to the floor in despair and broke the Circle. The lights and flames vanished, and I was left shivering in the dark, as tense and wary as a stricken animal. In that moment I would have done anything to go back to him.

I know now that I will never marry or have children. But if I had been lucky enough to have a daughter, I would have told her that if she found love, she should hold on to it and never let it go.

# Thirty-three

This is the moment. I am wide awake, tense and wary like an animal.

As soon as I am sure that the others are asleep, I fly down the familiar servants' staircase, not caring about the dark. I think only about seeing Sebastian again. I pray that he hasn't got tired of waiting for me night after night. I have to see him. I have to find out. Everything else has been leading to this moment. Now I will know the truth.

The great house around me is unnaturally quiet, as though everyone has fallen into an enchanted sleep, even the mice. I fumble with the fastening of the door into the stable yard. I am outside. The sky is clear and dark, thickly spread with hard, cold stars. Everything is still. Time has stopped. I begin to run. In my hurry I have forgotten to put on any shoes, and my feet sink into the damp grass. The ruins loom up ahead: so still, so dark. The lake glimmers. An owl screeches from the broken arches of the chapel. Sebastian said he would wait.

I listen and look, straining every nerve. There is no one there. So now I know.

It is over.

I mean nothing to Sebastian. I'm just another idiotic girl swept away by a handsome face. My breath is coming in quick gasps. My heart is beating so hard that it hurts. Then I see him, slumped against a low wall in the shadows.

"Evie?" He staggers to his feet. I fly over to him, and he folds me in his arms. We cling to each other without speaking; then he pulls away.

"Oh, Evie, I'm so sorry. I thought I would never see you again."

"It's all right, it's all right. I'm sorry too; it was my fault."

"No! Don't say that. I want to explain—"

"It doesn't matter; it's not important." I look into his face. He is unnaturally pale and gaunt. Fear cuts through me. "Sebastian, what's wrong? You look terrible. Are you ill?"

"It's not important." He coughs wearily. "Listen, all that stuff about meeting my parents. I should have told you the truth. My parents are dead. There is no one to meet. I'm on my own."

"Why didn't you tell me?"

"I didn't want you . . . feeling sorry for me." A glint of pride flashes over his face. "It was stupid. Please forgive me."

"There's nothing to forgive. I was stupid too. I've missed you so much."

"Have you?" he says eagerly, hungrily. "Oh, Evie, I haven't even felt alive without you."

"Well, I'm here now," I reply, hugging him tight. He looks so haggard and sick that I just want to take all his pain away. "I'll make you better. I'll never walk out on you again. Don't worry; I'm here."

He smiles like a fragile, wasted angel.

"Yes, you're here. Let's celebrate. What shall we do?"

"What do you suggest?" I laugh softly. "A picnic? Going to the movies? We don't have a lot of choices."

Sebastian's eyes gleam. "I know what I want to do. Let's swim in the lake together. We can pretend it's your wild sea. Would you like that?"

"But you're not well, and it's cold. . . ."

He touches a strand of my hair, as he had done when we had first met. I feel myself weakening.

"I don't care," he says, his eyes searching my face as if trying to memorize me.

"And I haven't got a bathing suit." Though I know that I can't resist.

Slowly Sebastian reaches out and unties my robe, letting it fall onto the wet grass. The cold air bites through my nightgown. I unfasten Frankie's necklace and drop it onto the crumpled robe.

"What's that?" he asks, glancing down carelessly.

"My grandmother's necklace. I don't want to get it wet."

He laughs, kind and tender. "You're always so sensible, Evie, even when you are swimming in a forbidden lake in the middle of the night." Then he pulls off his coat and his loose shirt. His arms and chest gleam like pale stone against his dark riding breeches. "Are you ready?" he whispers. He catches me up in his arms, as if I were a bride being carried across the threshold, and wades into the silent waters of the lake.

Its dark ripples spread out as we swim side by side. Then our hands touch, our eyes meet, and our limbs twine like clinging ivy. Our mouths reach for each other. In that moment a flash like an electric charge scorches through me. I gasp and swallow some water. I am being pulled under the surface. Panic grips me, and I can't remember how to swim. I'm no longer myself—I am Laura, choking with terror in the muddy waters of the lake.

Something—someone—is clutching me, dragging me down. I plunge deep below the surface of the lake. I'm surrounded by a ring of white faces hooded in dark robes: terrifying, monstrous women reaching toward me. They are screaming, calling out a name that rings through my head: *"Sebastian! Sebastian!"* Then another voice cries *"Evie, Evie . . ."*

It is my mother. I've never heard that voice before, but I know instinctively that it is her. With my last strength I kick out and reach the surface, struggling to break free.

"Evie! Evie!" This time it is Sebastian calling me. I am in his arms on the smooth grass by the side of the lake, retching and shivering. I push him away and lash out with my fists.

"Don't," he soothes. "Don't, Evie. You're all right now."

"Stay away from me; don't touch me!"

"What are you talking about? Evie, it's me, Sebastian."

I burst into dry, racking sobs.

"I . . . I saw them. I . . . saw those women."

"What? What did you see?"

I look straight into those angel eyes. Was this what the redheaded girl was trying to warn me about?

"Those women. They were trying to kill me. And they were calling your name."

He looks startled, afraid even; then his face hardens.

"There was no one there, Evie. And I won't let anyone hurt you. You've got to believe that."

"But they were there, under the water!"

"You just got a cramp and panicked."

"It's not just that," I rush on. "I've been seeing other things, people I don't know, hearing voices, imagining all kinds of stuff. I thought I could ignore it, but I think I'm going crazy."

"You're not, Evie; you're good and true and beautiful, and I won't let this place hurt you. I'll take care of you, I swear." He pulls me close to him, as though he will never let me go, and says, "I love you."

Everything else falls away. I am still, more still than I have ever been in my whole life. The world is no longer a terrifying place. I am not alone. Sebastian loves me. Nothing is more important than that. He begins to stroke my face and hair. "Stay with me, Evie. I want you to be with me—forever."

He lifts me up lightly and easily and carries me away from the lake. I cling to his neck and breathe in the smell of his damp skin. I want to call out to the hills, to the trees and the stars: *I love, I love, I love him, like the endless song of the sea.*

This is the moment.

He walks under the broken arches of the chapel and sets me down amid the deep and silent shadows. Through the roofless vault above me, I see the stars crown Sebastian's head with cold white fire as he leans over to kiss me at last.

It is joy, pure joy. We kiss again and again, then we open our eyes and gaze in wonder at the miracle of each other. And one by one the stars blink and are gone, and the birds begin to sing.

# Thirty-four

I floated down to breakfast the next day. I wanted to run instead of walk, to fly instead of run. Every doubt and fear had vanished. I had never been so happy in all my life.

"Here, this is for you." Sophie was standing by the table, helping to set out the morning mail. Since Celeste's accident she had been determinedly friendly.

"Thanks, Sophie." I took the letter eagerly, hoping it was from Sebastian, but the envelope she handed me was addressed to *Miss Evelyn Johnson* in unfamiliar handwriting. A printed crest on the back of the envelope said, *Beechwood Nursing Home.*

"I hope it's not more bad news," Sophie said, her lip trembling slightly. "Did you hear that Celeste has broken her leg really badly? She's not coming back to school for ages."

"Oh—I'm sorry. I didn't know."

"Poor Celeste."

"Yeah. Well, see you later, Sophie."

I hurried away, unwilling to open the letter somehow. Bad news, Sophie had said. I couldn't bear to get any bad news about Frankie. I didn't want anything to spoil my happiness about Sebastian.

By the time the midmorning break arrived, I was ashamed of my cowardice. I was being totally selfish. Of course I wanted to hear how Frankie was getting on. It might even be a letter from Frankie herself, back to normal, just like the old days. I decided to go outside to read it in private.

"Hey," said Sarah, coming up to me as I headed for the door. "Do you want to go down to the stables for a bit?"

"Sure."

I felt guilty that I had broken my promise to her not to see Sebastian. I would have to try to explain, but not yet.

"I've got a letter," I said with false brightness, pulling it out of my pocket. "It might be good news about Frankie."

"Okay. I'll go and see to the ponies and leave you to read it."

I sat on a low bench outside the tack room. Inside the envelope was a note, and folded with it was a piece of yellowing paper. As I read them both, the blood seemed to sing in my head.

"Sarah! Sarah!"

She came running over from the other side of the yard.

"What's the matter? What happened?"

I couldn't answer. I just handed her the note. She sat down on the bench and began to read.

*Dear Evelyn,*

*You don't know me, but I am one of the nurses who cares for your grandmother here at Beechwood. We are all very fond of her. Last week she seemed to be doing quite a lot better. She managed to indicate that she wanted this enclosed document to be sent to you. I asked the manager if that was all right, and she gave me your address at the boarding school. You're very lucky to be there, aren't you? But I forgot to mail it, because the next day your grandmother had a bad turn again. I am sure your father has been keeping you up-to-date. She is stable now, though I am not sure if she knows what is going on around her. It's a shame, but you mustn't be sad, as we are all doing our best for her, and I am sure she will be better soon.*

*Yours truly,*

*Margaret Walsh*

"So what's in this document?"

I passed her the worn scrap of paper.

"'The generations of our family,'" Sarah read, "'beginning with Evelyn Frances Smith, who was known as Effie. Born in 1884, she rightly belonged elsewhere but was beloved by everyone at Uppercliffe.' Then there's a list of women's names, all in different handwriting."

"Read out the names," I whispered.

"'Eliza Agnes, daughter to Effie, born in 1904, taken from the valley at the age of two. Frances Mary, born 1933.' Then it says, 'Clara—my dearest daughter. Drowned just before her thirtieth birthday.'" Sarah stopped reading and glanced up at me.

"Keep going."

"The last name on the list is Evelyn Johnson. Is that you?"

"Everyone always calls me Evie."

"So Clara is your mother, and Frances Mary must be Frankie?"

I nodded. I couldn't speak.

Sarah frowned over the paper again. "Eliza was your great grandmother, and the other Evelyn—Effie—was your great-great-grandmother."

The image of a little girl with bronze curls sitting in

the sun flashed into my mind. Was that Effie? Had I really seen her?

"There's a kind of drawing on the other side of the paper," continued Sarah. "A sketch of something. And it says, 'An heirloom of the daughters of Evelyn Frances Smith. May it never be parted from them or fall into darkness.' I don't know what that's about; do you, Evie?"

"I think I do," I answered slowly.

My hands shook as I pulled my necklace from its hiding place under my school shirt. The silver trinket was exactly the same shape as the sketch on the paper.

"Evie, we saw that on the doorway over the farmhouse—don't you remember? This paper and the house and your necklace—they're all connected."

"So the necklace must be the heirloom." I gazed at it in wonder. "And now it belongs to me."

A bell rang. Wyldcliffe didn't stop for anything. I hid the necklace away again.

"We've got to get back to class," said Sarah. "But we need to try to figure out if Lady Agnes fits into all this. Wait a minute . . . 1884—when this Effie was born—that would be the year of Agnes's death. Don't you remember that the painting of her was done in 1882, two years before her accident?"

"I don't see how this has anything to do with Agnes."

"But one of these women, your ancestors, has the same name. Look, it says here, 'Eliza Agnes.'"

"I guess it was a common name back then. It doesn't necessarily link this particular Eliza Agnes with Lady Agnes Templeton."

"It's a start, though, isn't it?" said Sarah eagerly. Then she frowned. "It's funny that Frankie managed to send this to you just now, almost as if she knew you needed it."

*Could Frankie really have known?* I wondered. As we went back inside, I wished with all my heart that I could see her and talk to her. There was so much more that I needed to know.

All that day my mind was faraway, with those women whose lives were part of my own. I even shared a name with one of them. Evelyn . . . Evie . . . Effie. She was the missing link, the grandmother that Frankie had never known. My great-great-grandmother. It was her name I had heard up on the moors by the ruined farmhouse. And I knew that I had really seen her sitting on a doorstep eating an apple on a long-ago spring morning. I didn't want to see things that other people couldn't. I wasn't like Sarah, excited by the idea of the unknown. I wanted to be sane, sensible Evie Johnson, safe in Sebastian's arms.

But something was bothering me, and I couldn't let go of it.

Why should Effie—Evelyn Frances Smith, a humble woman from a poor hillside farm—have been important enough to possess an heirloom that had been carefully handed down from daughter to daughter for five generations? The question haunted me all day. Where had the necklace come from? Was it valuable? And how could I find out?

# Thirty-five

THE JOURNAL OF LADY AGNES, MAY 23, 1883
*The silver necklace is all I have left. The Mystic Way is closed to me. I no longer have any power, not even enough to snuff out a candle. I can hardly bear to write about what I have done, but I must. I have to accept my new reality.*

*I watched S. many times in the flames, night after night. It was like a drug. I couldn't stop myself; I needed to know what was happening to him. Eventually I saw that he had recovered from his illness and was planning to come to London, desperate to find me. No, that wasn't true. It wasn't me he wanted to find, only a way to reach the Fire.*

*After much thought and suffering, I decided to put the*

possibility of giving him what he seeks beyond my own reach forever. Now, even if he does discover my hiding place, I cannot be tempted by his anguished cries and his pleading looks. I can do him no harm, and the Mysteries will be guarded for the girl who will one day use them well.

Once I had made my decision, I roamed the markets and parted with my last few shillings to buy a curious engraved trinket from an Eastern trader who spoke little English. There are so many different nationalities huddled in these crowded streets, all selling something. I haggled over the price; then we agreed terms, and he hung the bauble on a heavy silver chain. I returned to my lodging, well satisfied with my bargain.

That night I made the Sacred Circle for the last time. I did everything with great care, wanting to remember the beauty of the gift I was about to give back.

Once I had summoned the flames, I made them dance high around me, like a forest of silver trees rocking in the wind. For a long while I stood in delight, simply watching the light and colors, but then I had to begin my work.

I concentrated all my powers, until I no longer saw with my eyes but with my mind. I needed to go into the heart of the Fire, so I called to its guardian spirit, and the Spirit answered me. Then it seemed to me that I was in the cavern I had once dreamed of, where an endlessly twisting column of flame rose from the very center of the created world. I was not afraid. I was allowed to approach, and then I had a choice. All I had to do was to reach out my hand and I would be part of that immortal beauty and power forever. But instead I thrust the silver trinket into the column of fire. And now, for the first time, the heat scorched me, until I thought I would die. My life force seemed to be dragged out of me and into the silver jewel. I saw two beloved faces, his and hers, and I vowed to protect them. Then the pain became so great that I passed into nothingness. When I awoke I was alone in my poor, bare room, and the necklace was cool in my hand.

My struggle is over. My powers are now sealed in this gleaming talisman, far beyond his reach, or my own. I know that he never truly loved me, though I do not blame him for it. His feelings were those of an eager boy bound for some marvelous adventure. It was excitement and power he needed, not my love.

She will be the one to teach him the secrets of his heart.

And now I must put aside my love for him, like a wedding garment that is no longer needed. I have put my whole life to one side to save theirs. That is my choice. That is my freedom.

# Thirty-six

It was a long, restless day. I put aside my thoughts of Sebastian and secretly read the letters from the nursing home over and over again, hidden in the pages of my schoolbooks, and tried to make sense of everything. Eventually it was time to get ready for bed. I went to the bathroom and locked the door. Sitting on the floor, I undid the ribbon around my neck and examined the necklace carefully. It was made of twisting silver strands with a glinting crystal at its center, which seemed to glow different colors as I turned it in the light. It was pretty, though I hadn't thought about it much until now as a piece of jewelry, only as a link with Frankie.

Someone thumped on the bathroom door.

"Hurry up!"

It was India, impatient as usual and snappier than ever without Celeste around to soothe her ego. I sighed and got up. But as I looked in the mirror to fasten the necklace again, I swayed with shock. A different face, not mine, was looking back at me. A girl with long auburn curls, in a black gown, with a gleaming silver chain at her throat and a tiny baby in her arms. It was Agnes.

I clutched the side of the basin. Then I heard her singing:

*The night is dark, but day is near,*
*Hush, little baby, do not fear.*
*Hush, little Effie, Mama's here. . . .*

The hammering on the door began again.

"Have you dropped down dead in there or something?"

I flung open the door, pushed past India, and marched back to the dorm. Ignoring everyone, I drew the curtain around my bed and pulled the covers up to my chin.

*Agnes had a baby called Effie. Agnes had a baby; Agnes was Effie's mother. . . .* The words raced through my head. I couldn't ignore what I was seeing any longer. I couldn't explain it away. This was real. For the first time I began to believe that Agnes herself was trying to tell me the truth of what had happened to her.

She'd had a baby, but she hadn't been married. And her baby was little Effie with the vivid curls. I guessed that in those days Agnes couldn't possibly have kept her; the whole thing would have been a terrible scandal. So, what if Effie had been sent to live on a local farm? What if she had been given a name to hide behind—Evelyn Frances Smith—and had grown up as an ordinary farmer's daughter? Then she'd gotten married and had her own daughter, Eliza Agnes, my great-grandmother, whose middle name hinted at the connection with the Abbey. That was where Effie had rightly belonged.

My mind was whirling. With a sick feeling in my stomach I remembered the rumors about Agnes's death, saying that it hadn't been an accident. What if she had been gotten rid of to hush up the scandal about the baby? Lord Charles was rich and powerful; he could have hired thugs, squared it all with the authorities, spread that story about the riding accident. I imagined him as a cold, cruel Victorian father, caring more about his reputation than about his only daughter. No wonder Wyldcliffe had been cursed.

No, that was impossible. Now I was going too far; no

parent would allow such a thing. Besides, Sarah had said that Lord Charles had been heartbroken and had fled abroad after her death. But had he been driven away by grief, or by guilt?

I sat up in bed, my head almost bursting, desperate to work it all out.

Whatever the details, one thing seemed clear to me: Agnes had died under mysterious circumstances, and the violence of that death had left an imprint of energy at Wyldcliffe. And I had picked it up, tuned in to it, just as Sarah had said might be possible, because Agnes was my distant ancestor. Somehow it all made sense. My insights into her world were amazing, but quite logical, a kind of scientific phenomenon. I wasn't going nuts after all.

I wanted to dance with relief; then I remembered the gentle face of the young mother I had glimpsed across the barrier of time, and grieved for her. Poor Agnes, I thought. She would have been hardly any older than I was, and she must have been so afraid. I wondered what the man she had loved had been like. I hoped they had been happy together, at least for a little time. But he must have let her down, or she wouldn't have been left to face the consequences alone. Then it hit me: *Stay away from him.* Her words had no connection with Sebastian. She must have been thinking of the man who had betrayed her, not Sebastian at all.

The joy I had felt the night before came flooding back. It was okay. There was nothing to fear. I was right to love him.

It felt as though the last pieces of the puzzle were falling into place. Now I could share all this with Sebastian—in fact, he might even know something about Agnes's history. After all, he had told me stuff about Lord Charles and his family before. I had to see him, just as soon as the other girls had fallen asleep. And then, in the morning, I would proudly present the whole story to Sarah, like a detective who had just solved an impossible case.

I felt for the little necklace under my nightgown. Now I would always wear it—not just for Frankie, but for all those women who had come before me, especially Agnes. It was the least I could do.

# Thirty-seven

THE JOURNAL OF LADY AGNES, NOVEMBER 13, 1884

*It is more than two years since I began to keep this journal. I have not written in it for many months, but it is the least I can do now to pick up my pen and continue with my story, if only to make a record for my little daughter of these extraordinary times. As I look back through these pages, it seems to me that those old days in Wyldcliffe were another life, only half remembered, like sleepwalking. When I fled to London I was still a child, caught up in a great adventure, and even its dangers seemed like part of a romantic story I was living in. But now I have changed. I am a woman, with a child of my own to care for and protect, part of the long line of mothers who nurse hope for the future and remember the past.*

My child, poor mite, will never know her father. We buried Francis only four weeks ago. He was kind and good and patient to the very end. I knew when we first met that he was already touched by consumption, but I did not know how little time there would be for us. His decline, once it began, was rapid. It is almost too painful and private to write about, but I have learned that in a strange way, suffering has given me strength.

However terrible it has been to lose him, I am so grateful that we had these brief months of happiness. Our meeting was only by chance, when Polly told me about a young man, Francis Howard, lodging in her neighborhood, an artist who had been turned out of his wealthy family for pursuing his dreams, and who was now so poor that he would trade one of his paintings for a hot meal. He had sketched Polly one evening, and she was eager to show me the result. And so we met, and so my life changed. Was that chance—or fate? If I hadn't gone along that Sunday afternoon to admire Polly's portrait, would we have missed meeting each other in this world? I don't know, but I have faith that we will meet again in a better one.

After I had run away from Wyldcliffe, I thought that I would never love again. But I know now that there are different kinds of love. Francis taught me that loving someone does not have to be painful. He was tender and true and good. His paintings, as well as his gentle heart, were full of the joy of life. And now I don't suppose that anyone will ever appreciate his work. I had to exchange the last few canvases he left for food.

I am thankful that Francis lived just long enough to see our daughter. She is my heart's delight, and although I was so ill after her birth, she kept me alive. Everything about her is beautiful: her tiny hands, her bright eyes, the delicious smell of her smooth skin. I hold her close and rock her to sleep every night, singing as Martha once did to me:

> The night is dark, but day is near,
> Hush, little baby, do not fear. . . .

Now I am afraid, though. I cannot support us both with my needlework, and although the people around me have proved to be such good friends—Polly and her mother and the other neighbors—I cannot stay here. I have made up my mind to go back to Wyldcliffe. I will try to see my parents. It is not their money or their grand house that I want for my little one, only their love. I want her to know her family and the wild valley where she truly belongs. I don't deserve forgiveness for the hurt I have caused them, but my daughter does.

I will not go straight to the Abbey, however, in case I am not welcome. Instead I will stay with Martha, who has managed to write to me from time to time. She is living with her nephew on the farm now and says she is longing to see my "bairn." And I am longing to be home.

# Thirty-eight

I was longing with every atom to see Sebastian. I couldn't wait another second. Everything in the dorm seemed quiet, so I decided to risk it. I crept across the room as quietly as a cat and headed to the door.

"Evie!"

It was Helen, her eyes glinting in the dark.

"What is it?" I whispered back, trying to sound unconcerned.

"Don't go out tonight. You mustn't."

"I don't know what you're talking about."

"It's a new moon," she said. "They'll be out there."

"Who? Who will be there?"

"I . . . I can't tell you."

"Oh, you're driving me insane," I hissed. "But I'm not

going to let this place get to me; do you understand?"

"There are things about this place you don't know," she replied. "You need to be careful."

India stirred in her sleep. We were in danger of waking her. I leaned closer to Helen.

"Look, Helen, I'm grateful for the advice and all that, but I don't need your help. I can take care of myself."

I turned my back on her and slipped out, making my way as quickly as I could down the narrow back stairs. At last I flung open the old green door and stepped out into the cold night air.

Sebastian was waiting for me, pacing up and down in the yard. He pulled me into the shadows and kissed me, then hugged me tight. "Thank God you're safe. I've been so worried."

"Why? What's the matter?"

"Every time I have to let you go, I don't know when we'll see each other again. I'm in agony every second that I'm away from you." He kissed my lips, my eyes, my forehead, like butterfly wings brushing my face. "Dearest Evie, darling Evie," he murmured. "We can't stay here."

He led me across the stable yard into the walled kitchen garden. The beanpoles stood like sentinels in the moonlight.

"Why are we going in here?" I asked.

"I think someone is watching the lake."

"Who?"

He shrugged. "One of the staff patrolling the grounds, keeping out undesirables like me. Let's talk here instead." We found a stone bench in a shadowy corner. Sebastian breathed more easily, and smiled. "Have you missed me today?"

"Every hour, every minute, every second." I smiled back. He wrapped his arms around me and I snuggled against him, warm and safe. Everything was going to be all right. I trusted him completely, and there was nothing I couldn't tell him.

"Sebastian, I wanted to ask what you know about Lady Agnes."

"Agnes? What about her?" His body was suddenly tense and rigid next to mine.

"You were telling me all that stuff about Lord Charles when you showed me the old grotto, so I thought you might know about Agnes," I said. "I've been thinking about her a lot, and those weird things I've been seeing—I think they are linked with Agnes. She's sort of . . . close to me. Kind of connected. It's hard to explain, but I wonder if you'd ever heard anything about her having a baby before she died? I know it sounds completely crazy."

Sebastian let go of me and stood up. "It's true," he said slowly. "She ran away from Wyldcliffe and married some ragtag painter, a struggling artist. They had a baby. A daughter."

So the first part of my theory was wrong. Agnes had been married after all. So what about Effie? Was she really Agnes's daughter?

"Do you know what happened to the baby?" I asked eagerly.

Sebastian turned to me with tired eyes. "Why are you asking all this?"

"I thought I had figured out something about Agnes that led to a connection with my family, but I must have gotten it all wrong."

"What do you mean?"

It all came tumbling out in a rush: the letter from the nursing home; the baby girl, Effie, who arrived at Uppercliffe Farm in the year that Agnes died; and my notion that she might have been Agnes's illegitimate child. I told him about the paper with the cryptic message about the "heirloom" of Evelyn Smith's descendants, and about Frankie's last gift to me.

"A necklace?" Sebastian's voice grew urgent. "Is it the

one you were wearing the other day? I didn't really see it. Let me look."

"Okay," I replied. "Wait a minute."

Something rustled in the dark shrubs as I fumbled to untie the ribbon. I glanced around, feeling strangely reluctant to take the necklace off, even for Sebastian. But I held it out to him, its silvery shape glowing in the moonlight, and he reached out to take it.

There was a crack of blue light, and Sebastian staggered backward, clutching his arm. The necklace fell to the ground.

"Sebastian! What happened?"

His eyes were closed, and he didn't speak; then he slowly looked up and gave me a haunted, twisted grin. "Just a shock—static electricity. You have this effect on me." He collapsed onto the bench with his hands covering his face. I flew to his side and put my arms around him.

"What is it? What's the matter?"

He groaned. "What's going to happen to us, Evie?"

"Nothing's going to happen. I'll persuade Miss Scratton to let us meet properly—you know, on the weekends. I'll write and explain to Dad, and he'll sort it out with the school. There's nothing to worry about."

But even as I said it, I knew it was no good.

"It's not going to work," he said, staring at the ground. "It can't work. I have to go away."

My brain reeled. This wasn't happening. He wasn't saying those words. But he was getting up, walking away from me, getting ready to leave.

"You can't . . . not just like that, Sebastian," I cried wildly.

"Evie, you promised once not to think badly of me. I need you to remember that promise when I am gone."

"What about last night?" I stammered. "You said we would be together always."

"And you would regret it for all eternity."

"I wouldn't; I wouldn't!"

"But I would," he said harshly. "I would, Evie."

Tears burned in my eyes. A terrible weight settled on my heart. I must have done something wrong the night before. Yet I had only returned his kisses with honest delight. I felt lost on a treacherous sea with no one to guide me. I ran after him.

"Where are you going? Stay with me," I pleaded.

"I can't. There's something I need to know. Everything depends on it. Meet me by the school gates tomorrow night. I'll be waiting." He paced away, then turned for one last moment, a look of pain and desperation on his face.

"Remember that I love you."

In a few moments he had gone, and the night was dark around me, as though every light had been put out. I knew that when we next met, it would be to say good-bye. And I knew that, whatever Sebastian had said, that crack of blue fire had been no static shock.

My necklace still lay gleaming on the wet ground. I bent down and picked it up, and slowly made my way out of the garden like a sleepwalker.

# Thirty-nine

The necklace. The blue fire. The child. Sebastian.

How did it all connect? I didn't know why or how, but I sensed that Lady Agnes was at the center of it all. It was only after I had mentioned her that Sebastian had behaved so oddly, so anxious and strained. . . . I dragged myself back to the dorm, and as I fell asleep it seemed to be her face, not Laura's, that was watching over me. When I woke up I couldn't get her out of my mind.

I had planned to tell everything to Sarah that morning, confident that I had solved all the mysteries, but now I was confused and afraid. I kept quiet, worrying about what it was that Sebastian needed to find out. What could it be? And if he loved me, why was he talking about leaving?

The seconds and minutes seemed achingly slow. I

struggled to focus on what the biology teacher was explaining in mind-numbing detail, and narrowly avoided getting a detention in Latin for muddling up a whole passage of Virgil. But every tormenting hour brought me closer to the answers I needed.

The December sun had set in the dirty yellow sky like a hard, bitter fruit. It was dark outside, and the lamps were lit for supper. I kept looking at my watch. Soon I would see him. Soon I would find out. . . .

"Evie, what's wrong?" Sarah leaned across the supper table.

"Headache," I lied, but she didn't look convinced. I made an effort. "It's Frankie's birthday. It's kind of hard." That was true, but it wasn't the whole truth. It wasn't just Frankie who was tearing at my heart.

At last we stood for prayers, and the students were dismissed. Sarah gave me a quick smile, and I stayed behind as usual to set out the coffee trays with Helen. I deliberately said nothing as we worked side by side. I had enough on my mind without dealing with Helen. As we finished putting the last silver spoon into place, she shoved a piece of paper into my hand.

"What's this?" I asked curtly.

"It's something you need to know." She looked terrible, really jumpy and exhausted. "Just read it; that's all."

She slouched out, her head down. I unfolded the paper and spread it out on one of the tables. It was a clipping from the local newspaper. *Valuable Painting Stolen,* shouted the headline. I sat, mystified, and began to read.

*A recent break-in at a local historical building, Fairfax Hall, has resulted in the loss of an old family portrait. The oil painting had hung there since Victorian times. Burglars forced their way into the Hall, which is now a popular museum, and took the portrait of Sebastian Fairfax, the wayward son of Sir Edward Fairfax.*

A cold hand seemed to touch the back of my neck, and my eyes raced across the rest of the article.

*It was rumored that Sebastian had taken his own life, though his body was never found. Mrs. Melinda Dawson, the museum director, commented, "It's such a terrible shame to lose the only portrait we had of this colorful figure. And it's a mystery why nothing else was taken. The picture had no great value, but it's a great loss for the Hall."*

At the bottom of the article was a reproduction of the missing painting. It was an exact portrait of my

Sebastian. The same eyes, the same hair, the same mocking expression.

*Impossible.*

I ran after Helen, but she had already disappeared.

"Have you seen Helen Black?" I asked a crowd of twelve-year-olds on their way up the marble stairs to bed, but they just shrugged and shook their heads.

"Are you looking for Helen?" said a voice behind me. It was Miss Dalrymple, and standing next to her was the sour, heavily built math teacher, Miss Raglan. They looked like black crows in their drab clothes, but Miss Dalrymple was all smiles.

"Poor Helen has detention this evening, I'm afraid. Silly girl! She should know the rules by now."

"Some people just can't keep away from trouble," Miss Raglan said coldly.

"But I need to speak to her, just for a second," I pleaded. "Where is she?"

"Oh, dear, I'm afraid you'll have to wait," said Miss Dalrymple. "Unless . . ." Her eyes narrowed slightly. "Unless you'd like us to take her a message?"

"No . . . no . . ." I backed away from her. "No, thanks."

Lying on my bed in the dorm, I waited for Helen to

come back, but when the hours passed and she didn't turn up I couldn't delay any longer. Perhaps she'd been ill and had gone to the nurse's room again, I thought. But I had no time to worry about Helen. I had to find Sebastian before it was too late. *Too late, too late.* The words echoed in my mind like a warning.

Sebastian was there at the gates, as we had arranged. The newspaper clipping was hidden deep in my pocket. It would wait. I wanted to hear first what he had to say.

"Thank you for coming," he said, as though I were a guest at a surreal dinner party. His voice trembled, and his hand shook as he helped me up onto the horse. I clung to him as though I could hold on forever, but as we galloped away the horse's hooves seem to beat out the same grim message: *too late, too late, too late.* . . . A swirling mist crept over the hillsides, and the moon rode high above us. Sebastian urged the horse faster and faster over the moor. Soon I recognized the shadowy outline of a building below us. We had reached Fairfax Hall.

Sebastian pulled up, and the horse picked its way down the side of the slope, toward the old house. I could see the shallow lake where we had sat and sketched that silly, ornate fountain. The water had been turned off, and now everything was still and silent.

"W-why are we h-here?" My teeth were chattering with cold.

"I want to show you something."

He slithered off the horse's back, and I followed him across the grass until we reached a dark shape: a slab of stone half-buried under a tangle of thornbushes. It was the exact spot where I'd seen Helen, or thought I had, on our visit to the Hall.

"Come and look, Evie." Sebastian took my hand in his cold fingers, and we stood side by side in front of the granite tablet.

> In Memory of a Beloved Son,
> Sebastian James Fairfax,
> Born in 1865.
> It is thought he departed this Life
> In 1884,
> By his own hand.
> GOD REST HIS SOUL.

"This memorial is for me. This is who I am."

Fear broke over me like an icy wave. "Stop being so dramatic; it's a stupid—"

"It's true." He looked immeasurably tired and sad.

"My parents put this stone up for me within sight of their house. But they got something wrong. I didn't die in 1884. I never died."

*No, no, no.* I wanted to scream, but I did my best to stay calm. Sane, sensible Evie, calm and logical and reasonable . . .

"But you're not called Fairfax," I argued.

"Sebastian James, remember? I only told you my first two names. I conveniently forgot about the Fairfax. I'm sorry I lied to you. I had no choice."

"Please stop—"

"Poor Evie, you think I'm quite mad, don't you? And you're right. It was mad of me to allow myself to start seeing you, mad to carry on with it, and mad to let myself love you."

Love.

It seemed like a word from a different world. But it was all I had. Sebastian loved me. I loved Sebastian. I had to hold on to that and never let it go.

"It's because I love you that I have to tell you the truth," he said. "It's too late to continue pretending that it's all going to have a happy ending."

*Too late.* My heart felt empty, like a ransacked grave.

"When you go back to the school tonight you will never be able to see me again. I have to make you understand.

Please give me this one chance to explain."

"All right," I replied mechanically, though my words seemed to come from the depths of a dream.

We moved away from the granite stone, and Sebastian spread his coat for me on the grass. I sat down, but he walked about restlessly, as though he didn't know how to start. Then he pulled a small black book from his pocket and pushed it into my hands.

"You need to read this. If you don't believe what I'm saying, you'll believe her."

"Who? What are you talking about?"

"Agnes, of course. This is her journal. Everything you need to know is in there."

I looked in wonder at the musty, waterstained little book. Its pages were covered in small, sloping handwriting. Some of them were stuck together, and the ink had spread and faded. It certainly looked very old.

My voice cracked in panic. "Where did you get this?"

"Please, Evie, just read it—for me. For us. Please."

The words danced in front of my eyes. Was I really going to find out the truth at last? I began to read the faded, looping handwriting: *My news is that dearest S. is back from his travels at last.*

# Forty

I had finally reached the last entry of the journal. Sebastian and I had sat side by side through the night, taking no notice of time, as I followed Agnes on every step of her strange journey. And now she had almost finished telling her tale:

> DECEMBER 11, 1884
>
> *We have reached Wyldcliffe after an exhausting journey and have been here several days. Martha and her family have been sworn to secrecy about our presence until I find the right moment to approach my parents. Martha's people are all being so kind. Her nephew John is newly married, and his wife begs me to let her cuddle the baby, marveling over her tiny fingers and toes. I swear they are all in love*

with her already. Their love and understanding make my task a little easier, but I dread that first meeting with my family. I still haven't decided whether to knock boldly on the front door or to write to them first. I have been taking long walks at dusk, leaving my baby—and the other treasure that I guard—safely with Martha, while I wander in my old haunts, brooding over my memories.

Once, I thought I saw a rider in the distance on a black horse, and my heart leaped with the thought that it might be him. But Martha says she has heard that he hardly stirs from the Hall, and lives in almost total seclusion. It is better like that, though I confess I would love to see him one more time and know whether he has repented of his folly. I pray he has, for all our sakes.

If only we could go back to before all this began and have one more ramble over the moors, just as when we were children. And yet I cannot regret anything that has happened, for without this tangled tale I would not have my beautiful baby, my darling Effie. Only her life matters now. Soon I must find the courage to face my parents and find out my little one's fate and whether they will protect her when I have gone. For something in me whispers that I have come back to Wyldcliffe to die.

Despite this, my heart is full of hope. I feel sure my

*child will have a happier life than mine. And when I look into the future with what little force I have left, I know that after my daughter and my daughter's daughters have left this earth, then the girl I have seen in my mind will come from the wild sea and put all this great sorrow to rest.*

Tears blurred my sight. I could hardly see to read the last few lines.

*I dreamed of her again last night. She was standing on the top of the moors with her hair blowing free and my gift to her hanging around her neck. As I watched her, I saw her raise her hand, and the hills around her turned to high green waves battling in a mighty storm. I do not know what it meant. But she too is my daughter, my sister, my hope. I know that I am with her always, and will somehow help her before the end.*

All this great sorrow. I wiped my eyes, seeing Agnes in my mind as clearly as I saw the rough grass at my feet. She was bending over a low table, scratching away with an old-fashioned pen, and she raised her pale, serious face to me and smiled.

My head was whirling with images of fire and water, of meetings and arguments, of strange rituals and threatening shadows. And through it all was a dark-haired boy, passionate and headstrong and beautiful. A boy called Sebastian James Fairfax. I let the book fall from my knee and closed my eyes.

"So now you know," Sebastian said in a low voice.

"I know what?" I forced myself to say. "The diary must be fake, a joke." But I knew in my heart that it wasn't.

"It's no fake. This journal was buried in a lead casket next to Agnes's grave. For these many, empty years I have respected her resting place, but last night the thought of those hidden papers tormented me beyond endurance. Agnes had once spoken to me of a girl she had seen in some strange vision. I had to know if that girl was you—if you were part of our tangled tale." He looked away, as though he were ashamed. "I . . . I dug up the casket last night. I had to find out if Agnes had left a clue that would tell me the truth."

"Oh, my God . . ."

"You're the one she wrote about, the one she was waiting for. It's true. You are descended from her. The last time I saw Agnes she told me that the baby was dead, but in fact it was alive and well, hidden at Uppercliffe Farm with old Martha. After Agnes died, Martha's family secretly hid her journal and brought the baby up as one of their own. You'd guessed that part of the story already, and you knew it was Effie's necklace that you wear." A hungry look flickered across his face. "The necklace is the key to everything."

I tried one last time to run away from the truth.

"Agnes can't have told you anything, Sebastian. She died more than a hundred years ago, and you're here with me now. It's all in the past. It's all over. You're just confused; you're not well."

Sebastian shook his head. "It's no use, Evie. Think about what you've just read. What did Agnes warn her friend, her beloved, about? What did she tell him would poison his very existence?"

The sky seemed to press down on me, and the hills were watching, waiting for some catastrophe to happen. I didn't want to speak the words. But I had to. "She told him not to seek eternal life."

"And he ignored her. He went down those dark paths as far as he could without her help. Not far enough to achieve true immortality, but enough to live a hundred years, two hundred maybe. Enough to be able to talk to Agnes and then to you, five generations later."

"I have to go." I began to walk away. All I wanted to do was get back to the school, crawl into bed, and shut this insanity out of my head.

"Evie, wait—I can prove it. Wait!"

I turned unwillingly and saw Sebastian take something from his pocket. It flashed silver-gray in the moonlight as he raised it to his head.

"Watch me, Evie."

*"No!"* The noise of the shot echoed across the moors, magnified a hundred times in the still night. Birds screeched and flapped up from the trees. I hurtled over to Sebastian's slumped body. An old-fashioned silver pistol had fallen from his hand. Blood ran down the side of his face, and his eyes were staring up at the stars. I covered my face in horror, shaking and terrified. A few minutes later, a low voice mingled with the wind.

"Don't cry, Evie. I just had to prove I was telling the truth."

I looked up and screamed. Sebastian was kneeling by my side, trying to comfort me. Where that dreadful hole at the side of his head had been, there was no mark at all, as if it had never happened.

"You see? I can't die. I never died. I am Sebastian Fairfax. Do you believe me now?"

I couldn't answer. I got up and staggered away, then bent over the grass and was violently sick.

"Feeling better?"

I couldn't answer. Sebastian had wiped my face and wrapped me in his coat, but I was still shaking.

"I'm sorry I shocked you like that. It was the only way I had of convincing you."

"I know."

Finally I knew the impossible truth. Sebastian had known Agnes. He had been alive for almost a hundred and fifty years, yet he was still nineteen. . . . He could never die. . . . I needed to keep saying it to myself over and over again. I pulled the newspaper clipping from my pocket and gave it to him.

"You stole the painting from Fairfax Hall, didn't you, so that I wouldn't guess who you were?"

"Yes. I thought it would finish everything between us. And I couldn't bear not to see you again. I know it was selfish. But you were the only good thing I had, the only light in the terrible darkness all around me. I'm so sorry."

"Tell me everything, Sebastian. I want to understand."

He hesitated. "There's so much that I wish you didn't

have to know. And when I have told you, you'll understand why we can never meet again."

"But if we love each other—" I began.

"Love can be destroyed, Evie," he replied grimly. "I don't think you'll have any love left for me when I have told you everything."

I didn't think anything else would ever shock me again. "I just want the truth."

"Everything Agnes wrote in the journal is true," Sebastian began. "How I found the Book, how we started to follow the Mystic Way. At first it seemed like a game, but Agnes had an extraordinary gift. She was right: I was jealous of her. I was accustomed to being the adored one, older, wiser, more knowledgeable—or so I thought. I worked furiously hard to keep up with her, straining myself to learn more and go deeper, but she was a natural.

"You know now what happened next. My insane ambition took over. I bullied her again and again to give me what I wanted. I knew she loved me, but I was too selfish to feel real love in return. I wanted power, not love. I wanted to live forever. Agnes could have found a way to achieve what I asked, but she knew it would be wrong. It would have distorted her powers and taken her into dangerous realms. And yet it was a torment to her not to be

278

able to give me what I craved, so she ran away from me.

"When she had gone, I was furious. My pride forced me to prove that I could achieve my dreams without her, without even telling her. Oh, Evie, I can't describe what dreadful paths I went down! But I was pleased with myself; I thought I was doing something daring and brave and magnificent. Eventually I learned how to extend my life beyond the dreams of men. I would live for many generations, but one day my time would run out. True immortality eluded me. I still need the touch of the eternal Fire, which Agnes reached so easily with her incorruptible mind.

"Agnes had hidden herself away in the stinking streets of London, while her parents pretended that she was in Europe on some pleasure tour. They were terrified of the possible scandal, and filled themselves with the hope that their darling girl would walk through the door one day, as though nothing had happened. I tried desperately to find Agnes, with no success. But when she finally dared to come back to Wyldcliffe, my spies found her easily enough. She walked every night in the shadows of the Abbey's walls, plucking up the courage to return to her home. I waited for her, and one night we met again at last."

He groaned and covered his face with his hands.

"Oh, Evie, tell me you love me now, for the last time."

I took his hands in mine and looked straight at him. His beauty was clouded by fear and pain and exhaustion, but that didn't matter.

"I love you, Sebastian. I always will."

He kissed my hands and forced himself to continue.

"Agnes was more beautiful than ever, though thin and tired. After the first shock she was overjoyed to see me again. But I was unkind, as always. She told me about her marriage, and the baby. I accused her of debasing herself by marrying anyone but me. I made insane threats against her husband and her child. Then she told me that her husband—Francis—had died, and that the child was dead too. I believed her, so I begged her to come away with me, to start again. She refused, and said she could no longer love me as a husband, only as a brother. I got angry. I told her that I loved her, which was a lie. I told her that I needed her, which was true.

"You see, Evie, I still dreamed about gaining perfect immortality. Living for two hundred years, or even five hundred years, wouldn't be enough for me. I begged Agnes once again for her help. But she told me she had given up her powers and hidden them away in a secret Talisman that I would never find. My temper flared up, and I shook her roughly, demanding to know where this hiding place was. She tried to break free, but a blind, furious madness came over me. I wouldn't let her go. I wanted to hurt her for the pain she was causing me. I threw her down angrily, and she . . . she . . ."

He stopped.

"What happened? Tell me!"

"She hit her head against the wall as she fell. It happened so quickly, just one tiny moment. Her body lay on the ground, as still as a flower in the moonlight. I started to weep, asking her forgiveness, begging her to speak to me. There was nothing she could say." He looked at me with shame and misery burning in his face. "Agnes was dead. I had destroyed her."

# Forty-one

A bird had begun to sing, far off over the moor. The sky was starting to get light. The night would soon be over, but the dawn would bring no hope or comfort. Sebastian had killed Agnes, and we were left to carry on with the weary confusion of life.

"I hate and despise myself."

"Don't," I said. "You mustn't say that."

"Why not, when it's true?"

I didn't reply. I was incredibly tired. Nothing seemed quite real.

"So, what's going to happen now?" I asked, forcing myself to speak.

"I want you to leave Wyldcliffe as soon as you can," Sebastian said. "It's your only hope of getting safely out of all this."

"I've nowhere to go. And I want to be near you."

"Evie, that's the last thing you should want! I'm a freak and a murderer."

"You're not! It was an accident. You never meant to hurt Agnes; I know you didn't."

"Dear Evie. You're always so good, so trusting." He sighed. "But there's more. You haven't heard the whole story yet. I have to tell you now, while I have the courage. But let's get out of here."

We began to walk slowly in the direction of the distant Abbey, leading the horse over the rough grass. I was glad to leave the dark monument under the thorn trees. I glanced at Sebastian's tormented face. At that moment I couldn't tell whether I loved him or pitied him, but I knew that my heart was breaking.

"So what do you want to tell me? Is it something to do with Agnes?"

He nodded. "When I realized that Agnes was . . . that it was over . . . I couldn't leave her lying there. I lifted her up and carried her through a little gate in the Abbey walls, into the gardens. No one was around. I walked to the old chapel ruins and laid her on the green bed of grass where the holy altar had once stood. Even then I was more concerned about myself than her, worrying about my grief and my shame and my fears. It occurred to me that this Talisman she had talked about might be around her neck, and that I might be able to use the powers she had sealed within it to revive her. At least, that was what I told myself. She wasn't wearing it, though, so I searched her pockets. There was nothing in them except a scrap of ribbon. A memento of her baby, I guessed.

"Then I heard a noise in the trees. The night watchman had roused himself from his stove in the gatehouse to make an inspection of the grounds. He must have seen Agnes's dress fluttering on the grass, and me crouching next to her. He came rushing at me with a pair of silver pistols, calling for help. I knocked him down and grabbed one of the pistols, held it against his head, and threatened to shoot him. But I was sickened by the thought of taking another life. I let him go and turned and ran. By now the alarm had been raised. Servants were running out in their nightshirts. I dodged to avoid them, but the watchman aimed his pistol and shot. The bullet went straight through my heart."

He laughed suddenly, an odd, discordant sound.

"It was so strange, Evie. I was glad to die. After everything I had done to avoid death, I would have finally welcomed it. But it didn't work out that like that. I felt the blood spurting down my chest. I collapsed on the ground and then . . . I can't describe it . . . I was still conscious, but transformed. I had passed into a world of shadows. The pain left me and I stood up. The servants were running past me, shouting out, 'Where is he? Has he gotten away?'

"'I'm here, you fools!' I screamed. 'Come and get me.' But they didn't seem to hear or see me. I wasn't dead, but I wasn't alive. I felt no hunger or thirst or pain. The secret potions I had taken, the evil rites I had endured in pursuit of immortality had left me with this: I no longer lived, but I couldn't truly die."

He looked down over the valley.

"I would have accepted that, Evie, as a just punishment for what I had done. Endless existence without meaning or joy. Later, when I had fled the Abbey, it soon became clear to me that what I faced was even worse than that." A tremor ran through his body like a spasm of pain. "The dark masters I had served in my search for forbidden knowledge told me that a choice lay before me in the Shadow world that I now inhabited. I had one last chance to become one of the Unconquered like them, existing forever out of the reach of time and space and the rules of God and man. For that, I needed the Talisman."

"Why? What was so special about it?"

"Agnes had sealed not only her powers, but her love for me inside the sacred object. Nothing else could help me."

"But what if you couldn't find it?"

Sebastian grimaced, as though flinching from some dreadful memory. "Without the Talisman, I would not be permitted to stay as I was. I could no longer be killed by a pistol shot or the thrust of a knife, but without the Talisman I would eventually fade."

"Fade? I don't understand." I didn't think I would ever understand.

"To fade is to wither and decay, hour by hour and minute by minute, until one becomes an evil spirit of darkness, a slave, a torment to oneself and others. In other words," he said, "a demon. To fade is to lose any last spark of humanity, yet to be eternally aware of one's own degradation. And that is what would happen to me. Oh, it might take many years, more than a hundred, but it would happen in the end."

He shuddered. I felt sick at the idea of Sebastian— so beautiful, so full of life—turning into some hideous specter. I kept thinking, *This can't be true; it can't be happening.* But it was. The earth was under my feet, and the sky was above me. I was awake. And Sebastian's voice went on remorselessly, spilling out his dreadful secrets.

"I was afraid of such a fate. I had desired life, not a living death. I swore I would do everything I could to find the Talisman and unlock its powers. I gathered my coven of followers around me and commanded them to help me keep my tormented hopes alive. I tried to convince myself that if only I could find the Talisman, I would live not as one of the dread Unconquered, but as a man again; I would become the person Agnes would have wanted me to be; I would have hundreds of lifetimes to make up for the mistakes I had made. And so I searched for it for many empty, dreary years. And then something happened . . . something so awful . . ."

"What?" I asked, horrified. "What happened?"

"I . . . I can't bear to tell you. But I swear that it made me face my crimes at last. I gave up the fight for the Talisman. I turned my back on what had been . . . feeding me. I accepted my final destiny. To become a foul demon was no more than I deserved. And at that precise point, when I was weak and beginning to fade, that was when I met you."

Sebastian turned my hand over in his. He traced the faint scar where I had cut myself on the glass the night we had met. Now I knew how he had been able to mend it, and why he had looked so ill and pale when we had first met. Sebastian wasn't sick; he was fading out of existence, leaving me behind, leaving this world and heading for the dark. . . .

"That first night I was astonished that you could see me," he said. "I usually conceal myself from the innocent."

"How? And where did you live all that time? Where do you go when I'm not with you? How do you live?" There were a thousand things I wanted to ask.

"I walk in the Shadows—caught between life and death. I still have powers enough. I have learned how to show myself to the living, or I can choose to be hidden. At times I have entered life again to try to forget everything. I have been a laborer, a shepherd, a traveler. For a while I lived with some Romany wanderers. They were good to me, like brothers. But I could never stay too long in one place or with one set of people. A nineteen-year-old who never got any older, who didn't seem to eat, or sleep, or have any family connections? It was impossible to belong anywhere. So I always came back to Wyldcliffe.

"The night we met I knew there was something special about you, Evie. I had concealed myself and my horse through some simple charms, as usual. And yet you saw me. I no longer knew how to be kind, or even scarcely human, when I first spoke to you, but something in you made me feel alive, and it wasn't just because you reminded me of Agnes. I was desperate, so wretched and lonely that I couldn't resist the temptation of seeing you again. After all, I was doomed, so what difference did one last piece of self-indulgence matter? But you were young and trusting and good—everything that I had lost—so after a while I told myself I had to stop seeing you, for your sake. For the first time in my whole existence I truly knew what it was to care for someone. I had been obsessed with Agnes, bound to her in ways I barely understood, but with you it was different." His blue eyes met mine. "For me, there is only you. You taught me how to love."

"I'm glad," I said fiercely.

"So am I." A faint smile softened his face; then he sighed. "But I was too weak to carry out my resolution. I let myself keep seeing you. And the supreme irony was that it was you who led me to the Talisman."

"How?"

"It was so simple, but so like Agnes. There had been all sorts of rumors about both of us after Agnes's death and my disappearance, which her parents tried to crush. They said she had died in an accident. They wanted to believe it, and they wanted everyone else to believe it too. The stories persisted, though. The local people gossiped that Agnes had brought a great treasure with her from London before she died. Oh, they said all sorts of crazy things: that secret papers had been buried next to her tomb, that her ghost had been seen down by the old chapel, and that she would return one day as an angel of light to save Wyldcliffe from some dreadful doom. They even claimed that touching her grave could heal sick people."

Sebastian reached out to touch my hair. "When I met you, I thought you could heal me, girl from the sea." He smiled sadly. "Sane, sensible Evie, you wouldn't have listened to all that nonsense, would you? But I latched on to the story about the treasure. I was sure it meant the Talisman, and like an arrogant fool I gave no thought to her real treasure—her child. A little girl growing up unnoticed on a local farm with a pretty trinket around her neck was enough to trick the deep and cunning magician that I imagined myself to be. But last night I touched your necklace, and I realized how I had been deceived. In desperation I went over all the old stories again, scratching in the dirt for more clues. I forced myself to do the one thing I had been decent enough to resist: I recovered those secret papers from where her friends had hidden them on hallowed ground. And her journal told me everything."

Now I understood. It was hanging around my neck, this precious Talisman, passed down from each mother to her daughter, the descendants of Evelyn Frances Smith, the secret heirloom: *May it never fall into darkness.* All I had to do was to give it to Sebastian, to give him what he had always wanted, and save him from his terrible fate. Perhaps these "Unconquered" would let him be, I thought desperately, perhaps it really would be possible for Sebastian to be restored to human life with my immortal gift; we could be together. . . .

"Here," I said. "Take it. You can have it."

He looked at me with infinite tenderness. "Darling Evie, if only it were that simple. Just being near it has given me some strength and energy in these last weeks. But don't you remember what happened the other night when I tried to touch it? Agnes was no fool. She has bound her powers to you and you alone. And she knew that if I tried to lay a finger on it, its powers would work against me."

"Why wouldn't she want to help you?"

"She didn't know that I was already ensnared by my own folly. She thought she was protecting me from a terrible mistake by sealing the Talisman. But it was too late. I had already put myself into the hands of my masters, like a blind fool. And so she also sealed the only thing that might have helped me: the memory of her love."

"Can't you get these . . . masters of yours to unseal it for you?"

"No! They are pitiless. They do not help the weak." A flicker of pain passed over his face. "The Unconquered have achieved immortality with their poisoned arts, and can no longer be touched by death, or truth, or love. They rule the Shadows, and they are terrible." He shuddered and clasped his hands together.

For an instant I seemed to see with Sebastian's eyes: ghastly figures of men robed in black and red, with iron crowns on their heads. One turned his face toward me, and I saw his ravaged, inhuman beauty, and I felt that I would turn to dust under his withering gaze. I dragged myself away from the awful vision and tried to understand what Sebastian was saying.

"My masters have made it clear to me that there is now only one way that I can use the Talisman to halt the process of fading."

"How? Tell me!"

Sebastian looked paler than ever, and his breath came in a quick, stabbing sob. "By conquering the Talisman, taking it from you by force and claiming my immortal crown. And to do that I would have to kill you."

I knew by his face that he was telling the truth.

"I cannot be near you anymore, Evie. I know that as I fade further into darkness and become less than I am now, I will be tempted to come after the Talisman. To become one of the Unconquered, or their eternal slave—how can I be sure what I will choose when the moment finally arrives? I'm so afraid that in the end I will destroy you, as I destroyed Agnes. Now do you see why I cannot love you? My love is worthless."

"What about my love for you?" I cried. "Was that all for nothing?"

"You must stop loving me. Your life is in danger, and not just from what I might be tempted to do. There are other forces watching you, eager for what you possess. I can't control them any longer. I am not the only wretch who has searched for the Talisman. You mustn't stay here," he urged. "Run away. Don't go back to the Abbey—not tonight, not ever. There's nothing there for you but danger and trouble. There's nothing there for you but death."

In a sudden swift movement he lifted me onto his horse, thrusting the reins in my hands. He pulled my face toward his for one last, despairing kiss, then pointed the horse's head to the other side of the sleeping valley, away from the Abbey.

"But Sebastian—"

"You must do as I say! Leave Wyldcliffe now, while you can. From now on we must be nothing to each other, Evie. We must be strangers." His face was like death, and his voice was as hard as ice. "We must be enemies."

He slapped the horse's glossy flank, and the powerful animal tossed its head and surged over the grass. I pulled madly on the reins to make it stop and looked over my shoulder.

"Sebastian! Sebastian!" I called into the wind. "Where are you?"

There was no answer. The top of the hill was bare and wide, as empty of hiding places as the open desert. Sebastian had disappeared into the air. He had gone, and left not a trace behind on those desolate hills. I was alone.

I waited and waited, but he never came. I let the horse amble slowly wherever it wanted to go. I had no will left to make any choice, good or bad. By the time the glimmering dawn seeped slowly over the moors, the horse had reached the Abbey gates. I slid down and it cantered away.

I was back where I had begun, all those weeks ago. The peeling sign by the gates still picked out its bizarre message:

# WYLDCLIFFE
# BE COOL
# OR YOU DIE.

I pushed the iron gates open and walked wearily to the only home I had left. What did it matter what was waiting for me there? Sebastian had gone. He was my enemy, and I felt as though I had already died.

# Forty-two

I walked down the deserted drive. The Abbey looked like a vast prison in the first cold streaks of morning light. If I hurried, I might get back to bed before anyone noticed that I was missing. Avoiding the main front door, I crept down the path to the stables. As I passed the kitchen garden, someone stepped out of the shadows.

"Sarah!" I gasped.

"Thank God I've found you!"

She hugged me quickly, then dragged me into the walled garden.

"What are you doing out here?" I said in astonishment.

"Helen asked me to keep an eye on you last night. She saw me on her way to detention and said she was worried about you. I explained that you were upset about Frankie and told her not to fret. But then," Sarah continued, "after I had gone to bed, I got the weirdest feeling that something was really wrong. I had this image of you lost on the moors. I sneaked over to your dorm, but you weren't there, and neither was Helen. So I came out to look for you both. I was just about to tell Miss Scratton that you were missing." She looked at me anxiously. "So where's Helen? And where have you been?"

"You know you said I should find out more about Sebastian?" I took a deep breath. "Well, I did."

As briefly as I could, I told her everything. I saw her expression change from disbelief to revulsion to pity. And running underneath it all was fear.

"So he's a . . . ghost?"

"I don't think so." I shrugged. "He's between worlds. In the Shadows, he called it. He isn't alive, like we are, but he can't die either."

"And if he doesn't get help from this Talisman thing—your necklace—he's going to become some kind of demon?"

"Apparently," I said. There was no energy left in me for any emotion. "And plan B is that he kills me in order to get the Talisman."

Sarah looked at me in horror. "Evie, you've got to get away from here."

"How can I? Do you expect me to write to my dad and say, 'Please take me away from Wyldcliffe; my boyfriend has turned out to be a dangerous hundred-and-fifty-year-old spirit'? He'd think I'd gone crazy. Besides, I've nowhere to go. Dad's abroad; the cottage is rented most of the time. I've no family, just an old aunt in Wales, where I'll be shipped off to for the summer if I'm lucky."

"Can't you pretend to be ill or something?"

"It's no good, Sarah," I said in a blank, dead voice. "I can't run away from this. There's no escape. And I can never see Sebastian again." I burst into tears.

"Come on; you're exhausted," said Sarah. "Let's get you back inside." She took my arm and started to guide me toward the house, when I felt her fingers dig into my skin.

"Evie, look!" she called. "Look up there!"

Sarah pointed up to the high roof of weathered slate. Behind a pointed tower looking down onto the far side of the building was the figure of a girl. And there was no mistaking who it was this time. Helen's pale hair hung down her back over her nightgown, and she lifted her arms and face up to the sky, as if in worship of the pale dawn.

"What on earth . . . ? Helen!" I cried.

"Shhh!" said Sarah. "You'll distract her; she'll fall."

But it was even worse than that. The next instant Helen flung her arms out wide, stepped off the roof, and plunged downward. She fell, as light as a shadow, vanishing from our sight on the other side of the Abbey.

We ran to the front of the house, our feet flying across the gravel. "Please don't be hurt, please, please. . . ." I prayed blindly. All I could see in my mind was Helen's huddled body lying on the ground by the main door. But when we reached the front steps there was no one there.

*Impossible.*

We slipped into the entrance hall. There was no fire in the stone hearth, and none of the staff were about yet. Low voices were coming from the corridor to our left.

Sarah beckoned me to follow her. We stole as quietly as we could past the portraits and paneling and closed rooms. The voices seemed to come from Mrs. Hartle's study, and it sounded like an argument. The door was slightly open. We sneaked up to it and peered in, taking care not to be seen. Helen was standing in front of the High Mistress's desk, defiant, silent, but unhurt. How could she possibly have jumped off the roof without being smashed like a china doll?

Mrs. Hartle, however, didn't seem to be interested in Helen's fall. Her usually smooth features were ruffled by anger.

"How dare you pull a stunt like that? Didn't it occur to you that someone might see you? Do you want to give everything away?"

"Yeah, I do." Helen flashed back. "I want people to know what's going on around here."

"Don't waste your energy, Helen. No one would believe you. Throw yourself from the rooftop and you'll just land yourself in an institution again, and it won't be a cozy children's home this time. No, it will be better for everyone if you start to do as I tell you."

"I won't cooperate. And you can't make me."

The High Mistress seemed to switch tactics. She sat back in her chair, no longer angry, but coolly amused. "I think you will find that I can. Oh, you've done well to last this long against me, but you won't be able to go on like this much longer."

"I can. . . . I will," said Helen, but she looked faint, as if she was struggling for air.

"Don't forget, Helen, that we are many, and you are alone."

"I'd rather die alone in a ditch than have anything to do with you!"

Mrs. Hartle sprang out of her seat and stood in front of Helen, dark and glowering. There was some strange connection between them, some struggle going on. Then Helen laughed softly. Instantly Mrs. Hartle's hand whipped across Helen's face in a stinging slap.

"Get out!" she snarled.

Sarah tugged at my sleeve and we fled back down the corridor. She started to run in the direction of the marble stairs, but I pulled her into the curtained alcove that led to the old servants' quarters. I fumbled with the door; then we pushed our way into the musty passage. "We can go this way without being seen," I explained quickly.

"But what about Helen?"

"Shhh!"

I could hear light footsteps on the other side of the door. My heart was beating like a hammer. I was sure it was Mrs. Hartle prowling after us. Then the door opened and Helen stood there for a second, framed by the light. "Evie? Sarah?" she whispered. "Are you there? I've been so worried about you."

"What about you?" Sarah stepped forward from where we were hiding. "We saw you fall!"

"Good. I wanted you to, or you wouldn't have believed me."

"You could have been hurt, and Mrs. Hartle didn't care at all," I protested. "And teachers aren't allowed to hit you like that!"

"I know. But she's not just a teacher." Helen sighed in the dark. "She's my mother."

# Forty-three

A bell rang out, echoing down the corridor outside. The new day had begun.

"We have to go," said Helen, suddenly alert. "Meet me after class."

"Where?"

"Down in the old grotto. Do you know where I mean? Don't let anyone see you. And don't talk to me today. Pretend we don't have anything to do with each other. They're watching all the time."

"Who is watching?" I asked.

"I'll explain later. Come on; we need to go."

We fled up the stairs to our dorms.

I don't know how I got through that day. Sebastian . . . Agnes . . . the Talisman . . . Helen . . . Mrs. Hartle. I felt as though I were drowning.

To make things worse, Celeste came back from the hospital, her leg set in plaster. She made a great show of being an injured martyr, hobbling bravely up the marble stairs, demanding attention and sympathy. But when Sophie offered to lend me an atlas in geography, Celeste looked stunned. The idea that her friends might have stopped hating me quite so much seemed to infuriate her, and she picked on me all afternoon, until I wanted to scream, *Leave me alone, leave me alone. . . .* But nothing Celeste could do or say was as tormenting as my own thoughts.

As soon as we were dismissed from class I flew out of the building and ran down to the lake. Its waters looked dull and dark, reflecting the wintry sky above. A hundred memories flooded through me of being there with Sebastian: laughing, talking, swimming, kissing—everything we could never do again. I walked on, determined not to give in to tears, and slipped through the tangled shrubs to the grotto.

"Sarah?" I called in a low voice. "Helen?"

"In here," came an answering whisper. There was gleam of a flashlight ahead of me. I followed it and found the others waiting for me next to the glittering mosaics.

"Tell us what was going on this morning, Helen," I said

bluntly. "Did you really fall from the roof? And is Mrs. Hartle really your mother?"

"The answer to both questions is yes. And I'll try to explain. But you probably won't believe it."

"Don't worry. I'm getting used to believing the unbelievable. Just try me."

Helen started to speak in a rapid, monotone voice. "I was brought up in a children's home, and I never knew who my parents were. The people at the home tried to be kind, but I didn't fit in. I got a reputation for being difficult. If anyone tried to help, I'd yell that I just wanted to be left alone. So after a bit they stopped trying. I caused so much trouble at school that I was kicked out." She flushed self-consciously. I'd never heard her say so much before, but she plowed on.

"I kind of turned in on myself. My real life was in my dreams. When I was little I'd always had this fantasy about being able to fly, like kids do. But even when I got older I used to dream about it. Eventually, when I was about thirteen, I started to sleepwalk. One night I woke up and I was on the roof of the home. I didn't know how I had gotten there. I looked down and thought that if I just stepped off, I would be able to fly somewhere completely new and different, somewhere I would belong. Another voice in my head was saying, *Don't be stupid; you'll kill yourself,* but somehow I knew it would be okay. So I closed my eyes and stepped off."

Helen closed her eyes as though searching for memories. "I felt the air rushing past me, and the sound of wind filled my head like a roaring fire. I was expecting some kind of crash, but when I opened my eyes again I had landed on the ground as lightly as a cat. And the drop must have been forty feet. I couldn't quite believe it, so I did it again and again. Every time I landed safely. It was as though I could slide down the wind, or as if I could swim through the air as easily as swimming through water. I can't really explain it."

She looked at us, trying to gauge our reactions. "There were other things too. I found I could move stuff just by thinking about it. If I wanted to move a book, for example, I would imagine that the wind was blowing it, and it would move all by itself. I could make a gale spring up out of nowhere. I could even transport myself from one place to another, just by the power of my thought."

"The power of your thought?" said Sarah. "What do you mean?"

"That's what Lady Agnes wrote," I interrupted. "'I feel, I desire, and it happens. . . .' Only she was drawn to fire, and you were drawn to the air."

"Yeah, it was like that," said Helen. "Let's say I would be locked in my room after stirring up some trouble at the home and I wanted to get out. Well, if I wanted it strongly enough, it was as if I went into this kind of . . . oh, I don't know, like a tunnel of rushing wind. And I came out at the other end in the place I had imagined: the park or the streets or down by the old canal. No one seemed to know, or see me do it. I thought I was some kind of freak. It made everything worse, not better. I was terrified that someone would find out, that they would think I was insane." She looked up nervously. "I suppose you think I'm a total head case, don't you? I know what they call me: crazy Helen Black."

"We don't think that," murmured Sarah.

"No," I said firmly. "You're our friend."

Helen looked shy and awkward and pleased. "Thanks."

"So how did you end up at Wyldcliffe?" I asked.

"About a year ago a woman came to the home. She was very smart, well dressed, not the kind of person I had seen before. It was Mrs. Hartle. She explained that she was my mother and that she'd been very young—not married— when I was born. My father had run off, and she hadn't been able to take care of me. Later she had married an older man, a rich man. He was dead and now she was in a good position at a school, and we were going to be together again. And then she told me that she knew that I was in touch with special, elemental powers, that it was a family gift, and that she alone could understand me. It was weird hearing her say all that, but I was so glad that it wasn't just me being crazy, and that my mother had come for me at last."

I felt a quick pulse of envy. I had imagined so many times that my own mother would turn up one day, saying, *I didn't drown; it was it all a mistake; I'm alive. . . .* Just the way Helen's mother had suddenly walked into her life.

"I was ecstatic at first," said Helen. "But as soon as we got to Wyldcliffe she changed. She said I wasn't to tell anyone who I was, as it wouldn't be good for her reputation. I would simply be known as a scholarship girl, an orphan. I soon figured that my mother wasn't really interested in me, only in what I could do. She wanted to use my gifts for her own ends."

"How did she know about them?" said Sarah.

Helen flushed, as though the words burned in her mouth. "My mother—Mrs. Hartle—is a Dark Sister, the High Mistress of the Wyldcliffe coven. She calls upon the elemental powers wherever they are and tries to subdue them to her own will and that of her master."

"Who is that?" I asked faintly.

She looked at me with pity in her clear, bright eyes. "You know who her master is, Evie, don't you?"

Yes, I knew. It couldn't be anyone else.

"It's Sebastian, isn't it?"

"Yes." Helen sighed. "I'm sorry, Evie. I really am."

# Forty-four

The water dripped around the statue of Pan. There seemed to be a thousand eyes watching me in the dark, waiting to see what would happen next. I felt as though an invisible net had begun to close in on me, trapping me in every direction. Something moved in a far corner, and I jumped.

"What's that?" I said.

"Probably a mouse or a rat," Helen answered. "There are old tunnels leading from the grotto into other parts of the grounds. I guess they're inhabited."

I suppressed a shudder and tried to concentrate.

"So your mother is one of these Dark Sisters?" asked Sarah, her eyes wide with apprehension. "What's that all about?"

"There is a tradition of women who attach themselves to a master of the Mystic Way, feeding him, protecting him, gaining strength from their sisterhood. They can be healers and workers of good, bound by ties of loyalty and knowledge. But if the master is evil, the coven can turn to poison too."

"Go on," I said quickly. I needed to know everything.

"Evie, the Dark Sisters at Wyldcliffe are dangerous. They don't care about healing or learning. They follow a corrupt master, binding themselves to him for selfish purposes. After Sebastian quarreled with Agnes, he collected a group of followers and promised that if he discovered the secret of immortality he would share it with them. In return they had to serve him unquestioningly."

"But they would have died long ago," Sarah pointed out.

"The Dark Sisters passed on their places in the coven to their daughters, and their daughters' daughters. And through all the long years since Agnes died and Sebastian crossed into the Shadows, they have nurtured and supported him in secret. Their main purpose has been to help him search for the Talisman."

"So, do you know who they are?" asked Sarah.

"Not definitely, no more than suspicions. Even in their

rituals and meetings they are careful to hide their identities. They could be village women or farmers' wives—or teachers here at the school, like my mother. All I know is that they are murderers."

Sarah and I glanced at each other uncertainly. For a moment I wondered if Helen was making it all up. She sensed our hesitation.

"I'm sorry, but you have to know the truth," Helen said. "If you don't believe me, watch and listen. And don't speak."

She closed her eyes and raised her arms, drawing a circle in the air with the tips of her fingers. A cold wind sprang up from nowhere, and somehow, out of this rushing wind, a silvery globe of light appeared and hung in the air in front of our eyes. I cried aloud, and Sarah gripped my hand. Helen was chanting under her breath, and the weird globe of light spun faster and faster, until we saw figures, like living pictures, in its silvery depths. One of them was Helen, and the other was her mother—the High Mistress.

"You could be great amongst our kind, Helen," Mrs. Hartle was saying. "You're a natural. But you could learn so much more, if only you would let me teach you."

"What can you possibly teach me?" replied Helen.

"Our Rites can lead to great power," the High Mistress said impressively. "Even, for the favored few, eternal life."

"The only power I want is the power to be myself. And I want to be free to live this life, not mess with your twisted schemes."

"So you refuse? Let me tell you, I can make your life at Wyldcliffe very unpleasant."

"I won't let you! I'll tell people who you really are; they'll stop you!"

Mrs. Hartle laughed coldly. "Crazy Helen Black complaining about the revered High Mistress of Wyldcliffe Abbey School? What are you going to tell them—that I am some kind of witch? I don't think so. It will be you they'll be locking up, not me. You really have no choice, Helen. You are one of us. It's time for you to accept your destiny."

Then the scene changed. Helen was dressed in a long cloak and hood that showed just a glimpse of her bright hair. She was in a dark underground place with many other women, all dressed in black robes. They were chanting in a circle. I saw an eye, a mouth, the slant of a cheek that I thought perhaps I recognized: a teacher, a cook, a cleaner. These were the women of Wyldcliffe, gathered in the coven, and Helen was among them. My mouth was dry. I knew that I had seen them before, those terrible hooded women, or at least some kind of shadow of them. They had been reaching out for me in my frenzied panic in the lake that night with Sebastian. I wanted Helen to stop. I didn't want to know any more. But I had no choice but to watch the mesmerizing sphere of light and the scene that was being acted out inside it.

"Our Master has not yet found the thing we seek," intoned the voice of the High Mistress. "He is beginning to fade, according to the laws of the Unconquered. If we do not sustain him, an end will come of all our hopes. We have already fed him with our very life force. Each of the Dark Sisters has given a year of her own life to prolong his. That is all we are permitted to give. Now we must find other, less willing victims. We will become Soul Stealers."

The image dissolved and was replaced by Helen and her mother glaring at each other.

"I won't allow you to do this!" Helen shouted. "This soul-stealing stuff is evil; you're like vampires. . . ."

"Indeed," Mrs. Hartle sneered. "Just as vampires suck blood, the coven will suck life from whoever lies in our path and use it to feed our Master. Fortunately we have a source of fresh young life so conveniently at hand—the

Wyldcliffe students. Any girl foolish enough to acquire three demerits will be sent to me for punishment, but not for the detention that she expects. We will be ready for her. She will wake up the next day knowing nothing about it, but part of her life force will have been transferred to our Master."

"You're insane! And I won't help you do this; I refuse."

Then the pictures changed rapidly. I saw Laura being handed a demerit card by Miss Raglan; then she was knocking on the door of Mrs. Hartle's study, and then she was lying asleep in some kind of underground crypt, with the robed figures swaying and chanting around her. She was pale, as pale as death. Then one of the women pushed in front of the others and tried to shake her, but she didn't wake up. "Laura, Laura! My God, you've killed her. . . ." The woman's hood fell back. It was Helen, and she was crying uncontrollably over Laura's cold body.

"We drank too deep," said the High Mistress in an expressionless voice as she examined Laura's white face. "She is of no more use to us now. Take her body and throw it into the lake. It will seem as though she has drowned there."

"You can't do that!" screamed Helen. "I hate you, I hate you."

Then I heard the real Helen give a long, shuddering breath. She dropped her hands, and the globe of light vanished. She looked at us, red-eyed and scared.

"I was there," she said. "I couldn't do anything to stop it. I saw Laura's face; I saw her eyes after the life had drained away. I watched them throw her body in the lake." She was struggling not to cry. "And that's the woman I have to call my mother! She didn't care what had happened to Laura so long as no one discovered the coven's secret. I threatened to go to the police, but she just laughed."

I gasped. "So Celeste was right."

"Yeah," Helen said, wiping her face on her sleeve. "Celeste is mean and snobby and all the rest, but she was right about that. I tried to hint to her that Laura hadn't drowned, but she started to accuse me of all sorts of things, so I clammed up. But Celeste was right to blame me! I knew what was going on, and I should have done something to stop it."

"There was nothing you could have done," Sarah said quietly.

"At least I told her—Mrs. Hartle—that there was no way I would ever be part of her coven again, whatever she did to me. And she knows I'll never change my mind."

I felt totally sick. So that had been Sebastian's connection with Laura. "How could Sebastian have agreed to any of this?" I cried.

"Evie, I swear he didn't know about it. The coven had told him that the life force they fed him was their own and that they were willing to give it. They said they would be amply repaid when Sebastian found the Talisman and led them all to immortality. When Sebastian found out what had happened to Laura, he refused to take any more sustenance from the Sisters. He and my mother had a blazing fight. Sebastian said he was sickened by what they had done and that it was better for him to accept his fate and let himself fade into what he would become. But she screamed that he had promised them immortality and she would hold him to his promise. Since then the coven has been even more desperate to find the Talisman. Mrs. Hartle thinks she can force Sebastian to use its powers, if he's unwilling. As Sebastian gets weaker and weaker, I'm not sure he'll be able to control them."

This was the thing Sebastian couldn't bring himself to tell me—the cold-blooded destruction of an innocent girl. Agnes's death had been a terrible accident, but this was something else. Laura's death had been Mrs. Hartle's twisted gift to Sebastian. I didn't know who I wanted to weep for most: Laura or Agnes or Sebastian. I had no tears left for myself.

"Evie, when you arrived at Wyldcliffe, I knew there was something different about you. I couldn't afford to be friendly; I didn't want to draw Mrs. Hartle's attention to you. So I started spying on you secretly, following you at night, watching you everywhere you went. I'm sorry. I didn't mean to pry."

"So it *was* you that day at Fairfax Hall!"

"Yeah," she said with a rueful smile. "I thought myself over there to check on you without anyone knowing. And I'd gotten you into trouble the night before to try to frighten you into giving up your meetings with Sebastian. I wanted to warn you outright about him, but I never knew who would be secretly listening to us. Anyway, my efforts didn't work. I watched you get drawn in deeper and deeper. I heard what you and Sarah said about your possible connection with Lady Agnes. And I was almost crazy with worry when I found out you had the Talisman."

"How could you know—?"

"I was watching in the garden that night when Sebastian touched the necklace. After that I was sure what it really was. I'm terrified of what will happen if my mother or Sebastian find out that you have the very thing they have been searching for all these years. You mustn't ever tell him."

My heart was jumping. I looked at Sarah's and Helen's white faces. "He knows already," I confessed. "But he promised that he would stay away. He doesn't want it."

"Evie, you can't trust him! As he fades further the desire to cling to human life will grow until it's an intolerable hunger. In the end Sebastian's desire for the Talisman will be far stronger than any feelings he has for you." Helen looked at me with pity. "From now on, you have to treat him as an enemy."

"Tell me something I don't already know. Sebastian and his pack of Dark Sisters could kill me at any moment. And there's nothing I can do about it." My flippant tone was a poor disguise for my fears.

"There is," said Helen. "I might be able to help you."

I looked up, a stirring of hope fluttering inside me.

"There's only one thing you can do. You possess the Talisman. Use it to release your own powers, Evie." Her eyes glimmered in the shadows. "Follow the Mystic Way."

# Forty-five

I stared at Helen. "You must be joking."

"Of course I'm not."

"I'm not getting mixed up in all that stuff. That was what started all this trouble in the first place. And besides, I just couldn't do all the chanting and rites and dancing around the maypole, or whatever they do. . . ."

"You mean all that mumbo jumbo?" said Sarah with a faint smile.

I grinned back weakly, but it wasn't funny anymore.

"Evie, haven't you learned anything yet?" Helen said impatiently. "It's not mumbo jumbo. It's as real as the ground we're standing on. And you're already mixed up in the Mystic Way. It's in your blood."

I said nothing. The damp and cold of the cave seemed

to be seeping into my veins, freezing my mind. I couldn't think.

"So what are you going to do?" she persisted. "Just wait until Sebastian or the coven comes after you?"

I tore the ribbon from my neck and held up the innocent-looking necklace. "I'll stop wearing this thing. I'll send it away, back to Frankie. . . ."

"And put her in the same danger?"

"Then I'll just get rid of it! I'll . . . I'll throw it in the lake, or chuck it down one of those old mine shafts on the top of the moors."

"So that they can pick it up at their convenience? You can't abandon the Talisman, and it will be impossible to destroy." Her pale face looked more ethereal than ever as she stood in front of me, urging me to believe her. "Just open your mind, Evie. Learn how to use it."

"But I don't know how!"

Helen placed her hand on mine. A flash of blue light flamed out of the Talisman and lit up the cave, making the mosaics spring to life with a thousand reflections.

"You see? The Talisman is ready to awaken, if you'll let it."

"But I haven't got any powers," I argued. "I'm not like you."

"You saw Lady Agnes, though," said Sarah. "And you could see Sebastian."

I couldn't deny it. I looked down at the Talisman, lying there in my hand. What would it demand of me? Agnes had died because of the Mystic Way, and it had lured Sebastian to his doom. . . . Would I be able to do any better? Helen and Sarah were looking at me expectantly. I was standing on a precipice, hovering between two worlds.

"Can you really teach me what to do?"

"I can try," Helen replied. "Some things I have learned since being at Wyldcliffe; others I just kind of knew from the beginning. But I think that everyone has a voice inside them, telling them the story of their own power; it's just that they just don't bother to listen to it. Look at the girls here at Wyldcliffe. All they care about is being popular and getting invited to the right parties at the holidays. They don't listen to what's really going on inside them. Some people are naturally more sensitive, though, like you and Sarah."

"How do you mean?" asked Sarah.

"I've often felt your mind reaching out to mine. I had to work hard to keep you out sometimes. No one has taught you how to develop your instincts into power, but I know you could do it. And, Evie, you can't deny what you have experienced. You both have huge potential to awaken your real selves. And the Mystic Way is a sort of key that can unlock that potential."

"But not everyone can do this weird magic stuff, levitation and healing and all that," I said.

"It's not magic!" She laughed. "This isn't a fairy tale, Evie. The stuff I can do, and what Agnes could do—it's all part of the mystery of nature. We think we have all the answers, but our very existence is a miracle. What do you really understand about the universe and the stars and the ocean, and, oh, I don't know . . . electricity and magnetism and string theory and quantum physics? Isn't all that 'unbelievable'?"

"That's different," I objected.

"Is it? When people first taught that the earth went around the sun, and not the other way around, they were regarded as dangerous lunatics. But now it's accepted. And it's the same with this. People will understand it one day." She fell silent, then shrugged. "This isn't about some philosophical theory, Evie; it's about survival. How else are you going to protect yourself? Agnes left you the Talisman. She must have wanted you to use it."

"That's why she has been trying to contact you," said Sarah seriously. "I'm sure Helen's right. You've got to do this, Evie. Just open your mind to it."

*You can do it, Evie; you can do anything you want.* I seemed to hear another faint echo of my mother's voice, and the thought flashed through my mind that if I could use the Talisman to help myself, then maybe I could use it to help Sebastian. It was the tiniest chance, but it was enough.

"Okay," I muttered. "I'll give it a go."

"What about you, Sarah? Evie needs all the support she can get."

"Sure." Sarah quickly squeezed my hand. "I believe in the unseen world. Count me in."

Helen's beautiful smile lit up her face. "Great. We'll need to start from the very beginning, with the Circle. And we'll need some candles."

I groped in an alcove behind the statue of Pan, remembering my last visit. The candles and matches that Sebastian had used were still there.

"That's perfect," said Helen. She lit the candles, and their warm yellow light danced across the grotto's walls. Then she fumbled in her bag and found a piece of chalk in her art supplies.

"Put the Talisman on the ground."

I did as Helen asked. Sarah placed the flickering candles around it. Then Helen drew with the chalk on the floor, marking a circle to surround the three of us, with the Talisman in the center.

"Don't step out of the Circle, whatever you do. Now hold hands."

We linked our hands. I felt silly, like a child at a birthday party waiting for the magician to pull a rabbit out of his hat. But Helen looked deadly serious.

"Try to empty your minds," she said. "Concentrate on the Elements that we come from: the air of our breath, the water of our veins, the earth of our bodies, and the fire of our desires."

She began to chant it over and over, and we copied her: "The water of our veins . . . the fire of our desires . . ."

Then she raised her arms and face, just as we had seen her standing on the roof, and spoke in a low, clear voice: "We stand here, pure in intention, courageous of heart, young in spirit, united of purpose. We ask that the powers within us might awake. We ask Agnes to show us the truth of her Talisman. We call on our sisters: the wind, the earth, and the seas. We invoke the fire of life."

Even then part of me was saying, *Nothing will happen; I can't really do this. . . .* I wasn't prepared for what happened next.

The lights flickered to a ghostly glow. A wind sprang

up, wrapping itself around us, blowing our hair, taking my breath away.

"Hold out your hands."

Shaking, I held them out in front of me, and Sarah did the same. A column of bright white fire shot up from the Talisman, and tiny flames danced around the circle that Helen had drawn on the floor. I gasped. Water was flowing from my hands, spilling to the ground like a waterfall. I looked across at Sarah. Fine dust was pouring out of hers. Earth, water, air, fire . . . Then I saw a girl in white at the heart of the column of fire. *"Agnes!"* I cried as I went spinning out of control, falling into another world. . . .

Everything was black. It was over.

"Don't step out of the circle!"

I blinked and opened my eyes. The only light came from the candles, which were burning steadily. The Talisman lay cool and unharmed on the floor. I bent down and picked it up, and heard Agnes whisper, *I am with you always. . . .*

Helen quickly rubbed the chalk markings away with her foot. Then she turned to us with flushed cheeks. "The Elements have spoken. Earth for Sarah, water for Evie. I thought it would be like that." She smiled. "So now we are complete. Four friends, four Elements, four corners of the circle."

"But there are only three of us," said Sarah.

"No, there aren't," I said, looking up slowly. "Don't forget Agnes. She's in this too."

Now I had glimpsed her world, and I could never go back to being the girl I used to be.

# Forty-six

Agnes.

I was aware of her every day. She was by my side as I walked down the long, echoing corridors of Wyldcliffe. Sometimes she was as vivid and real as any other girl, sometimes just a shadow, like a sigh. I was afraid of what Sebastian had told me and of the things that Helen had shown us, but Agnes somehow gave me the courage to keep going in that place of twisted secrets. She even gave me the strength to deal with Celeste, who seemed more determined than ever to land me in trouble.

She must have had plenty of time lying in her hospital bed to dream up her pathetic campaign—stupid stuff like tearing pages from my books, or hiding my gym clothes, anything to make life uncomfortable. It wasn't enough for her to dislike me personally; she wanted India and Sophie and the whole of her crowd to hate me too. Sophie looked a bit awkward, but she was too weak to say anything, and soon fell back under Celeste's control. I didn't care. I knew who my friends were.

"Do you really think you're going to get me expelled by doing all this childish stuff?" I asked Celeste wearily as I came into the dorm and found my clothes scattered on the floor for the third time that week.

"Not for this, Johnson," she replied. "This is just to wind you up. It's kind of fun, though."

"You're sick, you know, Celeste."

"Really? How kind of you to tell me," she drawled. Then she laughed. "You're the one who's going to be sick when you're packing your bags to leave."

I walked out without speaking. I had to get away from her before I lost my temper. I mustn't draw attention to myself—hadn't Miss Scratton said that once? I ran down the marble stairs heading anywhere—the stables, the library, it didn't matter.

"No running on the stairs!"

I stopped and looked behind me. It was Miss Dalrymple.

"Where are you dashing to like that?" She looked smiling and cheerful, but she watched me unblinkingly, like a snake. She came closer to me and I started to feel sick. Lights seemed to press on my eyes until I saw a bright patch hovering in front of me. It was in the shape of a cross—no, a kind of sword, and then for split second I saw Sebastian as though faraway, his beautiful face taut with concentration, as he cut the air with swift movements, a silver dagger flashing in his hand. The silver dagger . . .

I tried to speak: "Sorry."

"Remember that running on the stairs can be dangerous," she said blandly. "We wouldn't want anything to happen, would we? Why, Evie, you look so pale. Are you all right?"

"I'm fine."

"But so untidy, dear." Her eyes were darting all over me. "Make sure your hair is tied back in the future. And you're not wearing jewelry, are you?"

Jewelry. My heart was big and loud in my chest. The blood sang in my head.

"N-no . . . no . . . of course not."

Was she an overzealous teacher searching for rule breakers, or a member of the coven searching for the Talisman? Either way I was trapped. She was standing so close to me now that I could see the fine veins in her cheeks, could smell the heavy, hypnotic perfume that she wore. I had to get away. I panicked and pulled open the first two buttons of my shirt, showing my bare neck.

"I don't have any jewelry," I stammered. "I don't have anything."

Miss Dalrymple's face fell as she stepped back; then she smiled again.

"Of course not. Why would you?"

She let me go. I was shaking, but safe. Miss Dalrymple couldn't have known that seconds before I had run down the marble steps, I had obeyed a blind impulse and hidden my necklace in a dark crack on the old servants' staircase. But I couldn't hide it forever.

"You have to make progress in the Rites, Evie," urged Helen. "Look at what happened with Dalrymple. She could be involved. I'm sure she is. If the coven finds out that you are hiding the Talisman, they'll close in on you. And Sebastian might attack any day."

"He won't!"

"Evie, you can't be sure about that." Helen sighed. "It's desperately important for you to be prepared."

"I'm trying! I've been practicing the Rites with you and Sarah every day. It's just that I . . ."

"What?" asked Sarah.

"I can't make anything happen," I said. "Not since that first time."

I don't know what I had expected. Perhaps I imagined that I would be able to wave a wand and perform miracles, turn back the clocks and make everything all right by magic. It wasn't like that, though. I couldn't dance on the wind like Helen or heal people like Agnes. I couldn't do anything.

I had brooded over the Talisman, called to it, turned it over in my hands, and hung it around my neck once again, but I had not been able to awaken it from its long sleep. And when Helen drew the Circle in our secret meetings, nothing happened to me. Sarah, on the other hand, was leaving me far behind. She knew how to perform the incantations, and when she placed her hands over a mound of earth that had been ritually scattered inside the Circle, a tiny green shoot would spring up from it before our eyes, like a fast-forwarded film. But I was completely useless.

So here we all were again, down in the grotto, trying everything one more time.

"You just need to trust yourself," Sarah said. "It will come."

They watched me anxiously as I waved my hands like an idiot over a bowl of water, trying to make it turn into steam, or create waves in it, or make it turn pink, or whatever I was supposed to be doing. . . .

"Open your mind," Helen urged. "Feel your Element calling you; harness its powers—"

"I can't!"

She looked up at me thoughtfully. "Or you don't want to."

"I do, I do," I cried. "I know it's important."

"It's not a question of knowing, Evie. You have to *feel*."

Perhaps that was the problem. I didn't want to feel anything. My mother's death all those years ago had shut something down inside me. I had grown up kidding myself that I was strong and independent, not needing anyone, but I saw now that I had simply been afraid to love, in case the person I loved vanished, as she had. And then Sebastian had come along, and I had stepped out of my protective armor. I had thrown myself headfirst into loving Sebastian, but he had gone, leaving me even more painfully alone than before. The boy I loved was a murderer, a wandering spirit, one of the doomed, and he was out there somewhere, beginning to fade. He was my enemy.

I was so unhappy that it hurt, like being cut with a knife. Of course I couldn't feel anything; I didn't want to, ever again.

"Evie, are you paying attention?" Helen's voice jerked me back from my thoughts.

"Try again, Evie," Sarah pleaded. "They're getting closer; I'm sure they are. You've got to be able to defend yourself!"

And another distant voice echoed across the years in my head, as light and quick as silver: *Find your powers, my sister, find yourself.*

"I am trying," I lied. Stretching my hands over the bowl of water, I closed my eyes and began to chant.

Water.

A single drop falling from a leaf onto the ground. The distant ocean, unimaginably vast, as deep and dark as the space behind the stars. Fine mist on the moors in the morning. Rain falling into the rich earth. A mountain stream singing as it raced down, down, down to the sea.

I couldn't do anything to command water, but I dreamed about it. The dream I'd had on my very first night at Wyldcliffe, of a great wave rising up to sweep everything away, haunted me night after night. And from the minute I woke and splashed my face in the bathroom, I was aware of how it was impossible to live without water. *Water of life, cleanse and refresh us. . . .* The half-remembered words of a hymn that Frankie used to hum under her breath drifted up from my memories. Every time I drank a glass of tepid water in the dining hall, I thought of those useless bits of information you pick up without noticing.

Fact: There are more atoms in a single glass of water than there are glasses of water in all the seas in the world. All I had to do was turn on the tap to touch a living miracle.

More facts: The world's surface is seventy percent water; a child grows in the womb in a sac of water; our human bodies are largely composed of water. . . .

Water. The world. A child. My body. My tears.

Water for Evie. The old craving to swim came over me again, but I ignored it. I shut out the rain and the mists and the dreams. *You have to feel,* Helen had said, but I wasn't going to be tempted. I didn't want to feel anything. My heart had been wrung as dry as a bone, and I was going to keep it that way.

# Forty-seven

"So what is this Memorial Procession actually for?" I demanded. "Is this another of your crackpot Wyldcliffe traditions?"

We were down at the stables on a chilly December evening, grooming Bonny and Starlight. Sarah stopped brushing Bonny's chestnut coat and glanced into the next stall to make sure no one was there.

"It's for Lady Agnes," she said. "At sunset on the twelfth day of the twelfth month, on the anniversary of her death, every girl in the school has to gather down in the old chapel ruins to say prayers for her soul. I get the feeling the staff would like to abolish the procession, but it was a condition laid down in Lord Charles's will when the school took over the Abbey, so they're stuck with it."

"Oh." I hadn't expected this. Part of me still couldn't accept that Agnes was dead. I had come to know her face, her voice, her smile, until they were part of me. I blinked and kept brushing Starlight's tail and tried to keep my voice steady. "Well, it's a good thing, isn't it? Honoring her memory and all that?"

"Yes, of course," said Sarah. "It's just that there was some trouble a couple of years ago. One of the juniors became hysterical and swore that she had seen Agnes's ghost hovering in the chapel. The whole thing turned into a kind of morbid drama, and the girl's parents removed her from the school. So the mistresses are always worried that things will get out of hand again. I'm worried too. I can't get rid of this feeling that we're being watched."

Just then someone came over with a bucketful of feed for the ponies. It was the boy I had seen working in the stables before.

"Hi, Josh," Sarah said, turning to him brightly. "Thanks for bringing that."

The ponies greeted the boy like an old friend. He laughed and set down the bucket. His clothes were scruffy, but he moved with the confident grace of an experienced rider.

"No problem." He smiled. "I thought Bonny was

dragging her hind leg earlier, but I cleaned out her hooves, and she seems fine now. I just thought I'd let you know."

He turned the warmth of his smile on me, but I looked away.

"Okay, I'll watch out for it," said Sarah. "Thanks, Josh."

"See you." He strode away, whistling cheerfully. I busied myself with the ponies, my thoughts racing. I could hardly bear the idea of hanging around in the ruins with all the other Wyldcliffe girls, trampling the ground where Agnes had been, where Sebastian and I had once walked together. But I mustn't think about Sebastian. . . .

Very soon the Memorial Procession became the only topic of conversation in the school. Uniforms were ironed and shoes polished to Miss Scratton's satisfaction. Tubs of white flowers from the greenhouses were arranged in the main hall, filling the corridors with their secretive, papery scent. The music master, Mr. Brooke—one of the few male teachers allowed over the Wyldcliffe threshold—insisted on extra classes every morning to practice the hymns. I glanced over at Celeste and her snooty blond friends and wondered what they would say if they knew they were going to be singing for my ancestor, Lady Agnes Templeton. I was part of the Abbey now, just as much as they were. Like Effie, I rightly belonged.

This was one Wyldcliffe tradition I would be proud to uphold.

We lined up on the winding marble stairs, with the younger ones in the front and the tall top class on the higher steps at the back. The whole school was there, except for Celeste, who had been excused because of her injured leg. We were all wearing our bloodred winter coats and holding a single white lily in our gloved hands. Excited whispers ran through the crowd of girls like little dancing flames. They didn't care a bit about Agnes, of course; the night's procession would just be a theatrical excitement, nothing more.

There was a clatter of heels on the black and white tiles, and the mistresses swept into view below us: Miss Scratton and Miss Schofield and Miss Raglan and Miss Dalrymple and all the rest of them. They were robed in their dark academic gowns and carried tall white candles in silver holders. Mrs. Hartle was holding what looked like a heavy prayer book, and she frowned as she looked up at the rows of girls waiting on the stairs. I tried to see any likeness to Helen, but although they were both tall, they couldn't have been more different. Mrs. Hartle's face was dark and smooth and heavy, and Helen's full of light, like a medieval angel. It was hard to believe they were mother and daughter. No wonder it had been easy to keep it a secret.

"Silence!" called Miss Scratton. Her eyes darted over us. "Elizabeth Fisher, your coat is unfastened." The unfortunate Elizabeth fumbled to do up her buttons. "We will proceed from the main door to the chapel ruins. There will be no talking. There will be no giggling. There will be no silliness. Let us begin. Mr. Brooke, are you ready?"

The slightly flustered music teacher gave us the note and we began to sing, our voices echoing high and clear. Then the High Mistress led the way down the steps of the Abbey. A few crimson streaks of sun were visible in the pearl-gray sky. The day was dying. We paced slowly, in time to our solemn singing, which floated across the shadowy lawns like the thin chants of the nuns in the old times. The black robes of the mistresses fluttered in the biting wind, and I was glad for my thick coat.

The procession made its way around the edge of the lake and up to the ruins. Then we fell silent and stood in a circle around the green mound of the altar. The broken columns and archways of the ancient church gleamed in the candlelight. The whole place felt like a stage waiting for something to happen. Mrs. Hartle handed the book to

Miss Scratton, who began to intone a kind of prayer, her voice carried away by the wind.

"'Man, that is born of woman, hath but a short time to live, and is full of misery. He cometh up, and is cut down, like a flower. . . . In the midst of life we are in death. . . .'"

The words washed over me. I watched each girl go up to the mound and lay her flower on it, whispering the words, "In memory of Lady Agnes."

"Whosoever liveth and believeth in me shall never die. The last enemy that shall be destroyed is death. . . .'"

It was my turn. I walked up slowly. This was where she had lain in death, killed by the man I loved. In a flash I saw it all again: the struggle in the dark, Agnes's pale dress, the fury in Sebastian's eyes, and the terrible, eternal regret. . . .

"For Agnes," I said. Then I remembered the other silent victim of this haunted place and added quietly, "For Laura."

I turned away and looked with surprise at the ranks of watching girls. I had forgotten that anyone else was there with me. Miss Scratton's dry voice was still chanting in the background. "'We give thee hearty thanks that it hath pleased thee to deliver our sister Agnes out of the miseries of this sinful world.'"

And then it happened: a scream tore through the still night air. "Look! Look over there!" Panic spread through the girls. "It's over there!" Fingers were pointing and eyes were raised to the jagged arch where the east window had once stood. A figure in a white gown was looming there, its face covered by a long, streaming veil. It suddenly swooped down over the terrified girls, and the screaming grew like a storm. "It's her! It's Lady Agnes!" There was a confused stampede as they ran, knocking down the candles and crushing the flowers.

"Girls, stop this at once!" Miss Scratton shouted desperately, but no one was listening. Everyone around me was running, but I was still, as still as the High Mistress, who stood like a carved statue under the archway, her dark eyes watching me in triumph.

Later, when we were all safely back inside, I was made to stand in front of everyone as Mrs. Hartle held up the bundle of sheets and nightgowns that had been rigged up to scare a bunch of schoolgirls.

"Evelyn Johnson," she said coldly. "Your name is clearly marked on these items. Your actions tonight show not only a deplorable lack of consideration for others and a blatant disregard for our Wyldcliffe traditions, but a considerable degree of stupidity. How did you think you would get away with this senseless prank?"

I stared at the floor and didn't reply. It was easy to guess that Celeste had organized the whole thing. She had used my stuff to fix up the scarecrow version of Agnes that had been enough to terrify the younger girls and ruin the procession. She had done it, but I knew that I would be blamed. Celeste would get away with it, but I wouldn't. Even before Mrs. Hartle spoke next, I knew what was coming.

"Your record at this school has been most disappointing. You have already acquired two demerit cards this term. This will be your third. Your behavior is a disgrace. The governors may wish to review your position at the school. In the meantime you will report to me for your detention and punishment."

*You mustn't get another demerit, Evie.* With a sick lurch in my stomach I remembered what Miss Scratton had said. Had she known something? I glanced up at the rows of curious eyes, staring at me as pitilessly as on the night I had arrived at Wyldcliffe. Helen saw me and turned away, but Sarah looked back, close to tears. I couldn't see Miss Scratton anywhere.

"That will be all. Girls, I apologize that tonight's

celebration has been spoiled by one unworthy member of our community. You will all go straight to bed. Evie, you will come with me."

I followed her in silence. It seemed that everything had been leading to this moment. I was in the hands of the High Mistress, and I was totally alone.

# Forty-eight

This is the moment.

I am in Mrs. Hartle's study. It reminds me of my first day at Wyldcliffe, all those months ago. But I have changed. I'm no longer the same person, though Mrs. Hartle is just as secretive and deadly as when we first met. I am afraid. Now, like Helen, I am afraid of the High Mistress. She prowls around the room, picking things up, glancing though books, ignoring me, making me wait.

Finally she stands tall and dark in front of me and speaks.

"I know all about you, Evie. I know who you are. The first time we met, I admit you startled me with your resemblance to the portrait of the one we call the traitor." Her eyes dart over to a corner of the room. A painting that I hadn't noticed before is hanging against the paneling, and I recognize the girl with the long red hair. . . .

"Don't call her that! Agnes was true to the Mystic Way. It's you who have twisted it into something vile."

"Agnes was a fool," Mrs. Hartle states calmly. "She should not have entrusted her powers to a mere girl who knows nothing of our deep arts. But we will soon relieve you of that burden. Give me the Talisman."

"I don't know what you're talking about."

"You don't really imagine that you can hide it from me any longer?" she sneers. "My poor crazed daughter has already given your secret away. Oh, not on purpose, but you were like children playing with matches when you tried to master the Rites. I soon became alerted to your feeble attempts to summon the Powers. The High Mistress sees more than you know. Your pathetic experiments led me straight to you. And now I have found what I have long been searching for."

"But the Talisman is no good to you," I hazard. "Only I can use it."

"You! Don't fool yourself. You have no powers. You didn't try hard enough, did you, Evie? And now you will be destroyed by your precious Sebastian." There is scorn in her voice when she says his name. It fills me with anger.

"He won't hurt me on your orders. He is your master, not your servant."

Her face flushes darkly. "Our so-called Master has betrayed us. He has refused our aid and is fading rapidly. But we will not allow that to happen. He promised us immortality, and he must be made to keep his promise. Now that he is weak and we are strong, we will take the Talisman to him and force him to wield it."

She holds out her hand. "Give it to me now," she commands. "I want it."

Something clicks in my brain. Sebastian has refused her help. That means he has decided to fade rather than hurt me. He doesn't want me to die. He's not my enemy after all; he never will be. My fear vanishes like a dream. I feel strong, stronger than she could ever be. I know what I must do.

I untie the ribbon around my neck. The necklace gleams innocently, a pretty trinket; that's all. I drop it into Mrs. Hartle's outstretched hand.

A crack of blue fire lights up the room. She staggers back, then slumps over her desk. I snatch the Talisman from where it has fallen. The High Mistress has been stunned, knocked out, but only for a moment. I have to get away before she comes to. I have to get the Talisman somewhere safe.

I run to the door and fling it open. Two women in dark robes and masks are standing guard. They lunge forward to catch me. I slam the door shut and lock it with shaking hands. I am trapped. Mrs. Hartle groans and stirs. In desperation I rush to the window. It is small and high and barred. I beat against the glass, but there is no escape. "Please help, please, Agnes," I sob. I'm standing next to her portrait. Her gray eyes are looking into mine. I reach up and touch the painting, and the piece of paneled wall it hangs on swings open like a door.

I see a rough passageway that slopes downward and disappears from sight. I remember Helen saying something about a maze of tunnels under the Abbey. Perhaps this will lead me out of here, but it's so dark, so narrow. The women outside are battering the door; the High Mistress slowly raises her head. I have to get away. Without stopping to think, I step into the passage and close the secret door behind me with a loud click. I am locked in.

I stagger along blindly, feeling my way by brushing my hands against the cold, damp walls. It is dark, so dark that I can taste it in my throat. Every faltering step takes me deeper underground. *You can do it Evie; keep going, one step at a time.* I can hear voices; there's someone behind me, the faint swish of skirts. *Keep going.* But I am imprisoned by the weight of the earth around me and the blackness behind my eyes. I can't breathe; I am suffocating in a tomb, waiting to die.

And then I hear the memory of a voice, high and clear like a girl's, warm and gentle as a mother's:

> *The night is dark, but day is near,*
> *Hush, little baby, do not fear. . . .*

A faint silvery light begins to gleam. I realize it is coming from the Talisman. I cradle it in my hand, and it glows like a star.

I am no longer alone. Agnes is with me. I will find a way out of here. Somehow I will make it through this night.

I have been wandering a long time in this maze, twisting and turning in endless passageways, going in circles, meeting abrupt dead ends. But now I seem to have arrived somewhere. This place feels bigger, like a wide cavern. My footsteps echo here. I know, without understanding how, that I am underneath the ruined chapel, and that somewhere above me the stars are shining.

I freeze. Sounds echo ahead. Someone else's footstep.

Then a quick, fresh breeze blows through the underground cavern, and there is the scent of harebells. . . .

"Helen! Helen, are you there?"

A flashlight dazzles my eyes, and then I am overwhelmed by the living warmth of Sarah and Helen hugging me and laughing and crying all at once.

"How did you find me?"

"I thought my mother might take you down here," replies Helen. "It's where she brought Laura. How did you get away from her?"

"She tried to take the Talisman, but she couldn't. She'll come after it again, though, and I don't know if I can hold her off this time."

"She'll summon the coven to help her," Helen says anxiously. "We mustn't get caught down here."

"I can lead us out," says Sarah. "We came down the tunnel from the grotto, Evie. Let's go back that way."

Sarah sweeps the flashlight around, and I see that we are in a low, wide crypt with a vaulted ceiling. It is the meeting place of many passageways. At the far end there is a rough kind of stone table, like an altar. A low passage leads off from behind the table, and we run down it, but we soon hear the shuffle of many feet ahead of us, and chanting, like the growl of thunder.

"Go back!" whispers Sarah. "We'll have to find another way out. The coven is gathering. They're coming!"

We go back the way we came, but a crowd of robed and hooded women is already filling the crypt, pouring in from every side. They have no individual personalities, no distinction, only a terrible, anonymous presence. Their chanting is building to a crescendo. Some of them hold flickering torches. They see us by the light of the red flames, and they scream out wildly, encircling us, hungry for the Talisman. There are too many of them. We are trapped and helpless.

A tall figure robed in black enters, and the Dark Sisters part to let their High Mistress approach. She is holding the silver dagger. Everyone falls silent.

"I said that you would give me the Talisman," she says. "And you will. There is someone here that you cannot refuse. Bring him in!"

The women shudder and sigh as a hunched shape is carried in on a carved chair.

"Sebastian?" I whisper. There is no reply. All I hear is the hideous moaning of the coven.

"Sebastian, Lord Sebastian!" they screech. "This is the moment! Fulfill your vow!"

The slumped shape in the carved chair moves and

raises its hand. The women fall silent, their breath rattling like dry leaves before a storm. I must have gotten it all wrong, so utterly wrong. Sebastian has decided to work with his Sisters after all. He is here to claim his prize. It is the Talisman that he wants, not me.

He gets up and walks toward me, halting and slow. His eyes are sunk and red, his breathing labored. He is fading. It is happening, just as he said. There is no escape, not for any of us. I can't bear to see Sebastian's haggard face. I can't bear to see him wrench the Talisman from me. I can't bear to feel him tear my heart out for it. This is the end, at last. I close my eyes.

He reaches out to me, and I steel myself for his attack, but all he does is touch a strand of my hair. "I love you, girl from the sea," he whispers. Then he turns to the waiting women and shouts with his last strength, "Stay away! If you harm her you'll be destroyed."

The High Mistress screams, "Don't listen to him. Take them both!"

They pour forward like a dark wave, and someone speaks to me in a voice as clear as the dawn: *An heirloom of our house, may it never fall into darkness. You can do it, Evie. You can do anything, my sister.*

I know what I have to do. Sebastian has collapsed to

the ground. Quicker than lightning, I stoop and draw a Circle around us both with my fingertips, seeing it bright and clear in my mind. Tiny white flames burst into life and run along the edge of the circle. I place my hand over the Talisman hanging from my neck and call to it with the deepest secrets of my mind. *I think, I feel, I desire. . . .* Dazzling white light suddenly fills the crypt and knocks back the High Mistress and her followers.

"I command you . . ." she screams, but I laugh at her. I will not live by her rules. I see Helen and Sarah in the confusion and grasp their hands to pull them inside the Circle. My mind empties itself of everything. I begin to chant: "The air of our breath, the water of our veins, the earth of our bodies, and the fire of our desires, come to us now."

Sarah and Helen join in: "The water of our veins . . . the fire of our desires . . ." We are holding hands, but someone is missing, the fourth quarter of the Circle. Then I open my eyes and she is there: Agnes, dressed in white, smiling at me.

I stop fighting my fate. *I think, I desire, I feel. . . .* Oh, yes, I feel and I'm not frightened of it anymore. I love, and I don't regret it. Love is the only thing that matters now: my love for Sebastian, and my no less precious love for Sarah and Helen. And finally I turn to Agnes, my ancestor, my friend, my Mystic Sister. . . .

I reach out for her. She takes my hand and we are complete. Helen raises her arms to where the unseen sky glimmers far above us, and Sarah kneels and presses her hands to the ground. But Agnes and I remain standing, with Sebastian lying at our feet. His lips are parched. He groans, "Water . . ."

Water. Of course. The water of life.

Everything around me fades like a mist. I see myself walking over the moors. Sebastian is with me. My sisters are with me, Helen and Sarah and Agnes. . . . I am climbing higher, walking over the strong green earth. My mother is there. *My darling Evie,* she calls me. I am swept along by a great tide of love. Frankie is there. *There are worse things than death.* She smiles. *Good-bye, my lamb.* Then they all vanish, and I am climbing alone, high up to the top of the ancient mound, where the fort once stood, a tower of earth under the stars. I look below and see every stream, every trickle of water in the dark valley. I see the lake; I see the ocean, black on the horizon. Now, at last, I know myself. This is the moment, and the power to be myself is within me. The stars have fled, the night is over, and when I lift my hand the water obeys me and rises up in one mighty wave.

I open my eyes. Down in the crypt there is a great rumbling and shaking. For the first time I see fear in the High Mistress's face as her followers turn in panic to desert her. The ground cracks, the walls break, the wind blasts through the darkness, and then the water comes. It cannot enter our Circle, but rushes through the rest of the crypt like a boiling sea. And it seems to me that our enemies are swept to one side like tiny pebbles on the shore.

# Forty-nine

The sudden flood in the old cellars under the ruins could be explained: a freak accident that had channeled water from the lake down through one of the many sluices and tunnels that had been built in the old days. An accident, nothing more. Any other explanation would be impossible, of course.

We kept our knowledge to ourselves. We had escaped from the torrent by getting out through the tunnel to the old grotto. I left Sebastian there, curled in his coat under the statue of Pan. I wet his lips from the spring, kissed his hands, and promised to return. But when I went back the next day he had gone. Helen and Sarah kept me company as we searched as much of the underground maze as we could, but we found no trace of him. There was no sign of the coven either. The water had drained away, leaving a rank smell of mud and slime, and I half dreaded coming across the drowned bodies of nameless women, their robes twisted and their eyes blank and empty. But there was nothing. They had escaped.

It seemed that no one was hurt, but something had changed. The day after the flood we felt a strange sense of relief. I knew that I should be apprehensive that the High Mistress could strike again, but the day passed quietly, like some sort of waiting place between one battle and the next. And then, as we stood for prayers after supper, Miss Scratton made the announcement.

"It is my painful duty to inform you girls that Mrs. Hartle has been reported missing to the police. She has not been seen since the end of the procession last night. While we are not sure of her whereabouts, I wish to reassure you that the authorities do not believe that she is dead. Let us pray that our High Mistress will be with us once again very soon."

It caused a sensation. Something to gossip and wonder over. Something that had never happened before in the whole history of Wyldcliffe. For us it was different. Helen broke down into silent, painful tears at the news, though no one took any notice. It was just crazy Helen Black. . . .

Only we knew why she wept, torn between love and hate.

Miss Scratton's announcement wasn't the only piece of news. Later in the evening a telephone call came from the nursing home to say that Frankie had passed away. At dawn, they said. Just as the day was breaking. Very peaceful, they said. I didn't cry. I felt for the silver necklace under my shirt and said, "I'm glad I said good-bye to her." The kind school nurse who gave me the message looked at me strangely, murmuring that it must be such a shock. . . .

*We all must die.* I believe Frankie knew that I wasn't alone anymore and that she could let me go. I didn't cry. *God does not take away life.* . . . *Good-bye, my darling.*

*Good-bye.*

The next few days passed incredibly slowly. I spent the time with Helen and Sarah, wondering what would happen next. Had we really destroyed the High Mistress? Or was she out there somewhere, biding her time and gathering her forces for the next attack?

As the whole school waited for news, it was Miss Scratton who took charge. She organized everything, protecting the students from the intrusion of the press and the questions of the police. She went from class to class making sure that everything still ran like clockwork and that Wyldcliffe would survive. If I hadn't remembered the masked faces I had seen down in the crypt, if I hadn't known not to trust any woman under the Abbey's roof, I would have drawn comfort from her calm presence.

We had won the first battle. I knew, however, that if Celia Hartle was really missing, or even dead, another High Mistress would soon emerge from the shadows to lead the coven. Like a starving dog hunting for a scrap of food, they wouldn't give up their quest for the Talisman. We had stopped them once, but while it hung around my neck I was in danger, as long as Sebastian was still out there to give them the faintest scent of hope.

Sebastian. My beginning and my end. A boy I was never supposed to meet had changed my life. And now that I had reached out and touched the Talisman with my mind, I knew I could not let it rest. Somehow, I vowed, I would master every secret that Agnes had bequeathed to me and wrench Sebastian's destiny into my hands. I would not let him fade in torment for my sake. I had to find him, before it was too late, because all I had left to cling to were the last words he had said to me.

*I love you.*

There was no power greater than that, no mystery so deep.

The December wind blew cold and bitter across the Abbey's lawns. It was the end of the term. Dad managed to get some leave so that we could spend the holidays together.

At home we went walking on the beach every day, watching the green waves tumble like dolphins, quiet in our shared sorrow over Frankie. I tried hard to be the girl he had said good-bye to in September, but he sensed a difference.

"Poor Evie," he said. "It hasn't been easy."

"No," I replied. "It's all right, though. I can cope."

He hugged me. "I know. But you'll be glad to get back to Wyldcliffe. You've got friends there now, haven't you?"

I nodded. Words were so inadequate. Yes, I had friends. Yes, I needed to get back to Wyldcliffe. My friends would be waiting.

My friends. My sisters.

My beloved.